THE CRUISE

THE CRUISE

A NOVEL OF MURDER AND ROMANCE

Maeve Binchy • Charlotte Bingham
Anita Burgh • Harry Cauley • Bernard Cornwell
Josephine Cox • Ken Follett • William Horwood
Susan Howatch • Matthew Kneale • Nicholas Rhea
Murray Smith • Eileen Townsend • Joanna Trollope

HarperCollins*Publishers*

All the characters in this book are fictitious
and any resemblance to persons
living or dead is purely coincidental.

HarperCollins*Publishers*

First published in UK in 1995 by Studio Editions Ltd, London.
First published in Australia in 1995 by HarperCollins*Publishers*.

HarperCollins*Publishers*
25 Ryde Road, Pymble, Sydney, NSW 2073, Australia
31 View Road, Glenfield, Auckland 10, New Zealand
77–85 Fulham Palace Road, London W6 8JB, United Kingdom
Hazelton Lanes, 55 Avenue Road, Suite 2900, Toronto, Ontario M5R 3L2
and 1995 Markham Road, Scarborough, Ontario, M1B 5M8, Canada
10 East 53rd Street, New York, NY 10032, USA

National Library of Australia Cataloguing-in-Publication data:

The cruise.

ISBN 0 7322 5636 4.
823.914

Front and back cover illustrations by Hans De Haas
Cover design by Darian Causby
Printed in Australia by Griffin Paperbacks, Adelaide

9 8 7 6 5 4 3 2 1
99 98 97 96 95

About the
DYSLEXIA INSTITUTE

The Dyslexia Institute (DI) is a non-profit making company, limited by guarantee and with charitable status, authorised in law to diagnose, treat and generally educate people who have dyslexia or specific difficulties with learning.

It is the only nationwide organisation providing a full service of assessments, teaching, teacher training and support to dyslexic people and their families.

For more information on the services offered to individuals and schools please contact:

Head Office
133 Gresham Road
Staines
Middlesex TW18 2AJ

The Authors

The authors of *The Cruise* had all kinds of reasons for wanting to be involved, ranging from "Saintliness!" to "Dyslexia seems such a cruel thing, eating away at people's confidence just at the age when they need it most." The following brief biographies outline their many accomplishments.

Maeve Binchy began teaching after she graduated from University College Dublin, but after using her long summer holidays to write travel articles, she joined the *Irish Times*. She has written two stage plays, and her television play, *Deeply Regretted By*, won two Jacobs Awards and the Best Script Award at the Prague Film Festival in the later 70s. Many of her books have been adapted for television and cinema and her last three novels were number one bestsellers.

Charlotte Bingham began writing at the age of 10, and continued to do so in the evenings once she began work at 16. Her first book was published in 1963 as *Coronet Among the Weeds*. Since then she has written numerous best-selling novels including *To Hear a Nightingale* and *Change of Heart*. She has written, together with her husband actor Terence Brady, over 120 television scripts including 'Upstairs, Downstairs' and 'Nanny'.

Anita Burgh was a working class student nurse who married a Lord. She has lived in Greece, France, Cambridge and Cornwall and has worked in the pop industry, at the Medical Research Council and ran a hotel, as well as having four children. Her first novel *Distinctions of Class*, published in 1987 and based on her own experiences, was shortlisted for the Boots Romantic Novel of the Year Award, and led to a series of successful novels, including *Advances* which was published in 1992 to great critical acclaim.

Harry Cauley has had two plays produced on Broadway. He was producer-director of the Apple Hill Playhouse near Pittsburgh, Pennsylvania for thirteen years until he went to Hollywood and started writing for television on the ground-breaking series 'Mary Hartman, Mary Hartman'. He won the Writers Guild of America Award for *And There Were Times Dear*, a film about a victim of Alzheimer's disease, and now lives in Cherry Valley, California.

Bernard Cornwell was born in London and raised in Essex. He became a BBC television producer in London and Belfast, but now lives in America with his wife. He is the author of the hugely successful 'Sharpe' series, set during the Peninsula War, which has been adapted for television starring Sean Bean as Richard Sharpe, and the American Civil War series 'Starbuck'. His contemporary thrillers have all been bestsellers.

Josephine Cox was born in a cotton–mill house in Blackburn and grew up in a family of ten children. Having gained a place at Cambridge University once her children had started school, she instead became a teacher and began writing her first full-length novel. This was accepted for publication in 1981, a year in which she also won the Superwoman of Great Britain Award, for which her family had secretly entered her. Now writing full time, her novels frequently appear in the bestseller lists.

Ken Follett first became a reporter with his home town newspaper in Wales, but left to join the London Evening News. His first novel had little success, but he continued to write whilst rapidly climbing the career ladder and becoming Deputy Managing Director of a London publishing house. He is now 45 and having sold a total of 40 million copies of his books worldwide, is one of Britain's biggest selling authors.

William Horwood has become one of Britain's best-loved story tellers with his successful *Duncton Wood* series, and a bestselling trilogy, *The Wolves of Time*. The 1993 publication of The Willows in Winter brought both critical acclaim and controversy, and widened his readership still further. It is now being televised, and *Toad Triumphant*, a new novel in this series, was published in 1995.

Susan Howatch obtained a law degree from King's College, London, before emigrating to the USA, where her first novel, a short mystery, was published. Five years and five novels later, she produced an international bestseller *Penmarric*. After living in Ireland for a time she returned to England. Her series of novels set in the fictional town of Starbridge have achieved book sales of over 20 million.

Matthew Kneale was born in London in 1960 and read Modern History at Magdalen College, Oxford. He has had three novels published, the first of which, *Whore Banquets*, won a Somerset Maugham Award, while the latest, *Sweet Thames*, won the John Llewellyn Rhys Prize. He also works as a travel photographer and has lived in Tokyo and Rome, as well as journeying widely in some 70 countries.

Nicholas Rhea is one of the pseudonyms under which Peter Walker writes. After 30 years with the North Yorkshire

Police, he retired with the rank of Inspector, to concentrate on his writing and has published more than 80 books. Among those written as Nicholas Rhea are the 'Constable' books, which were adapted by Yorkshire television as 'Heartbeat'. His non-fiction publications include police text books and articles on rural country life and folk lore.

Murray Smith was born in Scotland, and served as an officer in The Cameronians and, later, Special Forces. He has since written over 143 hours of television, including 'The Paradise Club' which won the Television and Cinema Exhibitors Award for the best TV series in 1990. He devised, scripted and produced the 'Frederick Forsyth Presents' series for LWT and has scripted several successful motion pictures including *Bear Island* and *The Sellout*.

Eileen Townsend is the Scottish-born author of many bestselling novels, including *Of Woman Born*, *In Love and War*, *Dreamtime*, and her latest work *Thine is the Kingdom*. Along with her two dogs and her husband Professor Colin Townsend, with whom she compiled the highly acclaimed bestseller War Wives, she lives in an historic old house on the banks of the Lough Derg in the west of Ireland.

Joanna Trollope is a fifth generation niece of Anthony Trollope. After reading English at Oxford University, she spent two years in the Foreign Office. In 1980 she became a full-time author writing a number of historical novels under the name of Caroline Harvey. More recently she has written six contemporary novels, three of which have been adapted for television – *The Rector's Wife*, *A Village Affair* and *The Choir*. She recently won the Booksellers' Association Author of the Year Award.

How *The Cruise* Came About

In 1990 Liz Brooks, Executive Director of the Dyslexia Institute, wrote to Roald Dahl and asked whether he would write a book for us. He agreed, and the result was a huge success – the rights for The Vicar of Nibbleswicke were auctioned at Christie's and raised an incredibly generous amount. Some three years later, now as a DI fundraiser but also the mother of a dyslexic son, it seemed sensible to pursue the idea of approaching authors and publishers once again, since these are the people who benefit from our success in unlocking the mysteries of literacy. I was aware of the success of The Vicar of Nibbleswicke and set about thinking of a similar way of creating a book. I resolved to adopt an old family motto: "No hide, no Christmas Box" – in other words, if you don't ask you won't get!

I had met the novelist Susan Howatch, a great supporter, when we served together on the DI Berkeley Ball Committee in 1993, so I began by asking her whether she would write a book giving the DI the copyright. Unfortunately, Susan's commitments prevented her from undertaking such a venture, but we tossed around some ideas, including a book of short stories, and eventually came up with the notion of creating a book by asking a group of well-known novelists each to write a chapter then pass it on to the next – rather like a game of consequences.

It was heartwarming to get replies from those brave enough to attempt the project. Soon we had Nicholas Rhea,

Maeve Binchy and Joanna Trollope 'signed up', but Susan was becoming concerned that with so many authors the book would need a strong linking mechanism to give it cohesion. During this time I sought advice from Sonia Land, a top London literary agent, who had helped the DI with the Roald Dahl project. Maeve was also extremely helpful and suggested setting the story in the 1990s, either in a school or on board a ship. We liked the idea of a cruise because we felt it offered myriad possibilities – not only a wide choice of characters, both passengers and crew, but also a series of exotic locations. It seemed a good base for either a romantic novel or a thriller and had obvious potential for publicising the book once it was ready to publish.

With this latter idea in mind, various companies were approached for help. P&O warmed most to the idea, particularly since they could see the book linking with the launch of their new liner, *Oriana* (then under construction) in April 1995. With P&O seriously interested, the next task was to sort out the logistics. With the help of Sonia and her tireless PA, Stephanie Lloyd, we drew up a complicated schedule based on publishing the book for Christmas 1995, which would be dispatched, together with reference material and dates that allowed each author sufficient 'thinking time' as well as writing time.

Slowly, it seemed, the final author list took shape. Many household names we approached were kind enough to praise the originality of the project and give it their blessing, despite being unable to participate. Many were too committed to other work to be available, but we appreciated that these people took the trouble to respond, often with handwritten notes, and all wishing us well. Every participant was then sent a huge package containing everything one could possibly want to know about cruising, P&O, *Oriana* and ports around the Mediterranean – with handbooks and videos to follow.

A couple of months later, Chapter One arrived and was dispatched to all the remaining authors with an invitation to author number two to start writing. At this point I began correspondence with all the authors to keep them up to date with progress while trying hard not to pester them. There was also crucial information to be imparted – P&O's insistence, for example, that in return for their involvement the ship must not, under any circumstances, be hijacked or sunk. After much soul searching they did agree to a murder on board, particularly since Murder on the Orient Express had done nothing but good for the appeal of that train.

Now the chapters began rolling in like clockwork from England, America and France – brilliant evocations of life on board a ship that hadn't even been launched, written by a group of authors who had never been cruising! There were also the most unexpected twists and turns of plot. One author would carefully set up a situation for the next to exploit only for the scenario to be totally and unexpectedly changed. Someone even suggested that Joanna Trollope should put an Aga in one of the cabins, which would identify her as the author of that chapter, but I didn't dare suggest it! If nothing else, the book was becoming an interesting study of the mind of the novelist. I decided that most of all they all like to have control over events and situations.

There were countless gratifying, frustrating and amusing moments along the way. Bernard Cornwell agreed at short notice to move up the 'batting order' when someone dropped out. Anita Burgh, who lives in France, told me that she was due in England to have an operation on her knee just before Christmas of 1994. As she was going to be incapacitated over this traditionally busy time she was happy to write her chapter then. She researched and wrote most of her chapter sitting up in her hospital bed and submitted it with a covering letter saying, "It was enormous fun and my knee is great, so it looks as if we can cancel the parrot."

Early in 1995 Richard Bates, producer of 'The Darling Buds of May' and many other popular television series, made a bid for the rights to a television series!

We knew that finishing the story would be tricky, but Ken Follett managed to tie up all the loose ends and write a conclusion that would satisfy the readers, the publisher, Sonia, Richard Bates, the DI and all the authors who had preceded him.

I want to thank them all. They were not only brave enough to take it on but gave so generously of their time and talent. I would also like to thank Stephanie Lloyd, who helped in so many ways, mostly by being at the end of a telephone with comforting words and reassurance whenever there was a crisis; Sonia Land, a very busy lady who gave a lot of time to the project and to me; Richard Bates for his invaluable advice; the DI for their unwavering faith in the book; Tim Stocker at P&O who has been so helpful in providing information on *Oriana*; Andrew Crofts who had the difficult job of editing the 'multicoloured' manuscript; and Studio Editions who finally pulled all the pieces together to publish this book.

Most important of all, thanks are due to everyone who has bought a copy of this book. While you enjoy reading it, spare a thought for those less fortunate than yourself who are unable to share the enjoyment. Every penny of royalties from this book will go towards helping dyslexic people, both children and adults, to read.

Sue Kilbracken, 1995

PLAN OF ORIANA

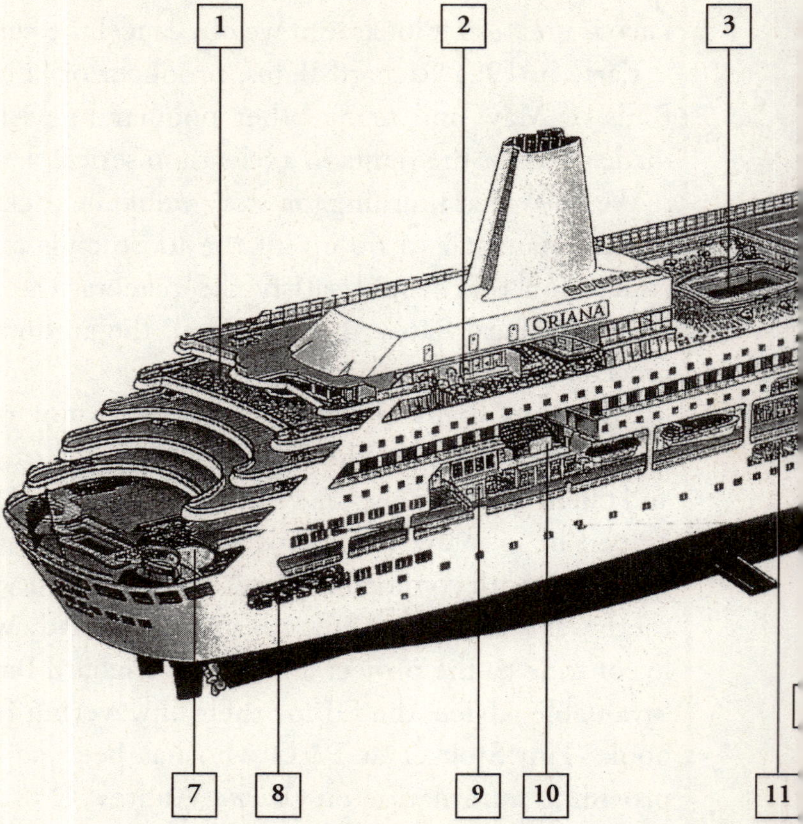

1 The Terrace Bar
2 The Conservatory
3 The Crystal Pool
4 The Riviera Pool
5 The Riviera Bar
6 The Crow's Nest
7 Pacific Lounge
8 The Oriental Restaurant
9 The Lord's Tavern
10 Chaplin Cinema

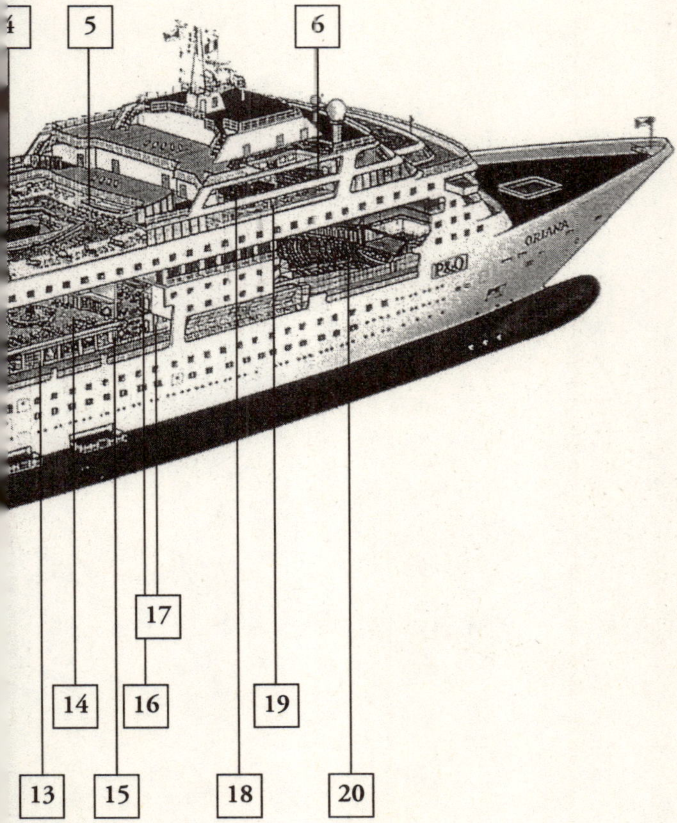

11 The Peninsula Restaurant
12 Harlequin's night club
13 Anderson's
14 Curzon Room
15 Monte Carlo Club
16 Tiffany Court and Bar
17 Royal Court
18 Iberia Room
19 Oasis
20 Theatre Royal

Courtesey of P&O

chapter ONE

"Of course I deserve to be castrated," said Simon, flicking a speck of toast from his crisp white shirt and pausing to examine his cuff-links as if he could not quite remember where he had seen them before. Brenda immediately felt an urge to grab the nearest knife. "Possibly," he drawled on, "I even deserve to be murdered. But I'm going to put everything right, and since I had the good sense to marry dear old you instead of some bimbo, I know you'll be relieved to hear that I've decided our marriage should continue – and don't think I don't intend to reward you for all your unswerving loyalty and devotion! I've got a wonderful treat lined up."

They were breakfasting in the kitchen of the London 'pied-à-terre' as Simon referred to it when he was with his constituents. Brenda thought of it as 'Simon's slum' and wished it was nearer Sloane Square and her favourite department store, Peter Jones. Dark and unloved, it was in an old-fashioned building five minutes from the Palace of

Westminster. At night the doom-laden chimes of Big Ben boomed through it like a death-knell – or so it had seemed to Brenda when she had lain awake worrying about how she would make ends meet if Simon abandoned her.

Simon was tall with eyes that were much too pale and the kind of hair that contrives to smother tell-tale flecks of silver beneath a mouse-brown sheen. He still had only one chin, although his fondness for nursery food, those English dishes which recalled boarding school at the height of the Empire, had not been beneficial to his silhouette. During the affair with Julia he had taken up squash in an attempt to burn up the flab, and Brenda had occasionally wondered if this violent exercise would result in him dropping dead, but he had survived. Worse still, he had even lost half a stone. Sometimes, after an encounter of her own with the bathroom scales, Brenda felt there was no justice of any kind in the world.

"I've planned a second honeymoon," he was announcing as she struggled to focus her mind on his revelation that the fruit of adultery was apparently to consist of a huge treat. "We'll be cruising."

Vague memories of articles on the gay scene surfaced at once to confuse her. "Cruising?"

"Yes, I thought we'd go on an Aegean cruise. Something very plush and up-market."

Brenda was now grappling with the horrific prospect of a second honeymoon. Surely she was dreaming?

"We'll take the girls away too, of course," he continued. "Say it's a reward for all the hard work they've been putting into their GCSEs. They'll love it."

"It all sounds very nice," she finally said, playing safe until she had time to analyse her options. "What a terrific treat!

I'm going to have a long bath and brood about what clothes I'll need."

She escaped from the kitchen to the hall. Scuffling noises beyond the closed door of the living room, where her twin daughters had spent the night on the sofa-bed, indicated that they had deviated from their holiday habit of sleeping till noon.

A quarter of an hour later, as she lay limply in the bath trying to avoid gazing at the roll of fat around her midriff, Brenda came to the reluctant conclusion that she had no choice but to go along with Simon's plan to junk Julia, appease his wife and ensure that he remained on course for a seat in the Cabinet. Julia had been another temporary blip in his great love affair with himself; in the end his ambition always ensured that self-interest triumphed over self-indulgence. And why did Brenda have to go along with his latest scheme? Because first and foremost, as she told herself, the twins were at a vulnerable age and their welfare had to come before hers. Second, she couldn't imagine being able to survive on her own when she had forgotten her secretarial skills and had no knowledge of word processors. She could not rely on financial support from Simon if she forced a divorce and wrecked his political future.

There was a third reason why she felt she had to humour Simon: she could not rid herself of the conviction that for a plain woman any marriage was better than none. Simon had long since convinced her of her inadequacy and lack of sexual attraction. If she lost him she would lose not only her home and her security but also her worth as a human being. The fact that Simon now wanted a reconciliation meant she had some worth at least. Without Simon she would have no worth at all as no man would ever want her again.

Outside the bathroom the telephone rang.

"Hello?" said Simon nervously, taking the call on the extension in the kitchen.

"Is that the Right Honourable Arch-Shit, Member of Parliament for –?"

Simon severed the connection and pushed the phone away from him as if it had suddenly transformed itself into a snake. Sweating lightly, he waited for Julia to ring again but nothing happened and after a while he regarded the silence as an omen, a hint that if he sat tight and kept calm everything would come right in the end.

Of course, he told himself as his self-confidence returned, Julia would get over being ditched. She would never go to the tabloids; she had to consider the welfare of her own high-profile career. He was absolutely safe, no question about it, but all the same . . . It was hard not to sweat with fright occasionally as he tiptoed around the abyss.

Simon began to think of the cruise. The trip lasted less than three weeks, which meant that it would probably end before he either went mad or suffered permanent liver damage. It was true that it was far more than he could afford, but he regarded it as an essential investment to safeguard his career.

"Are you sure it was her?" Sophie asked her twin sister.

"Oh yes," said Charlotte, who with an expertise born of long practice had picked up the receiver at exactly the right moment. "She called him the Right Honourable Arch-Shit."

"Wow, I can't wait for the double-page spread in the *Sun*!"

"Grow up, Soph. Would you really fancy being photographed by someone with a telescopic lens?"

"Do you suppose Dad's ever toe-sucked this woman?"

"Well, you can bet your bottom dollar he hasn't toe-sucked Mum. Why on earth doesn't she tell him to stuff his Greek treat and walk out, slamming the door?"

"This cruise could be just what we've been waiting for. God, if I don't lose my virginity before I'm seventeen, I'll kill myself. I don't know what's the matter with boys these days, all they want is to be friends! Why wasn't I born in those wonderful 1960s when everyone did it all the time and AIDS didn't exist? The nearest I ever get to an erotic thrill is watching someone put a condom over a banana in a sex-education class."

"Do you honestly think that once we get on board ship you'll be able to . . ." Sophie couldn't quite put it into words.

"I shall rise through the ranks and end up with the captain," Charlotte, who in some ways was very much her father's daughter, assured her.

"Wow!" said Sophie, reluctantly impressed by this rampant ambition. "Let's just hope there's no one with a telescopic lens on board . . ."

Julia Grant hurled her portable phone down on the scarlet sofa and looked around for something to smash, but since she had given up smoking there was not even an ashtray in sight in her bare, gleaming, modern Docklands flat. Julia believed in the minimalist approach to home furnishings because it cut down on the need for housework, a chore for which she had neither the time nor the inclination. She had tried employing cleaners but had abandoned them when they had done no work and drunk her gin. Cleaners, she had found, needed employers who could brew them tea and listen to their gossip.

Julia had no time for such things. She was the marketing director of a large independent television company; she earned a substantial salary. She had an accountant and a stockbroker. Her bank manager even knew her by name after she made a killing on the commodities market. (She had been sleeping with a City gentleman who shortly afterwards was arrested for insider dealing.) Her life was run with the maximum of emotional cost-cutting efficiency. Julia had a horror of emotional extravagance and took great pride in spurning such messy arrangements as marriage, motherhood and grand passion. Such hobbies were for unreconstructed females – poor creatures! – who led dull little lives. Thank God it was now quite impossible that she, at thirty-five, could ever sink to such a mundane level.

She had been introduced to Simon Daviot at a reception in the City. Simon thought she was stunning. He loved her independence, her insistence that she did not want to get emotionally involved, her emphasis on discretion, on emotional cost-cutting, on the necessity to keep one's public and private lives quite separate. As for Julia, she loved the world that he represented. She loved the excitement and eccentricity of life in the Palace of Westminster, the primitive thrill of being in touch with the centre of power.

Rather to her surprise she also found she liked Simon. She also admired him, but this wasn't unusual at all; Julia always admired men who wielded power and were overloaded with ambition. Wimps were for losers, not for Julia Grant; the last thing she wanted was a caring man who knew how to change a nappy. She wanted a daring man who knew how to make her happy – and happiness, for Julia, lay in participating vicariously in her lover's glamorous, macho, power-mad world.

Simon was fairly boring in bed, but that was all right, she didn't want Wonderman. Wonderman might have caused her to have an orgasm, and the one thing Julia feared was loss of control.

But now her job in television was beginning to bore her. She found she was becoming restless unless she got a regular fix of Simon's company. The strikingly minimalist flat began to seem very much less striking and much too minimal. Gradually she began to realize there was a void in her life that was demanding to be filled. She bought books on sex to try to improve her performance. She started to drink more. She even watched a pornographic video to see if it would ease the discomfort of Simon's many absences, but nothing filled the vacuum. Simon's mouse-brown hair and pale blue eyes were generating a longing that was becoming unbearable.

The climax of this devastating yearning came when she forgot to take one of her contraceptive pills. The amnesia shocked her, particularly when she found that a week later she had made the same mistake again. It was then that the truth finally dawned. She was desperate to be pregnant. She was craving to be with Simon all the time. She adored him, she worshipped him, she wanted nothing more from life than to be his perfect wife, his perfect parliamentary hostess and the perfect mother of his children. She saw herself in a smart little house in Lord North Street and in a country mansion – Dorneywood would do while they waited for Chequers – and in a multitude of glamorous locations with 'the people who mattered'. In short, she suddenly realized she had given birth to a thrilling vision, and she felt delirious with excitement.

"You're mad," said her brother Rupert, returning to England after a year in Australia and planting himself in her flat.

"No I'm not! Simon's going to marry me! It's my karma, my fate, my destiny – I tell you, I know this is going to work out! He'll ditch the drab wife very discreetly and continue on up the political ladder – it's been done before. The trick is to keep the adultery utterly under wraps and then after the divorce –"

"Christ, this is sheer fantasy! Wake up, girl! I bet you a fiver he leaves you flat."

Julia accepted the bet, but a week later Simon took her out to dinner at Chelsea Harbour and after two bottles of champagne he broke the news that he had decided to stay with his wife for the sake of the children. "Family values and all that . . ." He even had the gall to mention 'getting back to basics'. But he never once referred to his career.

Julia made a grand exit out of the restaurant, but was then sick in the gutter and had trouble finding a cab to take her home. When she finally arrived back at the flat, Rupert made black coffee and found a box of tissues to staunch the flood of tears.

At first she had no intention of begging Simon to change his mind, but she soon discovered that she was quite unable to let the matter rest. Her addiction to the power that Simon symbolized was too strong. She told herself that if she were to fight hard he might realize that he could not live without her. But Simon had reached the decision that at this point in his career he did not dare risk a divorce. He had also come to the conclusion that Julia was emotionally unstable and therefore thoroughly dangerous. Even if he did leave Brenda, he would never want to saddle himself with a woman like Julia who was hard to control.

"But Simon – darling –"

"It's over, Julia."

"But it can't be! We're made for each other! You can't possibly go back to Brenda now!"

"I've already done it," said Simon recklessly, and in his panic he then made a very unwise move. "We're taking the girls with us on a second honeymoon in August," he added at top speed. "We'll be sailing from Southampton on *Oriana* and heading for Greece!" Of course, as he contemplated later, he should never have disclosed all those details, but at that moment he was desperate to defuse Julia's fantasy.

"But Simon –"

He hung up. Julia stood listening to the empty line. Then at last she slowly replaced the receiver, turned to face Rupert, who was smoking pot and watching 'Neighbours' and said in her quietest, calmest voice: "The sod's taking his drab little wifey on a second honeymoon."

A shift had taken place in her consciousness. The fantasy had begun to fragment.

"My God," she heard herself say – her voice shaking with rage – "how dare he end it like this! And how dare he treat me like that! I want to bloody well disembowel him!"

"Hallelujah! You're finally getting angry. I've been afraid you were losing your marbles – all that sobbing and ranting and playing the tragedy queen."

"I'm going to make him pay! I'm going to make him wish he'd never been born! I'm going to –" She broke off as a brilliant idea exploded starrily in her brain.

The next day she went to the travel agent, and when she had obtained the P&O brochure she went straight to the section on summer cruises. There was only one that went to Greece during Parliament's summer recess. Back at the office she phoned Rupert, who was sipping Alka Seltzer and watching a morning chat-show.

"Do you still call yourself an actor?"

"What the hell do you mean? Of course I'm still an actor!"

"Okay, how would you like to play a young, handsome, virile television producer who's married radiant, sexy, dazzling me after a whirlwind courtship and is all set to sweep me off on an Aegean cruise?"

At noon Rupert decided he was no longer hung-over, and after making himself some coffee he went to the bathroom to check his looks. After five minutes of intense contemplation he decided that his designer stubble would have to go and that his pectoral muscles needed toning. He was keen not to let his physical appearance – his greatest asset – go to seed. He had now been in England for several weeks and depression was setting in. The episodes of the Australian soap opera in which he had played the part of the innocent young surfer had not yet been screened in England and no one knew him. He missed the recognition in pubs, he missed the Australian sunshine and the blissfully un-English way of life, and most of all he missed the groupies.

Having glanced at his clothes and recoiled, he began to wonder how much money Julia would give him to spend on acquiring the right designer casual-wear for the cruise. He did not like sponging off his sister, but there was no alternative. Julia had long ago appointed herself to be responsible for his welfare. He was seven years her junior and had been conceived in a last vain attempt by their parents to mend their marriage; his father had decamped soon afterwards to Canada where he had disappeared in order to avoid all claims for money and affection. Rupert's mother had accordingly been obliged to work, but the ordeal of retaining a full-time job while bringing up a family had taken its toll on her so that in the end it had been Julia who had cooked Rupert's meals, Julia who had seen he went to school in clean clothes, Julia who had taken part-time work from the age of fourteen and given him regular pocket-money. Finally their mother had managed to marry a man who got rid of Rupert by dispatching him to a minor public school and got rid of Julia by hitting her. Fortunately Julia had just graduated from university and she managed to get a good job. Rupert promptly dropped out of school and went to live with her. A year later their mother died. It was such a relief to know that they never needed to speak to their stepfather again.

Rupert started working as a television extra. He did wonder whether to take acting lessons, but decided against it. He felt it was a pity to waste his natural talent (so far untapped), but secretly he was afraid of applying to drama school and being rejected. Rupert was very afraid of receiving rejection of any kind. He wanted to be accepted, liked and loved – worshipped even – and the Australian groupies had given him a taste of paradise.

Julia had offered to pay for the drama lessons that were never taken. Julia had managed to get him bit-parts when he became bored with being an extra. And Julia had paid for him to go to Australia when he had declared that he would never get his big break in England and that Australian television was 'where it was all happening'. He had even been given the vital contact in Sydney as the result of Julia's efforts on his behalf, and certainly no one was happier than she was when he got the part of the innocent young surfer. By this time he had legally changed his name to Revell because he had felt that Grant was too ordinary, but he had kept his first name. Rupert liked being Rupert. It was the sort of name casting directors remembered. "RUPE, RUPE, RUPE!" chanted the groupies outside the studio. In ecstasy he told his sister he was now all set to live happily ever after.

"So what happened?" demanded Julia acidly when she phoned in response to his fax for the fare home.

Rupert could not quite bring himself to tell her what had happened, so he mumbled some glib story about how the new producer had taken a dislike to him. The money arrived from Julia but it was only enough to buy him the cheapest available seat on the plane. Meeting his flight at Heathrow he saw at once that she had decided to give him the coolest of receptions.

"I won't stay long, I promise," he said, but there was a note of uncertainty in his voice. "I just want an address to feed to the authorities so that I can get on the dole as quickly as possible."

He began to notice, with mounting horror, that the new man in his sister's life was no mere plaything but an idol who was inspiring her to seek immolation on the altar of marriage and motherhood. Rupert was appalled. He had taken it for granted that although lovers would come and go he would remain in Julia's life forever, but now he saw there was a real risk that he would lose that privileged position. Horrid memories surfaced, and he was just wondering if he could possibly hate anyone more than he now hated Julia's lover (whom he had yet to meet) when Julia stormed home from Chelsea Harbour with the miraculous news that the affair was over.

Rupert felt weak with relief, but the next morning he reached the conclusion that Julia was no longer to be trusted. If she had gone over the edge once she could do it again, and everyone knew nowadays that once a woman in her mid-thirties started to hear the biological clock ticking, she would stop at nothing until she had embraced motherhood hard enough to crush a rib. The time had obviously come for Rupert to make alternative plans for his nurture and support, but what was he to do? He only half believed that once his episodes of the soap were shown on English television they would generate any job offers. "The thing is," he said to himself as he surveyed the landscape of his unpromising future, "I'm terribly nice really." And he felt more convinced than ever that if he had a comfortable home with someone who was just as nice as he was he would be happiness personified. It would help if that person had enough money for them both to live on. The idea of going on an up-market cruise was growing on him.

A picture had drifted into his mind of a very tastefully rich woman, no longer young certainly, but by no means unacceptably old, who had a kind smile, a good sense of humour and a nice-natured personality, just like his, and she would be so absolutely delighted to have a well-spoken, well-dressed young man paying her such chivalrous attention that she would respond with great charm and – most important of all – generosity.

"Maybe you're right," he said meditatively at last to his sister. "Maybe the cruise is just what we both need . . ."

chapter TWO

Annie sat before the mirror. It had been a long time since she had really examined her reflection; two years in fact, ever since her beloved Lenny passed on.

The face that stared back at her was surprisingly pleasant. Though her long braided hair was now iron grey and her skin was sprinkled with fine lines, her heart-shaped face was still strikingly pretty and her large brown eyes still sparkled with vitality. She had a trim figure, full health and lately she was recovering a zest for life that would test a woman half her age.

As she sat there, her thoughtful gaze fell on a photograph standing in pride of place on the dressing-table; set in a plain wooden frame, it showed a couple in their youth. The tall dark-haired man was Annie's late husband. The young woman curved into his embrace was Annie herself. As she gazed at it, her smile deepened and the tears scalded her eyes.

Reaching out, she gently picked up the photograph and cradled it to her. "I miss you, sweetheart," she murmured, "more than you'll ever know." Closing her eyes she let the memories wash over her.

She talked with him a while telling him how she was going this very day to see his brother's children. "You'd be so proud of Mike," she said, "he has matured into a fine young man. Poor Chrissie could be such a beauty, but she seems to find life so difficult."

She let her gaze linger a moment longer on his face, then she replaced the photograph and began to delve about in the wardrobe. "Wear your best dress, Mike had said . . . but what? Shall I wear the blue skirt and waistcoat that Chrissie admired? Or should I wear that long grey dress with the lace neckline . . . that was your favourite, Lenny. Remember I wore it three years ago at your brother's sixtieth? Glancing at the photograph, she murmured fondly, "You were with me then . . . told me I was the loveliest creature there."

After almost emptying the wardrobe and trying on a dozen garments, she decided on a long wrap-around cream skirt, a white long-sleeved blouse with ruffles at the throat and cuffs, and a nutmeg-brown fringed gypsy waistcoat which Mike had bought her for Christmas. "I know how much you like unusual clothes," he'd told her, "and this is the same colour as your eyes." She remembered and smiled at the compliment.

An hour later she was ready. Her thick hair was woven into a broad plait which hung down her back to her waist; her cheekbones were lightly brushed with powder, and her round full lips touched with the palest pink lipstick. Her eyebrows and lashes, having retained their dark brown colour, needed no attention.

Going to the cupboard she scanned the lines of shoes and sandals that were neatly set out on the bottom racks. She settled for a pair of cream leather flatties with crossover straps and a pearl button to fasten. She was ready.

For the next ten minutes she busied herself about the house. She and Lenny had bought this house twenty-five years ago, moving into it when they returned from a wonderful honeymoon on the Isle of Wight. It had captured their hearts. "A perfect place to raise a family," Lenny had said. But the family never came and that was the only real regret Annie ever had. Still the house had been a haven for their love, a place where they could dream their dreams and grow old together. Now he was gone, leaving her to grow old alone, and she had spent the last two years immersed in her work.

The house had always been far too large for the two of them, but they could never bring themselves to leave it. Situated on the edge of the lovely village of Woburn Sands, and overlooking a vast expanse of woodland teeming with wildlife, it offered an oasis from a hectic world.

Here of a warm evening, Annie would sit in the conservatory and watch the deer roaming her garden. Playful squirrels ran up and down the trees and hedgehogs drank greedily from the saucers of milk that she always placed just outside the door; often, when she sat in the garden the birds would come and sit on the arm of her chair; no creature was ever afraid of her, she would give them all names and invent family histories for them, and eventually they would become characters in her children's books.

When it grew dark and the wildlife went away, Annie would turn on the television news and catch up on world events. Afterwards, she would read the daily newspapers from end to end, paying particular attention to any unsolved crimes and occasionally making notes in her little blue exercise books. Weeks, months or even years later when the culprit was eventually caught and the true facts reported, she would consult her notes to find that she had already solved the case. She was a bit of a Miss Marple with an eye for detail. “You’re a born detective,” Lenny used to tell her. She invariably pinpointed the killer ten minutes after a whodunnit had started on television.

Soon the house was in order and she was watching from the window for her nephew Mike. “Late again,” she mused aloud. “Been making rushed deliveries, I expect.” Mike had his own lorry and was fast on the way to building up a sound transport business.

Footloose and fancy free with no regular sweetheart, Mike still lived at home with his parents. It pleased Annie to know that as soon as the business was going well enough, Mike would be taking the house over from her so that she could move into something smaller. That way she would be secure in the knowledge that the home she and Lenny had created would go on being loved, and that she would still be able to visit whenever she wanted. Mike had said that he would pay her the market price but she had told him not to be so foolish, much better to use his money on other things. If he insisted on giving her something she would merely put it in the bank and it would come back to him whenever she passed on, along with the rest of her quite considerable estate. She worried about Chrissie, but felt sure Mike would take care of his sister if it proved necessary.

Mike cursed when the traffic lights turned red against him. The radio was playing a selection from years gone by. When the song began ‘That’ll be the day . . . when you make me cry . . .’ he turned the volume up, but not too much because he was in his precious black open-topped cabriolet and on a sultry evening such as this, the music tended to carry a long way, but there were no other cars in ear-shot. In a minute he was singing along, tapping his fingers against the wheel and closing his eyes as the lyrics carried him away.

The blue saloon turned the corner and quietly drove up to park behind him. The driver was a petite young woman in her early twenties with natural blonde hair and smiling green eyes. Wearing pale blue jeans and a white open-necked blouse, and with her long hair loose to her shoulders, she had a freshness about her that enhanced her childlike beauty.

At first her attention was drawn to the black open-topped car, a beautiful machine obviously much loved as the paintwork was gleaming and the chrome buffed to a mirror shine. Then, unable to resist looking at it just one more time, she picked up a typed document from the seat beside her. It was a contract, drawn up between her agent and P&O. For the next six months she would be singing to the passengers on board their newest luxury cruise ship. Delighted, she read it aloud . . . "Miss Roman Brindle . . . entertainer on board *Oriana*."

Strains of Buddy Holly's long-ago hit drifted towards her. She too had a weakness for songs from a bygone era and often used them in her act. Suddenly she was aware of a strong man's voice. Curious, she wound down her window and listened, a smile lighting her features when she saw how the driver in front was completely carried away by the music.

She guessed he was handsome from his dark, wavy hair and strong broad shoulders. "If I had time," she thought aloud, "I wouldn't mind getting to know you."

While she was wondering about him three things happened at once; the music changed to a classic rendering of Danny Boy, the lights changed to green and in that same minute Mike sensed that someone was watching him and turned round to look, his face, every bit as handsome as she had imagined, reflecting his acute embarrassment.

Smiling at him she shifted her car into gear and drew up alongside. "You've kept me entertained and it didn't cost me a penny," she said, laughing.

Mike laughed, too. "Didn't know you were watching," he admitted foolishly, "or I might have given a better performance."

"Next time we meet, I'll sing for you," she promised, pulling away.

"I'll hold you to that!" he yelled as her car gathered speed. "What's your name?" But she was gone, taking with her a slice of sunshine.

He was still thinking about her when he drew up outside Annie's house and she came out to meet him. "You look lovely as usual," he said, eyeing her up and down.

"Oh? And who was it said I was a frustrated hippie?"

"So you are!" he retorted.

"What kept you?"

"I'm sorry Annie," he apologized, "I had to make a late delivery."

Annie told him not to worry. In less than no time she was seated beside him. "I don't suppose you'd let me drive?" she asked wistfully.

He regarded her for a moment, a twinkle in his dark eyes. "Can I trust you not to go too fast?"

"No."

"Oh go on then!" he said.

Excited, she settled herself into the driver's seat. "Which direction?"

"Keep going straight until I tell you different."

"You still haven't told me where we're going," she reminded him.

"With your razor-sharp mind, I'm astonished you haven't already figured it out."

Grimacing, she suggested, "I believe I do have an idea of what you're planning but I wouldn't want to spoil it by making guesses."

"Go on. Let's see what you've come up with."

"Are you sure?"

"Can't wait!"

"All right." She concentrated on the few clues she had picked up over the last few weeks, ever since Mike said he was planning something special for her birthday. "I know you've been arranging something very special . . . and I know Chrissie is in on it."

"That's the easy bit. Go on."

"It can't be a day out because it's already half-past eight in the evening. It isn't a theatre or film because you know I can't sit still long enough to enjoy either."

"Very perceptive. Go on."

"It isn't bingo, or whist, because you couldn't sit still long enough for either. She grinned at him. "It's dinner!" Her pretty brown eyes lit up, "You devil, you're taking me out to dinner!"

"Nope."

Her smile fell. "Oh, how very disappointing."

The next few minutes were spent in silence, with Mike stealing a fond look at her and thinking how attractive she was. She was a one-off, an eccentric woman with unusual tastes. She looked years younger than her age apart from her grey hair. Annie never failed to amaze him. But then she was an amazing person, sharp-witted and observant, and with her infectious sense of humour she made wonderful company.

They drove in companionable silence and Mike's thoughts drifted back to the young woman he had met at the traffic-lights and the promise she had made . . . "Next time we meet, I'll sing for you" she had said, and he wondered if he would ever see her again. He hoped so. Oh, he hoped so!

Pointing to a filter road coming up on the left hand side, he instructed, "Turn off here then follow the road round to the right."

"Ah! We're making for the embankment then."

"Just follow the road, Annie."

As they came round to the main street he told her to turn down the embankment and then swing immediately left. "You might as well know we're going to the Swan Hotel," he revealed. "But that's all I'm saying. So you'll have to be patient until we get inside."

As they pulled up in the car park she put the vehicle out of gear and switched off the engine. With a coy look and a feigned shyness she exclaimed, "Oh Mike! Don't tell me you've planned a naughty weekend?"

Laughing aloud he shook his head at her antics. "Whoever said you were fifty-five years old," he remarked with disbelief, "they obviously don't know you."

As they opened the door to the dining room, the head waiter rushed forward. "Do you have a booking?" he enquired. The dining room was full and although he appeared composed, the beads of sweat on his forehead told another tale.

Mike assured him, “It’s a private party . . . booked under the name of Michael Young.”

The thin bony face expanded into a wan smile. “Of course.” Inclining his head, he gestured to the far end of the room, away from the diners, “This way if you please.”

As they made their way across the room, the luscious red carpet sank beneath their feet. The room was tastefully furnished right down to the very last detail; round tables dressed with pink undercloths and lacy tops; high-backed mahogany chairs with plush tapestry seats; expensive chandeliers and softly lit wall-lights; long polished dressers filled to bursting with silver trays and china tureens, each containing beautifully prepared salads and meats, and every wall lined with wonderful paintings.

Annie was impressed. “You have good taste, I’ll say that for you,” she told Mike in a soft voice.

“And you’re in for the best evening you’ve had in a long time,” he promised.

Mike was as good as his word. The other room was full of Annie’s friends and relatives. When Mike and Annie walked in everyone stood up and sang ‘Happy Birthday’. Hearing his cue, the waiter wheeled in the most beautiful birthday cake Annie had ever seen and all around her myriads of brightly coloured balloons floated to the floor.

“Oh Mike, this is a wonderful surprise!” Annie’s brown eyes shone with delight. Everyone gathered round hugging and kissing and she felt very special.

The evening sped by. The food was splendid; the music played gently in the background; they danced a little and Annie shared herself between them all. During a quiet moment, she sat herself beside Chrissie. “You don’t appear to be enjoying yourself,” she observed.

"It's your birthday, not mine," came the surly reply.

Used to Chrissie's abrupt manner Annie made no response. Instead she quietly regarded this petulant young lady, wondering how brother and sister could be so alike in looks yet so different in nature. Chrissie had large coal-dark eyes and long thick hair that was so black it shone blue in the soft light. Stunningly beautiful, she was tall and slim, with a figure that would grace any catwalk. Yet her nature was miserable. Arrogant and ungracious, she never had a good word to say about anyone.

Annie couldn't help but think how much more lovely Chrissie would be if that full sulking mouth was upturned in a smile. "Something's bothering you," she said softly, "do you want to talk about it?"

"No. You'd only say I told you so."

"I would never say that and you know it."

For the first time during the conversation Chrissie looked up, her dark eyes swimming with tears. "No, I suppose you wouldn't," she admitted grudgingly. "But I still don't want to talk about it."

She eyed Annie with blatant curiosity, thinking as she always did that here was a middle-aged woman who never let anything destroy her; not the disappointment of never having children, nor the death of her beloved husband Lenny. Chrissie envied her. She envied Annie's ability to look wonderful in clothes that might have better suited a Romany, she envied her calm nature and caring character. She envied her analytical mind, the way she took life in her stride and seemed always to be in charge. She envied the fact that her children's books were so successful when they seemed to Chrissie to be so simple minded and sickly. Most of all, she envied the fact that Annie was fifty-five years old with a thirst for life and an energy that shone out of her. It wasn't fair! Nothing was fair.

Later, when the dining room outside had emptied for the night, Annie thanked them all for such a wonderful evening. "One I won't forget in a hurry," she confessed.

"It isn't over yet," Mike said. Reaching into his jacket pocket he drew out a long white envelope. "For my favourite aunt," he said, handing it to her.

While Annie tore open the envelope she glanced up at the faces around her. They were all smiling, with the exception of Chrissie, who was lost in her own thoughts.

As she stared at the ticket, Annie could hardly believe it. "A cruise!" Open-mouthed she looked at Mike. "I've never been on a cruise before."

"Well, you're going on one now sweetheart," he told her with a grin. "The day after tomorrow you board *Oriana* at Southampton. From there you'll sail to Greece and Turkey . . . and . . ."

Springing out of her chair Annie threw her arms round his neck."I can't believe it!" she cried. She hugged everyone in turn and then she accused Mike, "You're trying to get rid of me, is that it? You want the nosey old crow out of the way for a few weeks."

"Chrissie and I are going with you," Mike grinned.

Annie swung round to Chrissie. "Is that true? Are you really coming with me?" Chrissie gave a sullen shrug and walked off.

chapter THREE

Sandra Van Horn was flicking through a pile of travel brochures in her forty-second floor triplex in mid-town Manhattan as she planned her summer schedule. She had already booked her suite on the QE2 and at the Savoy. There would be two weeks of hard, wise buying in London – all the leading galleries and auction houses had been contacted – and then a little relaxation, she thought, would be in order.

Sandra was a collector. Any beautiful object gave her a pleasure that was almost physical in its intensity. Her homes in Acapulco and Palm Beach were tributes to her excellent taste and her knowledge of the art world; she regarded these mansions as temples dedicated to beauty, and she visited them regularly to worship. The remainder of the year was spent travelling around the world and acquiring new objects to satisfy her desires.

After her second husband had been killed in his private plane, Sandra had vowed never to travel by air again, and although travel by sea had its restrictions, the comfort and luxury more than made up for them.

Sandra wrote some dates on her monogrammed Tiffany notepad before pausing to examine her calendar and make new calculations. She would cruise the fjords in June. On her return to Britain she could spend time, as she had promised she would, with some friends who had an estate in Scotland. A week would be more than enough, she thought, and then . . . and then, exhausted by the sight of falling rain, she would be hankering for warm clear skies. She was due in Istanbul in mid-August to inspect a collection of Russian icons, but how could she pass the intervening days? She picked up one of the P&O brochures and began to glance at the various cruises on offer.

Her first marriage had lasted less than six months and now she never thought of it. Indeed she had no idea whether he was still alive. Her second marriage had fared better, and ten years had passed before it had ended in tragedy; not only her husband had been killed in the crash but also her only child, the son of her first marriage. After the boy's father had revealed himself in his true colours it had taken her a long time to trust another man, and during this lengthy interval between marriages she had lavished all her love on her son who, if he had lived, would now have been twenty-six. How amazing to think of Jeffrey heading for thirty! It hardly seemed possible that she could be old enough to have a son of that age, but she had married at twenty-one and Jeffrey had been born eleven months later. He himself had been eighteen when he had been killed, and she could still see him so clearly in her memory: tall, slim, athletic, charming.

The telephone rang. It was Warren, her trusted 'walker', whom she had known for some years and who was, she considered, the perfect escort: wealthy enough not to be interested in her money, well-behaved, well-dressed, intelligent, civilized and homosexual. He was calling to confirm the details of their next visit to the theatre.

"And I thought that for dinner after we could go to . . ."

She listened to him and thought how restful he was, guaranteed never to overstep the line, never to involve her in any of the emotions she so feared. After Jeffrey was killed she had decided it was safer not to worship people. Much wiser instead to worship objects that could be arranged, controlled and if necessary preserved under glass cases.

". . . and of course it entirely depends on what you want to do, Sandi dear, and you know I'll fall in with your wishes . . ." Warren droned on, so pleasant, so restful, so eager to please, but she had trouble concentrating on what he was saying.

"Sandi darling, are you still there? Why the deep silence?"

"Sorry, I was just thinking of the theatre and wondering what'll be playing in London when I get there. Warren, I guess you wouldn't be interested in another trip to the Norwegian fjords in June?"

"Honey, I'd love it but I'm one hundred per cent committed to going to my mother's ninetieth birthday in Chicago, and –"

"Oh sure, I'd forgotten. Okay, how about July or August and the Aegean? It'll be hot, of course, but if we're cruising at least we can look forward to some sea breezes."

"P&O?"

"Of course." She read him the itinerary of the cruise.

"I'm gob-smacked!" screamed Jazzy down the phone to her very, very best friend Lisa. "My dream's come true! I've won a bloody cruise in a soddin' raffle!"

"My Gawd!"

"And since it's for two, you've got to come with me! Please, please, pretty please!"

"What about Den?"

"I'm not telling him," Jasmin giggled nervously, "I fancy just disappearing for a few weeks. Give him a chance to see how much he'd miss me."

"Are you sure, Babes?" Lisa was doubtful. Last time her friend had gone out without telling her lover she had ended up with a broken arm, and that was only for one evening. God knows what he would do if he found out she had gone on a cruise.

"Don't let's think about it," Jasmin said firmly. "I'm fed up with the whole thing; telling lies for him; the police knocking us up in the middle of the night, it's making me ill." She paused to compose herself, "And anyway, I want to be with you. We will have so much fun!"

"You're the best friend a girl ever had, Jazzy! Where are we going?"

"The Eye-Jan. A-E-G-E-A-N."

"Where's that?"

"Somewhere in Greece, I think. I haven't got a brochure yet, let's just start dieting right away so that we can have the biggest blow-out of all time as soon as we step on board!"

"What else happens on cruises apart from food?"

"Oh, it's all boozing and sex, of course, everyone knows that. There'll be loads of furry chests on board, Lisa. It'll be a sex-buffet-de-lux, a banquet, a –"

"Wowee! I'm having an orgasm just thinking about it."

"And the really nice thing about this cruise," said Rosamund to her mother during their weekly afternoon drive, "is that one's bound to meet such cultured, interesting people. They've invited Patrick to be a guest lecturer. Aren't we lucky!"

They were just approaching Sunnyfields sheltered housing development after a pleasant drive through the villages surrounding Cambridge when old Mrs Barlow suddenly chose to demonstrate that tact was no longer her forte. "You ought to put your name down for a flat here yourself," she told her daughter. "After all, you're over sixty now. Patrick will probably drop dead in his seventies, and you won't want to go on living in that big house on your own."

"We'll cross those bridges when we come to them, shall we?" Rosamund said jauntily.

Rosamund did not care to think of her own old age. In her mind's eye she saw herself as perpetually thirty-two, pretty and well-dressed, with a good looking, brilliantly clever husband and two happy and well-adjusted children. Of course she was aware of the fact that her children had long since grown up and that her husband was now white-haired, but she herself, lucky as ever, had seemed miraculously untouched by the passing years.

"Had a nice outing?" Patrick asked when she arrived home and peeped into his study to enquire if he wanted tea. He was laying out his collection of statuettes, trying to decide which ones to take with him on the cruise. He was very proud of them all and was loath to leave any behind. They were all perfect fibreglass reproductions that he had had made for him through his contacts in the museums of the world.

"Oh yes, we had a wonderful time, Mother was in great form," said Rosamund automatically. She glimpsed a yellow folder of photographs on his desk. "What are these?"

"Camilla dropped them in when you were out. They're the pictures of Poppy's sixteenth birthday party."

Patrick had been a professor of Byzantine Studies at the University and, since his retirement, he had been busy working on a book about the Empress Eudoxia's volatile relationship with St John Chrysostom. That afternoon he had resumed planning his talks for the cruise; the notes for a jolly little populist chat about Delphi were now on paper, and he was feeling intensely pleased with himself, a familiar feeling to Patrick.

Rosamund took the photos from the folder and sat down on the chair by Patrick's desk.

She looked at Poppy, so young, so pretty, so unlined, so slim-waisted, and suddenly the envy was so excruciating that she wanted to vomit. A voice in Rosamund's head shouted: "Sixteen years old!" And she knew that she hadn't been thirty-two for nearly three decades. Nor was she unlined and slim-waisted. She was an old age pensioner with bags under her eyes and no waist and hair that was dyed brown.

Aloud she said: "But I'm so lucky. I've got everything I could possibly want – a perfect home, a wonderful husband and family, a peaceful way of life . . ." But at that point in the familiar recital she broke off. What was so wonderful about her life nowadays? She went to coffee-parties and the occasional lecture, and she attended tapestry classes once a week and she did meals-on-wheels and she took her mother for drives – but she was just marking time, she could see that now, just filling the gaps until Patrick dropped dead in his seventies and Camilla eased her into Sunnyfields as tactfully as Rosamund herself had eased old Mrs Barlow in there two years ago. "No," Rosamund heard herself whisper, appalled. "No." And the next moment she burst noisily into tears.

"Hey, steady on old girl . . ." Patrick, unable to follow her train of thought and terrified of unrestrained emotion, gazed at her in horror. He was not uncaring. He was deeply upset, but women were such a strange species that he genuinely had no idea what he could do to help. Surely women weren't supposed to get hysterical once they were past that menopause-thing. "What on earth's the matter?" he said.

Rosamund grabbed the paperweight from his desk, hurled it at the nearest wall and stormed sobbing from the room.

Patrick decided that his best way forward was to adopt a policy of masterly inactivity. He had complete faith that Rosamund would soon be her sunny-natured self again, anxious to give thanks for their many blessings. All he had to do was wait. To pass the time he re-examined the photos to see if there was some vital clue he had missed, but he saw merely snapshot after snapshot of appallingly dressed teenagers having what appeared to be wholly innocent fun.

However, his glance did linger on the final photo in which there were two faces he had not expected to see. They belonged to the twin daughters of that MP fellow, the nasty right-winger who wanted the return of flogging and hanging – and had even mentioned the desirability of making adultery a criminal offence. Patrick, who was a devout old-fashioned liberal of the 1960s variety, took a dim view of Simon Daviot and was glad his constituency was some way from Cambridge.

Those twins were pretty little moppets, he could see that, but Patrick was more interested in their young male companions. His fondness for nubile male beauty was a penchant which he had always regarded as completely normal even though he had never mentioned it to a living soul. His desires had never been consummated. In his youth he had been afraid that any indiscretion would eventually be reported to his father, a conservative bishop who took a hard line on sin of any kind, and even after the old man died, the terror of being found out by the University authorities had remained with Patrick to ensure his fidelity to Rosamund.

Sighing, just as he always did when he thought of luscious young men perpetually beyond his reach, he slipped the photographs back into their folder.

Hilary Brown read the letter from her old school friend, Rosamund, for a second time. It was nine-thirty in the morning and her mail had already been divided into folders for her by Kitty, her secretary of over twenty years. Kitty placed all the bills, receipts, bank statements, appeals, royalty statements, insurance and pension details in the folder marked 'Finance'. She could cope with them all perfectly well herself but Hilary Brown always liked to have a glance at things before they were filed.

Then there was a file labelled 'Media'. This included cuttings and reviews and requests for interviews. There was the large file of problem letters to be answered. These would be dealt with mainly by Kitty and her assistants, but again Hilary liked to see the letters first.

There was a smaller file marked 'Personal'. This was where she had found the two closely written pages from Rosamund. The letter seemed quite casual and light but there was a shorthand between those who had soldiered together at Lady Harriet's for so many years. And anyway, it was her business to read between the lines. Hilary Brown, psychologist, long-standing Agony Aunt to the nation, could recognize a cry for help even if it was disguised as a brave little whimper.

Rosamund said she didn't want to impose on Hilary, who she knew was so frightfully busy, but she would be coming to London soon to buy clothes for this simply super Greek island cruise she was going on and would there be a minute or two to have tea and tiny sandwiches somewhere that still did nice teas?

Hilary had a series of rules that she lived by. These rules had made her one of the most successful columnists and business women of her generation. One of them said that if anything was worrying you, instead of brooding about it and wasting quality time that could be spent on something better . . . act at once. She flicked open her desk organizer; names, addresses, postal codes, phone and fax numbers, all immaculately coded in exact alphabetical and numerical order. She found the name and dialled the number. Patrick came to the telephone eventually.

"Hilary my dear," he boomed. He didn't even remotely like her, but Hilary did not object to his false enthusiasm. It was part of good manners. She used the technique herself. Patrick said that he hadn't a clue where Rosamund was . . . and then lowered his voice confidentially and said, truth to tell, his wife seemed not to be her usual self. "I'll tell the old girl to give you a ring, right?"

"Yes, tell the Old Girl that," Hilary retorted.

Something in her tone brought Patrick up short. "Sorry Hilary, what did you say?" he asked.

"What you've always been saying about Rosamund, 'Old Girl', it's what you call her. It's what we are, isn't it?"

"Well yes, no, not old, I mean in terms of age . . ."

"Bye Patrick," Hilary said and put the phone down. She sat for a moment breathing deeply. How she hated that stupid old man. He might be a brilliant professor but he had no idea about people and life. He had completely ruined Rosamund's life and had no idea that he had done it. She had been such a lively spirit at school, the one who everyone thought would do the most and go the farthest in the world, and within a few years of marriage Patrick had reduced her to a shell of her former self, a mere convenience, there to serve and provide him with the back-up he needed to shine in the University spotlight. So many times Hilary had imagined how Rosamund would benefit from an early widowhood, but it wasn't something she could ever say to her friend. Rosamund was far too loyal for any of that sort of talk.

Rosamund didn't call back until late that evening. "Hilary?"

"Rosamund?"

"You were asleep?"

"No I wasn't, as it happens."

"Hilary," Rosamund blurted out, "could I come and stay for a few days?" Hilary let the pause last too long and Rosamund began to backtrack. "I mean, of course, of course I can stay in a hotel. What I meant was . . ." She hadn't an ounce of self-confidence left.

"Darling Rosamund, of course you're going to stay here. Didn't Patrick tell you, that's what I rang to say this morning?"

"No he didn't . . ." Everything was going to be all right. Hilary reached for her glasses and her Filofax.

When they had sorted out their dates and Hilary had hung up on her pathetically grateful old friend, she got to thinking. The idea of a cruise to the Greek islands seemed rather attractive. She needed a break and it would be fun to spend some time with Rosamund after all these years. She felt that her friend needed her. There must be something she could do to help her throw off the burdensome yoke of marriage. They had known each other for nearly half a century, it would be good to take a break from her usual hectic schedule and reflect on the way her own life had gone. By the time she fell asleep the decision was made. She, too, was going cruising, and something had to be done about Professor Patrick Westcott.

chapter FOUR

Mike was on time. At exactly twenty minutes to seven he arrived in bright sunshine. "What a day!" he exclaimed, collecting Annie's suitcases. "If it's like this throughout our cruise you won't find me complaining."

"Where's Chrissie?" Annie asked.

"She's making her own way to the ship."

Annie decided not to pursue that topic; she would just have to wait and see what happened.

"It's best to leave early," he remarked as he packed her cases into the boot. "The motorway can be murder later on." Dressed for comfort he cut a fine figure in brown cords and a casual open-necked shirt. Though used to rising early, he still had that sleepy kid look about him and his dark wavy hair seemed more unruly than usual. "Had a bad night," he said, running his hands through his hair when he caught Annie quietly smiling.

She climbed in beside him. "I expect you're excited like me," she said, "though, being a man, you'd never admit it."

As they made their way along the lanes to the junction they chatted about the forthcoming holiday. “You’re right,” he admitted, “I am excited. You’re not the only one who’s never been on a cruise.”

Just as he predicted the traffic was not too heavy on the motorway, although a chauffeured Daimler Sovereign almost collided with them when it pulled in sharply at the Toddington intersection.

“Bloody fool!” Only by using his sharp-witted driving skill did Mike avoid hitting the other car broadside.

Enraged, Annie shook her fist at the sour-faced driver and found herself looking at an equally sour-faced passenger. Seated in the back beside a mousey little woman, the man bore the stamp of privileged authority. Dressed in a dark jacket and sober tie he was sitting bolt upright staring at her through angry pale blue eyes. He looked so stiff and hostile that Annie actually burst out laughing. “He looks like one of those dummies in a shop window,” she chuckled. It was funny though, she had the feeling she had seen the man before.

“I know who that was,” Annie said a few moments later. “His name’s Simon Daviot.”

“What? The politician?”

“The same.”

“Not of your political persuasion, eh?”

“Not bloody likely!” She had seen him on a number of interviews. “Arrogant bloke . . . talks out of his arse.”

Mike laughed. “I’m not sure I should be travelling with a woman who swears like a navvy.”

Annie laughed too. “I forgot myself, that’s all,” she said. “I promise I won’t do it again. As long as I don’t clap eyes on Simon Daviot again!”

They drove happily on to Southampton, both chattering with excitement about the adventures that lay ahead.

"Oh, Mike!" Annie's attention was drawn to the cruise liner as they drove into the docks. "Is that *Oriana*?"

Mike's dark eyes followed her gaze. "It is!" he exclaimed. "Look . . . there's the name on the side." A tractor and container had been blocking the nameplate but now it was in full view. "Isn't she beautiful!"

On board, *Oriana* was everything Annie had hoped. The sheer size of the ship was overwhelming. She smelt of polish and sea-breezes, the brassware shone so that you could see your face in it, and everywhere was sparkling clean. The crew were smartly turned out and each wore a bright welcoming smile.

There were lifts and shops and hundreds of people milling about. It was like a beautiful, dazzling, floating city. "I can't believe it!" Annie breathed.

They were greeted by a member of the entertainment staff, and cabins were assigned to them. They each had their photograph taken, "To keep as souvenirs," they were told, and finally they were shown to their cabins where their cabin stewards introduced themselves.

Annie, Mike and Chrissie had identical cabins right next door to one another. Each had a double bed, wardrobe, dressing table and cupboards, all in polished mahogany. They had private baths, mini-fridges, lounge areas and a large window through which Annie could watch the world go by. "It's wonderful!" she told Mike when he came to see if she was all right. "I'm so excited I can't keep still."

"It's some ship!" Mike agreed. "I could get used to this life."

"It must have cost you a fortune."

"None of your business," Mike grinned, "and anyway, you deserve it."

"I just hope you haven't taken money out of your business to pay for it."

He kissed the top of her head. "Don't worry," he said, "the business is doing just fine."

"Has Chrissie turned up?"

"Not yet," he shrugged and Annie bit her tongue before she said any more. She just hoped that Chrissie wasn't going to spoil the whole trip for them.

The two of them went to watch the luggage come aboard. Fascinated, Annie's brown eyes roved the quay, her inquisitive gaze scanned the faces there; people who were leaving, people who were staying, others who had come to watch the cruise ship sail away and those who had come to wave goodbye to loved ones. Every face told a story and Annie was in her element.

Taking out a blue exercise book from her capacious handbag, she began making notes. When she next raised her eyes it was to see the same Daimler Sovereign she had seen before draw in beside the ship and Simon Daviot step out of it. "Good God!" Turning to Mike she realized that he too had seen the new arrival.

"Looks like we're stuck with him whether we like it or not," he remarked ruefully.

"Never mind," Annie said bravely, "it's a big ship, perhaps our paths won't cross."

Not too far away in the Theatre Royal, Roman Brindle was going through her score. The pianist thought he had never heard such a strong and lovely voice, as she sang one song after another. He couldn't know that she was thinking of a certain dark-haired young man in an open-topped car, a man she thought she would never see again. The regret she felt emerged in her voice, giving it a soulful depth.

Alone in her cabin Annie hung up her clothes and prepared to meet Mike in fifteen minutes. She had left the door open and heard the sound of two people quarrelling. Peeping out she saw the man was Simon Daviot, but the woman was not the same one who had accompanied him in the car. She was younger, thirty-four or thirty-five, attractive, and forceful. The row was short but fierce. “I’ve a feeling this cruise is going to be the highlight of my life,” Annie whispered as she closed the door and with a smile made a hasty entry into her blue exercise book. ‘. . . Saw Simon Daviot again. He was arguing with a young woman whom he called Julia . . . and there was murder in the eyes of both of them.’

A gentle breeze touched the glistening surface of Southampton Water as the great ship moved sedately and almost silently out towards the open sea. Captain Richard Moore stood on the bridge enjoying the panorama of pleasurecraft, dinghies and yachts. As always, the sight filled him with a deep sense of both pleasure and pride and he allowed himself a small smile of satisfaction that he was in command of this most magnificent of cruise ships for the next two weeks.

For the first few days of the cruise Captain Moore was amazed by the smoothness with which the trip was going. The Bay of Biscay had been so tranquil he hadn’t even had to use *Oriana*’s massive stabilizing fins to ensure a smooth crossing. The passengers had become used to the sight, smell and swell of the ocean and had started to mix and relax as Lisbon, lying on the seven low hills at the estuary of the majestic River Tagus, had slid past.

"It's almost eerie," he confided to his staff captain.

"What is, sir?"

"Absolutely nothing has gone wrong. Seventeen hundred passengers, all thrown together, and no major problems. It seems almost unnatural."

"Long may it last, sir," the staff captain said, puzzled by the captain's words.

"Yes, indeed." Captain Moore pulled himself back from his thoughts. He was just being foolish, why shouldn't everything be going smoothly?

"May I?" So engrossed was Julia with her own thoughts that she had not noticed the approach of the tall, broad-shouldered man who was now standing at her table. She looked up and for one awful instant thought it was Simon Daviot. But it wasn't, thank God! She relaxed and managed to produce a brief smile. The man was carrying a glass of orange juice and pointing to one of the empty chairs at her table as, almost apologetically, he added, "I hope you don't mind, the other seats are all taken."

Wondering how she had not sensed his arrival, she nodded her consent and he eased the plush blue chair into a position so that he could use it. A big man, he needed plenty of space.

"The place is full, they've all come in here to cheer us into Ayios Nikolaos." His voice was deep and pleasant with just a hint of a Northumbrian accent. Julia also noticed the softness about his eyes which suggested calmness and contentment, but those same eyes bore just a hint of sadness. Some recent trauma perhaps? In his mid to late fifties, his hair was black and thick with just a hint of grey in places and not a sign of baldness, while his face was tanned and lean. Grey eyes without spectacles, clean shaven, good teeth – she was mentally assessing this newcomer who was casually but well dressed in a light blue shirt and pale beige chinos. A fit man. An interesting man. A man she'd not seen before; five days at sea and their paths had never crossed!

This morning they were in the Crow's Nest, staring out across the ocean while *Oriana* glided gracefully towards Crete and the clear blue waters of the Aegean glistened in the brilliant sunlight. In the distance, the square white buildings and red roofs of Ayios Nikolaos crowded onto a small hill which rose above a pale and sandy beach.

"You're not going to cheer us in?" The man had settled on the chair now.

"No," she shook her head. "No, I thought I wouldn't."

She did not offer any further explanation. She couldn't say she was sitting this one out because she was avoiding the Daviots. That's why she had selected this table. It was nicely out of the way but did offer a view of the entrance and of any incoming passengers. Simon Daviot was easy to spot, even in a crowd – at a distance, his height enabled her to see him long before he was likely to notice her and so, by remaining alert and secretive, she had managed to avoid him in Anderson's, in the Oriental Restaurant, the Conservatory and even in the crowded bar of the Lord's Tavern.

Ever since *Oriana* slipped out of Southampton Julia had been plotting and planning her revenge. She had staked out every area of the ship, so that she knew exactly how to make a quick getaway once she had decided how and when to strike. Her main problem now was her brother Rupert, who seemed completely unable to keep his mind on the assignment at hand. It was very irritating indeed to have your younger brother giving the impression that he was indulging you in a fantasy he himself actually found rather infantile. It was even more irritating when that brother was running up large bar bills at your expense and chatting up some sullen young woman he had taken a fancy to.

Julia was convinced that neither Simon nor Brenda had any idea she was on board, and for these few moments, therefore, she was relaxing with a cool drink, quite alone, quite content and quite prepared to miss the thrill of observing their entrance into the harbour at Ayios Nikolaos.

The arrival of this man had flustered her more than she liked to be flustered. She had been so lost in her own world of plans and vengeful thoughts that she found it hard to change gear and make polite conversation with a stranger, particularly an attractive one. Whenever anyone else had tried to strike up a conversation with her she had announced she had to go and meet her 'husband', but for some reason she didn't want to tell this man that she was married.

"And you? You're not watching her disgorge all these people into Greece?"

He shrugged his shoulders. "I've been before," he said. "We used to come here for our holidays . . . I've seen it many times – mind, it's always pleasant to come back."

"We?" She had picked up on his reference to someone else.

"My wife," he spoke gently. "Gwen. She loved Greece, but she died eighteen months ago. The family bought me this cruise as a present, they said I should get away for a while, be alone away from family and relations and unhappy memories. We were happy here, so it'll be strange, visiting our favourite places by myself . . ."

"I'm sorry . . ." her voice trailed away.

"Don't be." He smiled at her discomfort. "I'm Adrian Clarke." He held out a hand for her to shake.

She liked his old-fashioned courtesy and politeness, so rare in her world. This man was different, a man nonetheless but courteous and confident and gentle. She took his hand; he had a very firm grip.

"Julia Grant, I'm alone too." There, she'd said it. She'd dismissed Rupert in two seconds flat and endangered her whole mission. But she knew she would have to account for him if he turned up – and he was quite liable to suddenly appear. If Rupert saw Julia with another man he might go all protective and act the part of the jealous husband.

"Actually, I'm not entirely alone, my brother is on board, too. He's chasing every piece of skirt he can find. He's an actor – you can't take him seriously, so if he comes to meet you, well, just take everything he says and does with a pinch of the proverbial salt. Sometimes I wonder if he can tell the real world from the make- believe."

He nodded, although he had no idea what she was talking about. "What made you choose this cruise?" he asked, making polite conversation.

"I just wanted a break from my job. It was an impulse decision – and I'm enjoying it. I like the luxury of not having to worry about work every morning."

As Adrian seemed to know the island very well, Julia was about to ask his advice about which of the organized trips to take from Ayios Nikolaos or whether to avoid them altogether, when a middle-aged woman appeared and practically demanded, "Is that chair taken?"

Clarke, instinctively rising to his feet in the presence of a woman, sought some reaction from Julia. After all, it was her table, she had claimed it first, but she said, "Er, no. Help yourself."

"I've been standing over there, watching the island getting nearer and nearer but it's my legs, I'm not as young as I was you see, not as young as I'd like to be, so I just had to have a sit down . . . every seat's taken, do forgive me, I do hate intruding on couples . . ." She plonked her drink on to the table.

Clarke chuckled. "We're not a couple, I've just done the same as you."

"Oh," she looked at the interesting man and then at the attractive woman. "Oh. Well, so long as I'm not a nuisance." And she settled in one of the empty chairs at their table. Clarke then sat down again. Julia smiled to herself; it was years since she'd seen this kind of courtesy in a man. She guessed Clarke would hold doors open for ladies, stand up in crowded tubes to offer his seat . . . but he was no wimp, not with that deep voice and those wide shoulders. This was a real man. One she might enjoy, one who'd respect her and yet treat her like a real woman.

The older woman was chattering non-stop.

"My husband might be along later, and then again he might not, he's a bit of a dreamer, he's one of the cruise lecturers. Professor Westcott. Patrick. He spends his time preparing lectures and writing frightfully complicated and meaningful books. He's always got his head stuck in some old volume or other and sometimes forgets where he is. He'd forget his head if it was loose. I wonder if he'll remember to close the cabin door if he goes out? I left my camera there and I don't want it to go astray. I said I wanted to see the morning sun on the Aegean and try to count the houses on the hill behind Ayios. Did you know that every time you count them, you get a different number? Nobody ever counts the same number twice . . . somebody said that if you do count the same number twice in succession, you'll be happy for ever and ever. I do love legends, you know. I'm Rosamund, by the way. Rosamund Westcott."

"Adrian Clarke," smiled the big man and Julia said, "Julia Grant. Nice to meet you."

"He'll be working on his confounded book today which means I'll be at a loose end. Honestly, there are times when I could cheerfully murder him. I thought about another visit to Knossos but if I've heard the minotaur tale once, I've heard it a thousand times and Patrick always says they get it wrong, they rely on legend, not facts, according to him. It wasn't a man-beast, it was a man wearing a bull's head mask, so he reckons. Mind, I do love a good legend. And then there's the Dhiktaion Cave where Rhea gave birth to Zeus and fed him on goat's milk – they have taxis up to the cave, you know, but they're donkeys and mules. I mean, if I ask for a taxi I expect something on four wheels and an engine to propel it, not a scrawny mule costing a hundred drachmas a trip . . . poor things, they look worn out climbing that path day in day out with fat tourists on their backs. Then you have to scramble down into the cave with only a long brown candle to light your way between stalagmites and stalactites. Hundreds of people struggling down those rocks all carrying lighted candles . . . it's like a religious procession descending to hell. I suppose it is, in a way. A religious procession, I mean. It makes you want to sing or chant something, oh, and you mustn't miss the Plain of Lasithi with all those windmills. Fifteen thousand of them so they say. Can you imagine that? I wonder who counted them? They're supposed to pump water. Mind, they don't all work."

"I haven't decided where I'm going," Clarke took the opportunity to enter the conversation as Rosamund paused to take a sip from her pink drink.

"Well wherever you go, don't rely on local buses, they never run on time and don't ask for ice with your drinks. And never touch raki, that's a local firewater and do try to see the Samaria Gorge, but not if it rains. But I do love the olive groves, acres and acres of them . . ."

Julia looked at Clarke with a resigned smile and he relaxed in his chair as Rosamund wittered on and on about aspects of Crete.

Eventually, during a brief lull in Rosamund's chatter, Julia asked, "So if you've seen all these places, what will you be doing with yourself today, Rosamund?"

"I shall probably take a local bus to Elounda," she sighed. "A lovely run along the coast, and have lunch out. I do love Greek food, but I always give a bit to the cats. If they don't keel over, I know the food's all right."

"And a look at Spinalonga Island?" smiled Adrian.

"It smells," chuckled the voluble lady. "It was a leper colony, you know . . . there's a shed full of old bones that haven't been buried. Sordid stuff."

And then, as *Oriana* was making her final approach, Rosamund said, "Ah, there's my friend Hilary. Tootleoo, both of you. Sorry if I broke up the happy party." And with no more ado, she hurried away towards Hilary.

"I was thinking of a bus ride to the south of the island," smiled Clarke when he was sure Rosamund was out of earshot. "A local bus that is, not one of the organized trips. To Ierepetra, it's a seaside resort. The town's quite pleasant and the bus ride's fun; there are some lovely stops on the way in remote villages. Care to join me?"

"That would be nice," she decided with little hesitation. "Yes, that would be very nice. Without my brother, preferably!"

"Whatever you say!" he chuckled. "But I'm dying to meet this brother of yours."

She must find Rupert without delay and explain things to him; she didn't want him turning up on today's trip and pretending he was her husband.

Her lust for revenge had suddenly drained away. She just wished that she could make both Simon and Rupert disappear off the ship, leaving her in peace with this gentle man who had magically appeared in her life. Why could things never be simple? How had she ever managed to encumber herself with so much unwieldy emotional baggage? When she thought about a bus trip away from the ship with Adrian Clarke she was astonished to find herself blushing, and her air passages seemed to close up, like some foolish schoolgirl.

Then Julia began to wonder how Simon Daviot would respond to the sight of her with this tall, distinguished-looking man at her side. Perhaps there was no need to keep avoiding the Daviots. Perhaps Julia was favoured by the gods of ancient Greece. Perhaps they had dispatched Apollo or Zeus to aid her in her mission to rid herself of Simon.

For Simon Daviot, the choice of outing was difficult, particularly as he'd been recognized by several people on board. On the one hand, he did not wish to partake of a general tourist outing. He didn't think that a potential cabinet minister should be seen on a coach, but then again he should be seen taking a scholarly interest in classical history. "Perhaps we could hire a private car?" Brenda had suggested innocently.

"Oh don't be stupid," he had snapped back. "That would make me look the most appalling snob."

"Then you'll just have to put up with coach travel like everyone else," Brenda's voice had trembled with anger, but she had managed to keep the tears back. She hated her husband for talking to her as if she was an idiot all the time. He seemed to think that she should be grateful to him for giving up his mistress and agreeing to stay with her. It was almost as if he was trying to goad her into walking out on him, leaving him free to do as he pleased.

Having reinstated himself in a 'happy-marriage mode', Daviot was able to give more thought to politics and the 'big picture'. He might be able to capitalize upon today's outing and so the decision had to be made with care – there was certainly some appeal for a politician to have his photograph taken in the famous labyrinth, providing that it reflected the dilemma of the opposition rather than the policies of the current government. Perhaps a picture of him taken by his wife when speaking to a beggar in the ruins – or even handing over a few drachmas to a needy person . . . Now that was an idea. He was sure he could make Brenda agree to that.

On the other hand, a man of his standing might best be seen in the Archaeological Museum at Iraklion followed by a tour of the town, a walkabout almost, along with his faithful wife and daughters. If he could produce the image of happy family life coupled with an appreciation of ancient cultures and a dash of generosity towards the poor, then that would be all to the good. It would be nice if some of the other passengers witnessed him in action – after all, you never really knew who was among them. People were there to be used and cultivated.

Both Sophie and Charlotte, however, had emphasized they had no wish to spend their holidays in gloomy museums full of dreary artefacts and stuffy old people. But after some persuasive talk from Simon both agreed the Palace of Knossos would be acceptable. Charlotte had visions of losing her virginity in the labyrinth and, after reading about some favourite Greek sports, had dreamt of bull leaping and visions of Dionysus, the sex-mad son of the elder Dionysus.

There were statues of him all over Greece, she'd heard, naked with his erect secret bits as big as his entire body . . . he'd have a job jumping over a bull with that equipment to hinder him. The thought of it made her excited and nervous at the same time. Now that she had told her sister of her plans to 'become a woman' before the end of the cruise, the idea of failure was completely out of the question. She couldn't quite understand why nothing had happened so far. She was sure she had made her intentions very plain to virtually all the men who had crossed her path but none of them had shown any signs of wanting to do anything about it. The whole male species was proving to be an enormous disappointment to Charlotte, nothing like the tribe of potential rapists and sex maniacs that her mother had warned her and Sophie about when trying to educate them in the ways of the world.

Simon felt sure he'd seen Julia Grant on board, not just once but several times. He'd tried to tell himself it was all imagination, but it wasn't. He had seen her, he was sure of that. The first time had been just after boarding at Southampton – that experience had really shaken him. But afterwards, and quite distinct from that awful confrontation, he'd emerged two nights ago from the Peninsula Restaurant on E Deck and had been in time to see the shapely rear of an attractive woman descending the stairs to F Deck. She had been walking beside a man, though, and talking to him; it was a man he thought he'd recognized from somewhere, and she had been on the half-moon shaped stairs which led from Queen's Court down to Garden Court. Although he'd galloped in a somewhat ungainly manner towards the stairs, he'd been too late and he'd missed her. She and the man had disappeared. Since then there had been several more sightings and he swung between being certain she was on the ship and certain he was losing his mind.

The incident at Southampton had made him think that perhaps he had not yet escaped unscathed from the whole affair. He still blushed at the recollection of what had happened. He had come up behind that woman, totally convinced it was Julia, sure she must have followed him on board. He'd seized her by the shoulder and had shouted her name, demanding to know why she was here. When she'd refused to turn round and just kept walking, he'd grown angry, very angry, and had tried to halt her in her tracks by brute force. But when she'd turned around to face him, it had been someone else. It was not Julia. It was a total stranger. He was astonished by the vehemence of her response to him. It had, after all, been a simple case of mistaken identity which he tried to explain as she called him every name under the sun. He had never seen such cold, angry eyes and had she had a gun he was sure she would have shot him on the spot. Women were so touchy these days, seeing offence in everything a man said to them. It was just a mistake for God's sake, he hadn't intended to assault her. She screamed that he was a nuisance, that her name was not Julia and that she'd call a steward if he pestered her again. His stuttered apologies had been brushed aside – but she'd been so like Julia from the back; if Julia had had a twin, that woman could have been her. From the back, they couldn't have been more alike; the colour and style of their hair, and even their way of walking.

Although he had apologized she continued to loudly deliver a powerful and embarrassing lecture about sexual harassment by strange men, and about the standards of conduct expected from Members of Parliament even if they were on holiday. Her dressing down of him had been witnessed by several passengers, including one old woman who had stared shamelessly from her cabin door. He'd felt humiliated, like a schoolboy caught cheating. For a few hours afterwards he'd sat alone in the cabin, smarting with embarrassment and hardly daring to venture out in case he met her again. It was during those quiet moments that he'd first begun to wonder if he was paranoid about Julia and whether he was going to be able to give her up quite as easily as he had first imagined.

Surely, his common sense told him, she would not have followed him on this cruise? She couldn't! Could she? Then he was sure he'd caught yet another glimpse of his Julia in the Conservatory, standing alone at the opposite end. By the time he'd struggled through the crowds she had vanished. She'd disappeared like a wraith. On that occasion, he was absolutely sure it wasn't the other woman he'd mistakenly accosted, he was positive of that but it could have been the same one he'd seen on the staircase. The real Julia? It occurred to him that he was seeing 'Julias' in every crowded place, on every busy beach, in every nook and corner of *Oriana* and wondered if he was losing his mind.

Determined to discover the truth he had toured *Oriana*, visiting all the places where he thought she might be found.

But looking for one's elusive cast-off mistress among nearly three thousand people on board was worse than looking for one's wife in Harrods. He'd even seen the woman he'd accosted, the one who looked so like Julia from a distance. She'd been standing at the rails above the Crystal Pool and he had kept well out of her sight. But of Julia, there was no sign. Had she come to announce she was pregnant, God forbid! Was she alone? If that had been her on the stairs, who was the man? Somebody she'd picked up on board? A member of her family? He'd heard her talk about a brother but such references had been very few and very fleeting, almost as if she'd never wanted to mention him. He recalled that conversation with her in which he'd told her about the second honeymoon cruise, disclosing enough details for her to manoeuvre herself on board. But why would she do that? Did she intend to publicly embarrass and humiliate him and his family in front of the other passengers? To set him up for a compromising picture? Was Julia unstable enough to exact her revenge in some spectacular way?

There were times in the past when he'd thought she was unstable, times he'd thought she would behave like a woman scorned – with all the hellish fury that that could induce.

If she had manipulated herself into a holiday on board *Oriana*, he began to ask himself whether he should keep out of her way and not try to locate her. Right now he could do without confrontation and threats. What he should do was to catch her alone, away from crowded places, and then have a final showdown with her. His mind wracked with indecision, Simon tried to formulate some plan to deal with Julia if and when she did make herself known.

If he really wanted to know whether she was on board, he could ask at reception and even leave a letter for delivery to her cabin. But that was exactly what she would want him to do, and letters could be compromising; they could be used in evidence or sent to the *Sun*. So he discarded that idea. The more he brooded over the problem, the more he decided it would be sensible to keep out of her way, at least for the time being. Stop hunting her. Make her seek him out, play with her like playing with a large trout, let her make all the moves until she gave up, let her chase him . . . forget she might be on board, forget she might be out for revenge . . .

While considering his activities during the day ashore, therefore, he would endeavour to go somewhere that would not appeal to Julia Grant. After some deliberation and a short discussion with Brenda and the twins, he decided to visit the Palace of Knossos, home of the oldest flush water toilet in the world, and to compare its history and legends with the Palace of Westminster so that he could incorporate comparisons in future speeches. There were some pretty ancient loos in Westminster, too, he recollected.

"We're taking the Knossos outing," he announced to his family.

"Yippee!" shouted Charlotte, who could dream only of bull leaping and Greek members.

chapter
FIVE

Zeus was in one of his better moods, so the weather was fine, sunny and dry and a visit to the Samaria Gorge could safely be undertaken. Several of the passengers opted for this outing, including Sandra Van Horn and her friend Warren, Annie Young with her blue notebook always to hand, and her nephew Mike, and niece Chrissie. Chrissie was with Rupert Revell. They had met in the Lord's Tavern earlier in the cruise and had become fascinated with one another. Annie was puzzled, having thought Rupert was with another woman, but assumed she must have misread the situation. She wondered if she should say something to Chrissie about this other woman, but decided that her interference would not be welcome. Chrissie had also seen Rupert with Julia and was not sure what the relationship was, but did not feel ready to enquire. There was something mysterious and deceptive about him which she found very attractive. Annie and Mike were just pleased to see her smiling and making an effort to be pleasant to someone.

Sandra Van Horn had also noticed Chrissie, since she was a very noticeable young woman, if not always a very attractive one. Sandra had seen how the girl sulked, appearing almost to glow with resentment, when in the company of her aunt and brother. She had also seen her deep in conversation with Rupert and had watched how her whole face seemed to change. The two of them appeared to take an almost demonic pleasure in one another's company. The woman called Hilary Brown was also on the trip. Warren, who was able to find out something about everyone, told her that Hilary was a famous agony aunt. Sandra could see that she was a woman who might be worth talking to if Warren's company became too tedious.

Roman Brindle had also thought about joining the tour, but at the last moment decided to remain on board because she needed to rehearse some recent hits which she was adding to her repertoire. While passengers were preparing to leave *Oriana*, she decided to head for the Crow's Nest and its gorgeous white grand piano, where she could play to the memory of that dashing young man in the open-topped car, still having no idea how close he really was.

The heat, the dry and dusty air, the physical effort of being on one's feet for such long periods and the demands of organized outings all combined to produce some very tired people by early afternoon. For most of them their only thought was to return to the comfort of their cabins for a relaxing bath or shower before dinner. The ship was due to sail at six o'clock and so, as they made for the high seas, they could relax over the meal and enjoy the on-board entertainments.

Most had achieved their objectives that day – Simon Daviot had had his picture taken while handing money to a beggar, and although Charlotte had not lost her virginity, nor had she seen any bull leaping, she did manage to buy a small statue of Dionysus with his massively erect member which she intended to admire every evening before sleeping. Brenda, surprisingly, had enjoyed the outing too, finding it one occasion when the whole family had been happy, united and free from angst and argument, even if there was a cucumber strike in Iraklion. Thus the Daviots were all in an unusually happy mood as they returned to *Oriana*.

Even if she had not yet said 'yes' to a visit to his cabin, Rupert had continued to charm Chrissie with some of his acting specialities and stories of mixing with the rich and famous. It wasn't that Chrissie wasn't interested in him, she was very attracted indeed, but she wanted to make sure that she didn't appear to be an easy lay. She had made that mistake too many times in the past. She wanted to hold Rupert's attention for as long as possible, if only to give her someone other than her aunt and her brother to spend time with. Jazzy and Lisa had passed the time being chatted up by a Greek waiter in a taverna on the beach at Ayios Nikolaos and Rosamund, leaving Patrick behind to concentrate upon his learned book, had taken her bus ride to Elounda where, among the boats and water sports facilities, she'd met a charming Italian count who was painting watercolours of Greek Orthodox churches.

Julia Grant and Adrian Clarke had boarded a rickety old bus which stopped frequently in the middle of nowhere to take on board people standing at the roadside, bore them through breathtaking countryside, on roads hewn from solid rock between the mountains, past hill-top churches and tiny isolated communities such as Gournia, Episkop and Kato Khorio. They passed windmills, spaghetti-like arrangements of irrigation pipes in cultivated fields, ancient chapels and modern churches. And as they came down from the mountains in the bus, there was fruit galore – pomegranates, oranges, olives and apples with cucumbers, tomatoes and other vegetables growing in profusion nearer the coast.

In the town, Adrian had led her through the chaotic traffic and among the host of little shops, then down to the beach of grey shale, showing her a kingfisher perched on a rock, before taking her to lunch in a taverna. There she had talked as she had never talked before. She had felt so at ease with this man, telling him about herself, about her work, her ambitions, her lifestyle. He had listened patiently, drawing from her a good deal of emotion. She had even ventured a comment about a recent love affair that had gone wrong – although she had not mentioned Daviot by name. She liked Adrian because he did not press her for information, he let her talk as she wished, telling him what she wanted and not what he wanted to know – he was almost like a counsellor, she decided. But who was this man? She found him quite beguiling.

"I think we'd better leave soon," he had glanced at the sky. "Zeus is growing angry, look."

He was pointing to the black clouds that had appeared over the mountains behind the town. "I think we're in for a downpour! Besides, it's time we were getting back to *Oriana*."

They'd had to run for the bus because the heavens had opened, and he had taken her hand, ignoring the rain as she tried to shelter her hair with her free hand. Like laughing children, they had dashed through the streets. Then the rain had stopped as suddenly as it had started, and by that time they were firm friends, drenched but happy. He had eased her into the bus with a tender hand in the middle of her back, after which they had settled in a seat at the rear, like a courting couple. Now, they were waiting for the bus to depart.

"You haven't told me anything about yourself," she ventured as they awaited a driver. "You let me gabble on. I've talked as I've never talked before, and to a complete stranger!"

"So, perhaps you needed to talk?" he smiled. "And I'm happy to listen. It's often easier, talking to strangers. You've clearly had a bad time, pressures at work, this lover letting you down like he did. If you want to talk again, I'll be around for the duration of the cruise."

"Tell me about yourself," she leaned towards him, resting against his strong shoulder as the driver climbed aboard and started the engine. Now the conductor, a short happy woman, was coming to issue tickets. It was 250 drachmas each for the single trip. Adrian said it was his treat and she allowed him to buy her ticket – and, much to her surprise, she liked this feeling of being looked after.

It seemed such a long time ago that she'd been the object of such gentlemanly behaviour, such old-fashioned courtesy. Adrian was a natural leader, she decided, and she was following most willingly.

"There's not a lot to tell," he said with his gentle Northumbrian lilt.

"You're a widower," she pressed him. "You told me that. But what else? Family? Job?"

"Two sons, both grown-up, in their twenties. One at university studying English literature, the other working in a bank and studying for a banking qualification. Neither at home. I've three brothers and Gwen has – er had – two sisters and one brother. We're a big, happy family; we all get on with each other. Hobbies – travelling, eating out, reading. All very boring, all very ordinary."

"And the job?" she persisted. "Let me see, let me guess. One of the professions? Solicitor? Doctor? Surgeon?"

He laughed and added, "Your kind of men, are they? Like airline pilots, company directors, marketing supremos, international bankers, architects – no, I'm nothing quite so fine. I'm a very ordinary chap who's never wanted to strive for those heights. Have another guess?"

He was gently teasing her and she was enjoying the banter as the bus settled into its journey. "I don't know, you're too down-to-earth to be involved in something like television or publishing, you've got a north-eastern accent so you might be something to do with ships, ship-building maybe, or town planning."

Adrian allowed her to guess for a few more moments and then said, "When I'm on holiday, I never tell people what I do for a living. But for you, I'll reveal my occupation on one condition."

"What's that?" She was even more curious now.

"That you don't tell anyone else, none of the other passengers. When I'm on holiday, I like to keep my work quite apart from my leisure. I don't want to end up like that agony aunt who's going to have every crank on board chasing her for advice, or that MP who behaves as if he's waiting for an election to be announced."

"You are being mysterious," she laughed. "All right, mum's the word, and I can keep a secret, you know."

"I'm retired," he beamed. "I don't work."

"Retired? But you're too young. Redundancy was it? Disguised as early retirement?"

"No, a genuine retirement. In my job I could retire early, and after Gwen died that's what I did. Packed up with a nice pension so I could travel the world and meet lovely interesting people without any of the hassle connected with my line of work."

"So the job?" She was not going to allow him to escape without telling her.

"I was a policeman," he smiled. "A detective, actually. Ex-Detective Chief Superintendent Adrian Clarke at your service, ma'am."

"A detective? Oh my God . . . I had no idea . . ."

"You're shocked?"

"Surprised," she recovered herself. She was stunned in fact, but would never admit it. "Yes I am surprised. You seem too, well, gentle to be a detective."

"I'm from the north-east of England, Julia, not from Scotland Yard and besides I'm retired now. I'm not a policeman any more. That's why I don't want anyone to know what I did for a living – I get those silly people coming up to me and complaining about getting parking tickets or being caught for speeding . . . like doctors always get people telling them about illnesses and operations. Right, that's me."

"But, I mean you must have dealt with all sorts of things, murder and rapes, even, that kind of sordid crime."

"Yes I have. I've dealt with horrible crimes and horrible people, but let's not talk about it. I've finished being a detective, I'm on holiday, and tonight I fancy a long, relaxing bath followed by a long cool drink or two before a long and very leisurely dinner. Perhaps you will join me at my table?"

"I've never been entertained by a policeman before . . ."

"I'm not a policeman," he interrupted her, "I'm retired."

"Look." She had to say this. "I'm from a world where policemen are seen on television, either in drama or documentaries or being complained about by serving prisoners or left wing politicians or dodgy town councillors . . . in my world, no one ever has a good word for the police. I've never met a real, living policeman, retired policeman I should say, in a holiday situation . . . damn it all, you don't even have enormous feet."

"So there's a first time for everything," he chuckled. He was enjoying her discomfort. "Meet you in Lord's, say half past seven? Dinner to follow? Second sitting?"

"Yes," she said. "Yes, all right. I'd like that."

And so, as all the passengers were ending their day in Crete, the bus carrying Julia and Adrian rumbled on towards the town of Ayios Nikolaos where the gleaming white *Oriana* awaited their return.

Adrian Clarke occupied a two-bedded cabin on the port side of A Deck. He was pleased he had taken this cabin – the nomenclature was somewhat misleading because it had a double bed.

Whistling happily he pondered the next stage in his relationship with Julia Grant. She had obviously been badly bruised by the ending of her last relationship. He was used to listening to people talk and drawing his own conclusions and he was pretty sure that she still felt strongly about the man who had betrayed her, even though she professed that it was all over. He knew just how long it took to recover from relationships. He was quite happy to wait, to nurse her gently through a period of emotional convalescence. Gwen was still much too fresh in his mind for him to be able to think about becoming entangled with someone new just yet.

It would be very pleasant to be able to get to know Julia slowly and gently, away from all the pressures of normal everyday life, and just see what happened. He stripped, shaved and bathed, then dressed in a clean fresh shirt, tie, blazer and light trousers. Satisfied that he looked smart, he left his cabin, making sure he had the computer key card in his pocket – without that, he would not be able to regain entry.

Already *Oriana* was heading for the open sea – the next stop Paros in the morning. Before going to the Lord's Tavern, he decided to climb up to Lido Deck for a breath of fresh air and a final view of Crete. He had plenty of time for that before meeting Julia. Making for the staircase, he was passing one of the cabins when a middle-aged woman burst out screaming and shouting. He recognized her instantly. It was the woman who'd come to his table earlier, the one calling herself Rosamund.

"Help, please . . . oh, somebody please help me . . ."

Adrian ran towards her, calling, "All right, all right, Rosamund, calm down . . . I'm here . . . what is it?"

"Oh, thank God it's you. Look, in there, a woman . . . on my bed . . . I think she's dead."

"Right." Immediately Adrian's police instincts and training snapped into action and he said, "Wait outside, Rosamund, don't say anything to anyone. I'm a retired detective. I'll have a look at her."

"Thank goodness for that! I have no idea where Patrick is," she was muttering, "no idea at all. I've just come in, I've just found her . . ."

"It's your cabin?"

"Yes, mine and Patrick's."

"And the door? Was it open?"

"Yes, standing open just a little, they lock automatically don't they, with these computer card keys, but Patrick had left it standing open, so I thought. He's always doing that, leaving doors open . . . anyway, I just went in and called 'Patrick', as I do to let him know it's me coming in, and I found her. I thought she was asleep at first but then, well, oh dear, it's so horrible, all that blood on our bed . . ."

"Stay there Rosamund." The authority in Adrian's voice was such that Rosamund stood stock still outside the cabin, awaiting his initial investigation. He went inside, pushing the door open with a forefinger instead of touching the knobs and lock, and then easing it partially closed behind him. He let out a gasp of shock at the sight of the woman on the bed. "Julia?" he whispered and then saw it was not her. "Thank God!" The likeness was extraordinary; same reddish-brown hair, same hair-style even, same intriguing figure, same age, similar casual clothes – she wore a white sun-top and blue shorts. He stared at her face for a few seconds. Although it wasn't Julia there was still something about her which was familiar, he was sure he had met this woman before, although her hair had been a different colour. He searched his memory and then it came to him. It only took him a few more seconds to decide that he would say nothing and continue as if he was dealing with the murder of a complete stranger.

With professional detachment returning, he viewed the scene, knowing better than to touch anything at this point, and then, having absorbed a mental picture of the minutiae of the room, he touched her. She was still warm; he listened for breathing, tested the pulse on her wrists and neck but found nothing. Again, without moving her, he saw the bed cover was soaked with blood which had apparently come from her chest area. Carefully, he lifted her head – she was positioned chest down on the bed with blood having oozed from her, but he could not yet see whether the weapon was there. Maybe she was lying on it, but he mustn't move her, not yet. That she was dead was not in doubt. Whether that death had come from her own hand or from the hand of a murderer was yet to be determined, but it seemed an unlikely method of suicide.

Adrian picked up the telephone and dialled reception.

"My name is Adrian Clarke," he said. He told the receptionist his own cabin number and then gave that of the cabin he was calling from. "This is an emergency. I need the ship's doctor and the captain to come here immediately, to this cabin. Please treat this with confidence – but with great urgency. I am a retired detective chief superintendent. I will wait here until the officials arrive."

Then he went outside. "Rosamund," he said. "I fear this is going to be traumatic for you, but I can't let you back into the cabin just yet. I've called for the doctor and the captain. I think the cabin will have to be locked and sealed until a course of action is determined. Now, I forgot to ask – do you know the woman in there? Who is she?"

She shook her head. "Sorry, I have no idea. Perhaps it's a friend of Patrick's? She is rather like your friend, isn't she? That's who I thought it was at first . . . what a shock, I can tell you . . . look, I need to go to the toilet and get changed and have a bath and get ready for this evening . . . oh dear, this is awful, the poor thing." Rosamund was fighting to regain her normal sunny composure. She didn't like anything that caused her to lose her self-control. If she could just keep going, she told herself, this terrible event would do her no harm. She must maintain appearances.

"I'm sure another cabin will be put at your disposal. Please keep calm for just a little longer and remember we must not set off a panic of any kind. There might be a perfectly logical explanation for this woman's death and her presence in your cabin . . ."

Adrian Clarke didn't really believe that! He knew he was dealing with a murder, the signs were all there. With the door about an inch ajar, he stood outside and talked to Rosamund, awaiting the arrival of the doctor and the captain.

People were passing constantly, all trying to hide their curiosity as to what might be happening. They moved on when Adrian asked them to do so. Within less than five minutes, Captain Moore arrived, slightly breathless, and asked, "Mr Clarke? My name is Moore. Captain Moore. The doctor has been called as you requested, and is on his way. Now, can you please tell me what's happened?"

"I'm a retired detective chief superintendent," said Adrian. "I was called to have a look at a woman who is on the bed in this lady's cabin; she's dead, I fear, and from what I can see at this juncture, you might have a murder on your hands."

"Oh Jesus!" breathed Moore. "I thought it was going too well."

"I won't be totally sure until the doctor has examined her," Clarke went on. "We need to get death certified, then the cause of death established. It might be suicide, but I doubt it, the cabin door was open and it seems the woman – and her killer – gained entry."

"So it's not her cabin?"

"No, it belongs to this lady and her husband, Professor and Mrs Westcott."

"Rosamund Westcott. My husband is one of the lecturers on board. He's not around, Captain, I don't know where he is. I just returned to my cabin and found her, I've been out all day, at Elounda, luckily this gentleman was just passing."

"We need to get the deceased identified," said Clarke. "She's not dressed in much – a sun-top and shorts. And I suggest photographs of the woman *in situ*, and of the cabin. They'll be needed for the investigation."

"All right, one thing at a time," said Moore. "Mr Clarke, please show me the cabin."

Exhorting the captain not to touch anything, Clarke led him inside. Both men stood and looked, Moore remaining surprisingly calm in the face of this drama. "The cabin does not appear to have been disturbed," Adrian said. "No drawers and cupboards ransacked, no bed searched beneath the mattress, no damage to fittings, none of the damage you might expect to follow a burglary or a fight to the death." A white linen jacket, a man's jacket, was hanging over the back of a chair which was tucked beneath the dressing table, while one of the woman's shoes, a slip-on canvas sandal, a green one, lay close to the corner sofa. The other was on her right foot. In spite of her flimsy clothing, both men noticed she had not been undressed, a fact that tended to rule out a sex motive. When Clarke examined her fists visually, without touching them, he saw no items of cloth, no fibres, no pieces of hair or skin clutched in her tightly clenched fingers. It seemed she had not fought for her life. Perhaps the first stab wound had disabled her, the rest being delivered in a frenzy of violence or hate.

"The killer should be heavily bloodstained," Clarke said.

"We'll notify the laundry," Captain Moore nodded. "So, Chief Superintendent, what can we make of this?"

"I'm not sure." Clarke was honest. "We need to look at the chest injuries but we mustn't move her until the doctor's carried out his examination. If this was a murder under natural circumstances on shore, the room would be sealed and then forensically examined in minute detail before the body was removed for a post mortem."

"There is a medical centre on board," said Moore. "We can take her there. We can even conduct a post mortem."

"Good, then I suggest that once the doctor has certified her dead, we seal the room so that the necessary forensic examination can be carried out. An on-site examination of the body should be done, really, although I appreciate there are restrictions on board a ship . . . but I don't think your air-conditioning will cope with a dead human body for very long. And don't forget the photographs. You'll need photographs of her as she is now, and as she will be when we turn her over to examine the wounds. You've got a professional photographer on board?"

"Yes, but this is not in his usual line of business, Mr Clarke."

"I can explain what is required, that's if you need my help. I don't want to push in and be a nuisance if you can cope without me."

"Mr Clarke," said the captain, "believe me, we do have our procedures for most things, major crime included, but I'd welcome any advice you are able to give us."

Just then, there was a gentle knock on the cabin door and a sombre face peered around, saying, "Hello, good evening. I am Dr Patel, I am wanted here?"

"Come in, Doctor," invited Captain Moore. "I fear we have a problem. This is Detective Chief Superintendent Clarke, who happens to be one of our passengers. The woman on the bed is dead, we believe, and worse still, we think it might be murder."

“Oh goodness, I’m a general practitioner, gentlemen, not a police doctor, not a forensic scientist, not a pathologist.”

“I need you to certify death, to begin with,” said Clarke. The doctor listened to Clarke’s account and then conducted a very skilful preliminary examination of the body before pronouncing life extinct. He estimated she had been dead for no longer than three hours, but could not be more precise. Meanwhile, the captain had summoned the official photographer and a young man arrived, turning green around the gills, as Clarke explained the requirements. The unfortunate woman had to be photographed from all angles without moving her, and the position of her body had to be related to other objects in the room, such as the bed, the chairs and settee, her discarded shoe, and the coat hanging on the rear of the chair.

While the photographer was working under Clarke’s guidance, the captain summoned a steward by telephone and asked him to find a replacement cabin for Rosamund, who was still waiting outside. Clarke, having noted the undisturbed state of the cabin in which the body was found, agreed that she could be handed some of her personal belongings. Toiletries, fresh clothing and valuables were retrieved from the cabin by Clarke and handed to her as she waited outside. Minutes later, she had been allocated an empty cabin just a few doors along the deck and those inside said they would inform Professor Westcott of the change to his routine if and when he arrived. No one seemed to know where he was. Now that her composure was returning, Rosamund was surprised to find how unconcerned she was about her missing husband. The thought even crossed her mind that he, too, might have been murdered and still she didn’t feel anything. The moment she got to her new cabin she rang Hilary Brown and told her all about it, swearing her to secrecy. For the first time ever Rosamund felt that she actually had something of interest to talk to people about.

By the time the photographer and doctor had completed their work, Adrian realized he was late for his dinner engagement with Julia and said to Moore, "Look, I have an appointment now, I'm late. Can I just pop out and find her. Then I can return if you wish."

"What else needs to be done, Mr Clarke?" asked Moore.

"If I knew your procedures, I could advise you. What are your duties now?"

"As we are not in port, I must contact our offices at either Southampton or London and they will decide upon the appointment of an investigator. But we can't leave the body here, can we?"

"Might I suggest we allow Dr Patel to disturb the remains now, only slightly though, just enough to turn her over so that we can see the source of the blood? After that, and after we have taken more photographs, we can take her to the mortuary. You do have mortuary facilities?"

"Yes, of course."

"Right, well Dr Patel, shall we turn her over?"

"Yes, of course, yes indeed."

Carefully, Clarke, Moore and Dr Patel turned over the body, allowing the woman to remain on the bed, and it didn't take an expert to see that she had multiple stab wounds to the heart, chest and neck area. It had been a frenzied attack but the weapon was missing. She had been stabbed through her sun-top, the blood gushing from her arteries as she had collapsed onto the bed.

"Nasty one," said Clarke. "I reckon a post mortem will confirm death was by stab wounds, Doctor? I'll guess that at least one has pierced the heart. Can you do a post mortem for us?"

"Yes of course. As I said, I am not a pathologist but I think this one should not hold too many difficulties."

"Right," said Clarke. "Once the photographs have been taken, close-ups included please, the body can be taken to the mortuary. And we'll need photographs of the post mortem, if your man is up to it, Captain. Now, we need to see if she has any documents on her – passport, credit cards, cheque books, anything that will tell us who this woman is."

Clarke, experienced in searching corpses for items of identification, found nothing. The woman was not even wearing a ring of any kind, nor any other jewellery, although she did have a watch on her left wrist. Clarke, using writing paper from the room's supply, noted down details of the make and style, then drew a quick sketch of the cabin showing the position of the furniture, the bed and the woman's body as it had been found.

"I can arrange a cabin check of all passengers," said Moore. "It'll take time, but it will tell us who is absent."

"Right, do that," said Clarke. "Now, gentlemen, I will leave you to remove the body to the mortuary and lock the room upon leaving. Call me if you need help."

"I'm sure we will do just that, Mr Clarke, and thanks for your guidance. Let's hope we can clear this up quickly."

"I don't think the murderer will be far away," said Clarke, "unless, of course, she was killed while the ship was at Ayios Nikolaos. With all that blood around, the killer's clothing is bound to be bloodstained. The laundry may well turn something up."

"They may," Captain Moore agreed, "but there are also facilities for passengers to do their own laundry. Besides, it would be so easy to throw any bloodstained clothing overboard."

"Yes, I appreciate that," said Clarke. "But the killer and his or her clothes might have been seen. If we can find someone who saw a person wearing bloodstained clothing while rushing from this room, then we'll have found a good witness."

"Yes, of course. Lots of passengers left the ship this morning, Mr Clarke, and unless that woman had good reason for remaining on board, then she would have joined the other passengers in exploring Crete. She may have died upon her return or, of course, she might have remained on board all day."

"Or could she have brought someone back on board with her?"

"Nothing's impossible, Mr Clarke, as you will appreciate, but it would be highly unusual. I think our security system would have identified anyone coming aboard who was not authorized."

"I'm sure you are right. But the task is yours. Now, I must keep my appointment. Oh, you will need to make a detailed search for the murder weapon, but I fear it will be on the bed of the Aegean by this time."

And so retired Detective Chief Superintendent, Adrian Clarke, found himself at work during his holiday. Had his wife been alive, she would not have found that in any way unusual. Throughout their married life, Adrian had been called out at the most inopportune moments. Leaving the task of dealing with the corpse to the ship's crew, as was the procedure, Adrian hurried to the Lord's Tavern. He needed a good stiff drink now and hoped Julia had waited for him.

Although he was late, Julia was waiting. She had bought herself a sweet martini liberally laced with cool tonic but

Adrian was dismayed to find Rosamund Westcott sharing her table. She was sitting with a double whisky in front of her as she harangued Julia with the story of her dreadful discovery. She was in full flow when Adrian arrived.

Having learned of Adrian's part in the affair, Julia's face showed her concern for him. There were blood stains on his cuffs and trousers. He'd washed his hands in his own cabin but had missed those unsightly marks. Julia did not draw immediate attention to them, but said, "Sit down, Adrian, you need a drink. Let me get this one." She was accustomed to the art of ordering drinks. "A nice malt? A double?"

"Thanks," he said, settling down beside Rosamund.

"And what about you, Rosamund? Shall I get you another? Whisky again? Let me get you something."

"Another double whisky would be lovely – and necessary!"

And as Julia went to the bar, Rosamund, now somewhat subdued, continued, "Thank you for coming to my aid as you did, Mr Clarke. I really do appreciate it. I know Patrick would not have coped like that, he'd have panicked, got into a state, he hates blood anyway."

"Have you found him yet?"

"No, and I shall not trouble to look," she snapped impatiently, "If he can't get into the cabin, he'll come and find me. He'll have forgotten it's dinner time too, but he might turn up later for his meal when he notices what time it is . . . but that poor woman, Mr Clarke, how dreadful. To think she was killed in our room, on our bed . . ."

"Try not to dwell on it," he said. "And she might not have been killed there, she might have been placed there after death, that's always a possibility. So, how is your new cabin?"

"Just like the other one," she managed a weak smile. "Same colours, same side of the deck, there's no difference –

but I'll be afraid to open the door when I return. I made sure it was locked this time, no leaving doors open for me any more. I must tell Patrick. I wonder where he's got to? It's very mysterious. You don't think anything could have happened to him, do you?" A similar thought had been occurring to Adrian, but he assured her that she shouldn't worry, that Patrick was bound to show up sooner or later.

"He's obviously so involved in whatever he's doing," Adrian said. "He's probably just forgotten the time. Now, about this murder, I think the less we say about it to other passengers the better, at least until the formal investigation gets under way. P&O's head office is being notified and they will decide how to proceed, probably by appointing an investigating officer. It's really out of our hands now, we've done our bit." He paused and then changed the subject. "Have they moved all your belongings over from the cabin all right?"

"Oh yes," Rosamund nodded. "The only thing I can't seem to find is one of the statuettes that Patrick uses for his lectures, but he's probably got it with him."

"Is it valuable?"

"Oh my goodness, no. Patrick just has them made up for him . . . I really thought it was your friend, Mr Clarke, lying there. That woman is so like her."

"Julia, you mean?"

"Yes, Julia. It was an awful shock . . . I'm not sure I can cope with it," and quite surprisingly, Rosamund began to weep. They were soft tears, not sobs and she produced a handkerchief from somewhere and began to dab her eyes.

"I'm sorry, I don't usually do this, but it was going to be such a nice holiday, so carefree and happy. That poor, poor girl and I know I won't sleep tonight . . ."

"If Patrick doesn't turn up for dinner, you may join Julia and me," Adrian heard himself say. "It's best you are not alone."

"Thank you, but you'd be much better on your own with Julia than coping with neurotic old me. Besides, I have a friend on board, Hilary Brown, the psychologist. We've agreed to meet for dinner if Patrick doesn't show up."

"Well, the offer's there," he repeated. "Ah, here's Julia."

"What offer?" smiled Julia, having overheard part of their conversation. She was followed by a steward who bore a tray of drinks which he placed carefully on the table.

"I was inviting Rosamund to join us at dinner if her husband doesn't appear," Adrian said. "She's rather shocked by what has happened, but she thinks she would rather talk to her friend Hilary."

Julia smiled. Even though she did not really know Adrian, she knew this gesture was in keeping with his character and replied, "Yes, of course, Rosamund. It must have been terrible. Do join us if you wish."

"You are both very kind. But honestly, I thought it was you, Julia, I really did. She was your age, with your hairstyle and colouring, and her figure was just like yours . . ."

"Oh God!" Julia wasn't sure she wanted to hear this. There couldn't be a remote possibility, could there, that the attack had been meant for her? And if that had been the case, who might the attacker be? She found herself shuddering at the thought that it might have been her lying there in a pool of blood.

"Look, let's have no more talk of murders and deaths and unlikely scenarios," Adrian's voice was strong and commanding. "Right, Rosamund, tell us about your day. What did you get up to and what excitements came your way?"

She took a long draught from her glass and said, "Thank you Adrian, I can call you Adrian, can't I?"

"Of course." He winked at Julia and noticed the look of deep concern on her pale face.

"Are you all right?" he asked her.

"Yes," said Julia. "But please don't leave me, will you?"

In spite of attempts to maintain secrecy about the murder, news spread through the ship within hours. The dramatic summons of the captain and the ship's doctor, the removal of the body from the cabin, its transportation beneath white sheets to the mortuary, the dreadful task faced by the ship's photographer and the ordeal of Rosamund Westcott had all combined to create a wave of gossip and speculation.

The official approach was to try to maintain calm and to reduce speculation that a maniac was on board, but the ongoing gossip generated tales of screams in cabins, blood flowing beneath the doors, savagery unbridled with undreamt-of brutality, attempted rapes and sundry other fearful happenings.

For the alert Annie Young, notebook always at the ready, it took but a few discreet enquiries of stewards and bartenders for her to confirm that the rumours were true. A murder had been committed on *Oriana*. She'd felt something awful would happen, there'd been an air of tension on board for quite some time. She had even noted it down in her book. After ordering a White Lady from the cocktail bar, she settled in a corner of Anderson's to study the notes she had already made. Annie always made notes during her holidays – she recorded observations, snatches of conversation, behaviour and attitudes, facts about the countries she visited, names of local drinks and dishes, names of people she saw and met.

Since boarding *Oriana*, she had recorded several items of interest – of interest to her, that is. There was that man Rupert Revell for example – on the very first evening, she'd heard him say to one of the male passengers that he was a television producer and had then referred to his wife, Julia. Later, though, when Annie had been standing at the rail above the Crystal Pool, he'd told Chrissie, her very own Chrissie, that he was cruising with his sister and that he was an actor about to be launched into international stardom. Annie, of course, had not quizzed anyone, least of all Chrissie, about these discrepancies because, at the time, they had been of no real consequence, but, well, now that a murder had occurred, every lie, every deceit, every attempt to falsify one's image, might be of relevance. She highlighted those falsehoods in her book.

During her perambulations of *Oriana*'s many decks, though, Annie had seen Rupert talking in earnest to a young woman, on one occasion at breakfast. Were they man and wife? Or brother and sister? Certainly their conversation, as interpreted by the observant Annie, did not appear to be that of a man and wife. It had seemed more like a big sister trying to persuade a little brother to behave himself.

The woman had her back to her and Annie couldn't see her face. Her chief interest in that woman arose because she was sure it was the one she'd seen arguing with Simon Daviot. Did Revell have a wife called Julia who was a problem, one who'd been involved in some unsavoury escapade with Daviot? Daviot had used the name Julia when arguing with the woman, she'd heard him shout the name quite clearly. So was Julia involved with more than one man? Were both on board? It was a good question, Annie decided, the sort that might lead to the discovery of a murderer.

And the victim? Who was she? No one seemed to know who she was. During Annie's eavesdropping and gentle questioning, however, she had learned that the victim was a young woman in her mid or early thirties, slightly taller than average, slim build with a beautiful face and light auburn hair cut fashionably short. Just like the woman Daviot had been arguing with. Another factor that had emerged during Annie's investigation was that a retired detective chief superintendent, who happened to be on board, had been helping the ship's crew to cope with the drama.

He had apparently been very courteous, very helpful and highly professional. Annie decided that she should impart some of her snippets of information to him. It might just help to find the killer. Leaving Anderson's, she made her way to the Oriental Restaurant on E Deck because it was almost dinner time, and hoped she might catch the ex-policeman for a quick chat. She already knew which one he was – the steward who had found the new cabin for Mrs Westcott had been able to point out the man who had been present in the murder cabin. She'd seen him in the Lord's Tavern but had decided not to accost him in such a crowded place – she'd seek him out and ask for an appointment.

When she arrived at the restaurant, a small queue was waiting to be seated and she noticed Clarke was not among them; accordingly, she decided to wait just outside the door and then, even as she was deciding which was the best place to position herself, she saw him heading her way. And he had a beautiful woman on his arm – very like the one the MP had assailed, and the one who had been talking to Rupert Revell.

Taking a deep breath, Annie went to meet the big, handsome detective.

"Mr Clarke?" She was slightly nervous, not sure what his reaction might be.

"Yes?" He was polite but restrained, she felt.

"It's about that murder," she whispered in what she hoped was a discreet manner. "I would like to talk to you about it."

"Me? Why me?" he asked. "The matter is now in the hands of the captain."

"Yes, but, well, I understood you were investigating it, you see . . ."

"No, sorry." He was endeavouring to be firm with this woman. "I just happened to be present when the crime was discovered. Now, if you have any significant information . . . Mrs . . . ?"

"Young, Annie Young," she spoke quietly, thinking that he would have been much more interested.

"Yes, well if you have any useful information, Mrs Young, the proper channel of communication is to contact the bridge and ask for Captain Moore. I am not a policeman, you see, not any more. I have no jurisdiction here."

"Oh, well, in that case I will speak to Captain Moore. But I did see an argument, you see, between that Mr Daviot and a woman called Julia and well, I wondered if it was important. And then that Rupert Revell man, well, he's supposed to have a wife and then he says it's his sister . . ." Annie watched Julia's expression carefully.

"Julia?" Adrian looked at the woman before him and then at Julia. She was struggling to remain calm at these references to two of the men in her life. "This Julia, you mean?"

"Oh, no, I'm sure not that lady, but one very like her."

"Adrian," said Julia. "I think we had better find our seats." She wanted rid of this woman before she said too much.

But while Adrian's gut reaction had been to dismiss Annie as a silly interfering old nuisance, he now felt that she might well be a valuable witness. After all, what she had said could be important because even he, Adrian Clarke, had thought the dead woman looked like Julia Grant. So had Annie Young witnessed a prelude to murder? Had Annie seen the deceased in a state of conflict before her death? Had she seen the killer, indeed?

"You'd better come and view the body," he said. "If the deceased woman is the person you saw involved in an argument, it will be very relevant to this investigation. Come along, I'll contact the captain and we'll do it straight away."

"Not before dinner, Adrian!" cried Julia, desperately trying to win him away from this annoying woman.

"It'll only take a few minutes," he said. "Do you want to come and look at her, Julia? You might know her, everyone seems to think she looks like you!"

"Oh, no, I couldn't, I couldn't . . ."

"Can you find a table then? Save a seat for me and I'll join you in ten minutes."

Having contacted Moore by telephone, Adrian agreed to meet him outside the mortuary immediately, along with Annie Young. She was extremely nervous about this ordeal but Adrian assured her it would be just like looking at someone who was sleeping because the white sheets would cover everything except the face. Certainly, there would be no blood or wounds to examine. And so, with Moore and Clarke accompanying her, Annie Young was led into the disinfected atmosphere of *Oriana*'s mortuary and shown the white shrouded figure on the slab.

Gently, Clarke eased back the sheet covering the waxy but once beautiful face and Annie looked down upon her.

"I don't know her name," Annie's voice was trembling now, "but, yes, gentlemen, that is the woman who had a violent argument with that MP, Simon Daviot. I heard him, he shouted at her, calling her Julia. I saw them. She told him to stop harassing her, to leave her alone, to behave like an MP should, with propriety. I have a note of the time and place."

"Then our Mr Simon Daviot MP has some very important questions to answer," said ex-Detective Chief Superintendent Adrian Clarke.

chapter SIX

"This is my office," Adrian Clarke said wryly.

"Very nice," Simon Daviot answered in the tone of a man used to paying false compliments about his constituents' ill-decorated living rooms. The ship's purser had provided Adrian with an unoccupied suite, pushing aside the coffee tables and sofas in the lounge area to make space for two desks and a pair of uncomfortable chairs. The functional office furniture looked incongruous against the backdrop of blue sea beyond the suite's balcony, but Adrian Clarke was accustomed to such makeshift offices since much of his career had been spent in the sad, transient atmosphere of village halls transformed into murder headquarters. In fact he had never worked in such luxury before.

"They've given me a coffee-maker," he said. "White?"

Simon Daviot looked at his watch, a Rolex. "No thank you. I might be on holiday, but my time is still precious."

"Then sit, please." Adrian waited till his unwilling guest had taken one of the two uncomfortable chairs, then crossed to a fax machine that stood mute on a desk. He took a sheet of paper from its tray and handed it to the MP. "My credentials," he said.

"It's complicated," Adrian continued speaking while Simon Daviot read the paper. "Greek waters, of course, but the ship's of British registry. We could ask the Greek police in, but what with the language problems . . ." He raised his hands. "Besides, if we assume the crime was committed on the high seas then I don't think anyone will complain if the British police take responsibility. And as I happened to be here," he shrugged modestly as though New Scotland Yard's decision to allow him temporary charge of the case was an inexplicable privilege.

"It says here you're retired," Simon Daviot said, handing the paper back.

"Reinstated. Temporarily. And if I can't solve the case, then the Yard will send a full team." And the sooner the better, Adrian thought, because if this interview turned up nothing the case would need money and manpower – constables going from cabin to cabin, sophisticated forensic skills; all the paraphernalia of a modern murder investigation – instead of which it had one retired widower who everyone hoped could wrap up the murder with the minimum of fuss and publicity. "I'm sure you'll approve of my trying to save the British taxpayer the expense of New Scotland Yard conducting a Mediterranean murder investigation," Adrian said, and received not even the flicker of a smile in response. "You're sure about the coffee?" he asked.

"A whisky would be better." Simon Daviot crossed his legs and fastidiously plucked up one knee of his beige linen trousers. He was in his holiday uniform; blazer, blue shirt, linen trousers and deck shoes.

"Sorry, no whisky," Adrian said. "No whisky at all, alas." He sat behind the desk and leafed through his notebook while he surreptitiously took stock of the MP. He saw a tall, middle-aged man whose good looks were spoiled by pale watery-blue eyes that gave his face a petulant expression. This was a man, Adrian Clarke surmised, who had never quite reached as high as his aspirations, but then, who did? And was disappointment enough to make a prominent MP capable of murder? "You heard about the murder, sir?" Adrian asked.

"The whole ship has."

"Did you know the victim, sir?"

Simon Daviot gave a glimmer of a smile as if he recognized the innocent looking trap laid for him. "I don't even know who the victim is, Chief Superintendent."

"Forgive me, sir." Adrian Clarke liked to play his interviews this way. He would let Simon Daviot score all the debating points he wished and would respond with nothing except a false humility that he hoped would lull his opponent into complacency. "I've some pictures here," he said, and pretended to fumble through a file. He wanted to give the impression of a man easily confused, a tactic that had fooled many of his interviewees into a false confidence and loquacity. "Here," he said, taking out a glossy ten by twelve inch colour photograph of the dead girl. "A bit upsetting, I'm afraid."

An initial grimace flashed over Simon Daviot's face as he saw the shocking picture, but he disguised his reaction swiftly. The photograph showed the body after it had been turned over on the bed. The sheets and the girl's white suntop were soaked in blood while still more blood had splashed up to her mouth that hung slackly open. Daviot blinked twice, then put the picture back on the desk. "Don't know her."

"Her name is, was, Olivia Harman," Adrian Clarke said. "She grew up in Bristol, but emigrated to Australia five years ago. Now she works, worked, as a graphic designer for an advertising agency in Sydney. She came back to visit her parents and travel round Europe." That at least was the information which Adrian had been given by the crew, and it was the information he intended to work with for the moment, at least until he had discovered more about what was going on.

"A tragedy," Simon Daviot said without any sincerity at all. He was staring straight into Adrian Clarke's eyes, almost daring the man to make his allegation.

Adrian Clarke was not enjoying the interview. In truth he had ceased to enjoy the cruise the moment that death had intruded so gruesomely on his holiday, but now he was beginning to feel foolish. Simon Daviot was so very cocksure, so confident, and perhaps that was a politician's pose, but Adrian Clarke had the sixth sense that all good policemen need and it was telling him that this man was not his murderer. He felt the frustration of a professional denied his proper facilities; he needed facts and all he had was Annie Young's tittle-tattle. Crime writers might be convinced that middle-aged ladies made natural detectives, but Adrian had yet to find a single spinster or widow who could save any police force the huge cost of a Criminal Investigation Department. If only life was as simple as authors believed, he thought, then looked up into Daviot's infuriatingly smug face. "Did you know Miss Harman?" he asked abruptly.

"No." Simon Daviot took pleasure in the curt, unhelpful answer.

Adrian Clarke turned another page in his notebook. Not that there was anything useful in it, but its presence might suggest he had more facts than he did. "Forgive me, Mr Daviot," he said, "but I have a witness, a reliable witness, who saw you arguing with . . ." he hesitated, for Annie had not been entirely certain that it had been Olivia Harman whom she had seen arguing with Daviot, but then Adrian decided to take the plunge, "who saw you arguing with Miss Harman. That was at Southampton."

"Your witness," Simon Daviot corrected the detective, "saw Miss Harman arguing with me."

"But you said –"

"I said I did not know her. Nor did I. Nor did your witness see me arguing with her, for I did not. I mistook her for an old acquaintance, greeted her and was quite unjustifiably accused of harassment. I apologized, she refused to accept the apology and continued to imply that my motives were dishonourable. I explained I was a Member of Parliament, mistakenly believing that that might convince her of my respectability, but the woman simply went on shrieking at me until I managed to shake myself loose. And that was the extent of our meeting." Simon Daviot paused. "Feminism has much to answer for."

"Does it, sir?"

"Or maybe it was PMT?" Daviot said with a sneer.

"Pre-Murder Tension, sir?" Adrian Clarke asked, and when he received no answer went on to his next question. "You said that Miss Harman reminded you of an old acquaintance. Who would that be?"

"She reminded me of the wife of one of my front bench colleagues, Chief Superintendent, and I approached her in the hope that her husband was on board. Alas, not so." Simon Daviot told the lie smoothly.

"And the argument at Southampton," Adrian Clarke went on, "was your only meeting with Miss Harman?"

"Thankfully, yes." Simon Daviot shot a cuff of his blazer to look at his Rolex again. "Is this going to take long? We were hoping to visit the church in Paros."

Adrian Clarke turned to see that the ship was coming to a harbour crowned by the remains of an ancient fort. "One last question, sir," he said, turning back. "Might I know where you were yesterday afternoon? All afternoon?"

Simon Daviot sighed as though he was merely indulging the policeman's tiresome wishes. "I went with my family to Knossos. I imagine most of the other people who chose that tour can vouch for me. I remember one particularly tiresome fellow who insisted on lecturing me about the government's plans for the Post Office and I suppose he can assure you that I was at Knossos and not, as you plainly hope, murdering impertinent Australian tourists. It rained while we were at Knossos, which we weren't expecting. I was photographed by a number of different people. We were back on the boat by five o'clock. Brenda wanted to take a bath and a rest, so I changed into dry clothes and went for a drink in the Lord's Tavern. We had dinner at the second sitting. Do I need to go on?"

Adrian Clarke felt his first flicker of something wrong. A faint scent, to be sure, but he had picked up a very slight undercurrent of nervousness that he needed to exploit. "Brenda is your wife, sir?" he asked, using an innocuous question to buy a little time while he worked out exactly how to probe the nervousness.

"Of twenty-three years," Simon Daviot confirmed.

"Lord's Tavern, sir?" Adrian Clarke said in a slightly harder voice than any he had used so far. "That hardly seems your style, sir, if you'll forgive me. You look more the kind of man who might enjoy Anderson's. Doesn't the Lord's Tavern attract a younger crowd?"

Simon Daviot played the difficult ball with practised ease. "One of the drawbacks of my job, Chief Superintendent, is the need to stay in touch with all shades of opinion. Even the opinions of callow youth."

"Quite, sir." Adrian said. "And you were in Lord's, sir, from five until eight?"

"Not all the time, no." Suddenly the nervousness was back and even more evident than before. Simon Daviot paused a long time, recrossed his legs, forgetting to hitch up his trouser knee, and then gave Adrian a long, speculative look as though he was at last trying to gauge the strength of this troublesome opponent. Finally he shrugged, reached forward, took a pen and an empty piece of paper from Adrian's desk and wrote something down. "I was in Lord's for maybe twenty minutes," he said, "and afterwards, until I changed for dinner, I was there." He indicated the piece of paper that he slid back onto the desk.

Adrian took the paper and saw that the MP had written down a cabin number. "This is not your cabin, sir?"

"No. Brenda and I have a suite like this." Simon Daviot waved his arm round the stateroom. He could not allow anyone to think he'd settle for less than the very best.

"I see, sir," Adrian Clarke said, then tried to slip a question past his interviewee's guard. "And the wet clothes you discarded after the rainstorm, sir. Have they been washed? Dried?"

"These are they, Chief Superintendent," Daviot was not in the least disconcerted by the question. He gestured at the clothes he was wearing that were palpably free of even the faintest trace of bloodstain. "The service on this ship," he said, "is really astonishingly good."

"Quite, sir," Adrian Clarke said, then looked back at the piece of paper. "Might I assume, sir, that you were not alone in this cabin?'

Daviot answered in a tone every bit as dry as that of Adrian's question. "You might assume that, Chief Superintendent."

"So –"

"So, Chief Superintendent," Simon Daviot interrupted forcefully, "I will take it as a courtesy that the information I have given you remains confidential. I have a career and a marriage to consider, and though neither might be of importance to you, I cannot see what advantage you gain by jeopardizing either. You will doubtless talk to the lady in question, and she will confirm my account." He stood up and plucked his double-breasted blazer straight. "And if there's anything else I might do to help your enquiries?" The sarcasm in the last three words was palpable.

"No, sir," Adrian Clarke said sadly, "not at this moment, sir. And thank you."

"Thank you, Chief Superintendent." Simon Daviot, victorious, left the office. The ship trembled as the engines slowed. Adrian Clarke looked at his notes and swore. The arrogance of the man surpassed belief and Adrian would have liked nothing better than to have been able to lay the murder at his door. As it was he had been patronized and then included in the MP's sordid little man-to-man confession. He had wasted his time on a man who picked up girls in bars while supposedly on holiday with his family, time that he could have been spending with Julia, and he was still no nearer to solving the case. The trouble was that he still had no real idea of the time of Olivia Harman's death, though judging from her body temperature when she was discovered he suspected that she must have died earlier than five o'clock, which put Simon Daviot MP well in the clear. But if the murder had been just after five o'clock then Daviot could have hurried from his suite to the Westcott cabin, murdered Miss Harman, then gone on to Lord's, but how would he have hidden the inevitable bloodstains? And why jeopardize a political career by murdering a virtual stranger? And where were the murderer's clothes? Not in the ship's laundry. And where was Patrick Westcott? The murder had taken place in his cabin, yet the professor seemed to have disappeared entirely. If Westcott was not dead then he must have gone ashore in Crete, which meant that he must be a prime suspect, yet Adrian knew hardly a thing about the retired Cambridge professor.

"Damn it," Adrian muttered, "damn it, damn it, damn it." He had failed, and that meant the heavy mob from Scotland Yard must pack their murder bags and fly out to *Oriana*. The ship and her seventeen hundred passengers deserved better than that; they had come expecting the holiday of a lifetime, but a murderer had thrown a shadow over that dream and Adrian no longer knew how to protect it. He picked up Daviot's piece of paper and knew he must speak to the woman, but his instinct told him it would prove futile. He had come to a dead end and so he opened the drawer of his borrowed desk, took out the bottle of scotch the purser had given him and poured himself a very large drink. Damn it, he thought, damn it.

It was back to square one, wherever the hell that might be.

"Dear me," Annie Young murmured, "dear, dear me!" She was rubbing a hand across a marble column in the small shrine of St Nicholas, the oldest part of Paros's famous Church of a Hundred Gates, and the antiquity of the church was giving her a feeling of exquisite sadness for all the world's beauty that was gone and would never be recovered. She sometimes felt that the modern world was so brutal in its carelessness about beautiful things, a fact driven home by the sudden eruption of noise caused by some wretch on a motor bike outside the church. "I think I made a mistake," she said to her nephew Mike when the sound of the bike had faded enough to allow a human voice to be heard.

"Fallible, Aunt Annie?" Mike said. He was leafing through a guide book, trying to discover how old the church was. "600 AD, it says here."

"With my will, Mike," Annie said. She was feeling uncommonly tired. Perhaps it was the heat, or else the long walk to the church. She had insisted on walking, otherwise, she said, she would miss half the island's delights; the cats, hens and donkeys in the alleys, women in their black dresses, the olives, the smells of the shops open to the street with their intriguing piles of fruit and salted fish and unfamiliar vegetables. All those things Annie loved, but the walk had left her weary.

"So who gets the loot now?" Mike asked lightly. "The cat's home?"

"No, nothing like that. I've still left everything to you."

"Oh yes," Mike was temporarily embarrassed. "Thank you."

"No dear, you don't have to thank me. It's just that I haven't left anything to Chrissie. I rather assumed she would still be your responsibility and I don't think she's quite ready to handle things herself."

"You must do whatever you think best," Mike assured her, keen to change the subject.

"That's the problem. I think I may just have added to her belief that everyone in the world is against her."

"Does she have to know?"

"I told her, last night."

"Oh Annie, why did you do that?"

"She asked me, straight out, and you know how bad I am at lying. I was so taken aback I just blurted it out, then I tried to justify my decision and ended up making the whole thing far worse."

Mike fell silent. Another party from the ship came through from the main church. Mike recognized the irritating MP, Divot or Davit, who was always on television ranting about how if workers did not want to work then no wonder jobs moved abroad. He was with a woman who was too dumpy and flustered to be anything but his wife.

"If it was a mistake, then change the will," Mike said. "Give her something. She needs it more than I do. The lorry business is fine! Except for the taxes, of course." He raised his voice. "Every politician seems to think that a man with a lorry is a man capable of paying more tax."

Annie, alerted by the sudden vehemence in her nephew's voice, glanced around and saw Daviot. "I can't stand that man!" she hissed in a voice that carried easily in the small church. "Come on!" She grabbed Mike by the elbow and pulled him towards the exit, leaving not quite quickly enough to escape Simon Daviot's drawling comment about mutton dressed as lamb. "I'm surprised he hasn't been locked up for murder!" Annie said.

"Is he the murderer then?" Mike asked, amused by his aunt's insistence that she was 'a born detective'. He suspected she was a born gossip and a born romantic and a born hippie and probably a born busybody too, but he doubted that Annie would have much patience with the detailed minutiae of real detective work. Annie would simply arrest the nearest person she disliked and be done with the case.

"I saw him with the victim!" Annie said. "They were arguing!"

"Everyone argues with Simon Daviot, it's why he was born. Do you want to walk back? Or wait for a bus?"

"We can walk." Annie pulled on her wide brimmed straw hat. She would not give in to fatigue. Good Lord, she could walk farther and faster than people less than half her age. It was probably the heat, she told herself, nothing but the heat. She would stop in one of the more interesting food shops and buy something distinctively Greek to drink for refreshment. "Do you think fig juice will give me the runs?" she asked her nephew.

Mike laughed. "How would I know?"

He walked silently beside her for a few paces. Chrissie, he thought, must be livid, or rather she must be even more than livid, for his younger sister had been in a constant rage against life almost from the moment she had been born. To be told that she had been disinherited by her one affluent relative would ensure that the rage would last for the rest of her days. "Can't you change the will?" Mike asked his aunt. "I'm really quite competent, and if the politicians let me I shall probably make a more than decent living. Don't think I'm not grateful, but I'm not sure I need your money."

She had stopped to smell some oleanders. "Do you think oleanders would grow at home? A warm spot in the garden?

By the greenhouse wall, perhaps? I suppose not. It's like that dwarf holly I planted. Just didn't take. Wrong sort of soil, I think." She walked on a few paces, then gave Mike an annoyed glance from under the brim of her hat. "Why should I give any money to Chrissie? She doesn't even like me. She never visits me, never phones me."

"It's your will, Aunt Annie, so your choice, but why in God's name did you have to tell her you'd changed it? You're only fifty-five for heaven's sake, you'll probably outlive us all."

"Shall we go and see the fortress?" she said, changing the subject.

"Not if you want to reach the ship before it leaves," Mike said. "Naxos tonight."

"A night in port!" Annie clapped her hands. "A run ashore! The bright lights!"

Mike reckoned the lights aboard *Oriana* were a good deal brighter than anything Naxos would have to offer, but he knew his aunt would love finding a small restaurant serving some disgusting foods that no one else could stomach. Mike would have much preferred one of *Oriana*'s delicious dinners, but he knew his aunt's tastes and wanted her to enjoy every minute of this holiday. "We're eating ethnic tonight, are we?" he teased her. "Roast jellyfish in garlic?"

"Octopus, certainly. And ouzo and lots of retsina. Do you mind?"

"Of course not," Mike said. Then stopped dead in the street. "Oh my Lord," he said in a voice filled with awe. "I don't believe it!"

"What?" For a second Annie was worried, then one look at her nephew's excited face assured her that the news, whatever it might be, was good.

"There. That girl. See? Coming out of the café?"

Annie looked. "Lovely," she said, "very lovely." And if there was just a hint of doubt in Annie's voice it was because she had a decided preference for free and rebellious spirits, whereas the petite blonde coming out of the café looked very neat and composed. She had on trim blue jeans, newly laundered and immaculately pressed, a white open-necked blouse and a modest string of pale-green blue beads that matched her eyes. She looked a touch too conventional for Annie's taste, but that probably made her perfect for Mike who, Annie knew, yearned after respectability. And he was clearly struck with the girl. "You know her?" Annie asked her nephew.

"Not in the least," Mike said, then, astonishing his aunt, for he was not a particularly uninhibited man, he began singing That'll Be the Day loudly enough to attract the attention of the crowds in the street. One young man wearing a rucksack so full that it stretched high over his head even danced a few steps, while most of the other passers-by either smiled and hurried on or else pretended not to notice the impromptu concert. But the girl's reaction was quite different. First she froze, then she turned with a look of expectancy that was initially replaced with surprise and then with a look of such delight that Annie's doubts about her evaporated instantly. The girl smiled, shook her long blonde hair in disbelief, then walked up the street. "I said I'd sing for you next time," she said reprovingly.

"Was it that bad?" Mike asked, then blushed. "My name's Mike," he added, "Mike Young, and this ageing hippy is my Aunt Annie."

"Roman," the girl answered, "Roman Brindle." She shook hands with both of them.

"Roman?" Mike asked, thinking it was the most beautiful name in the world.

"From Beaconsfield, not Rome. I think I was born just after my mother had watched Ben Hur. It's a good job it wasn't Lost Horizons or else I'd be Shangri La Brindle!" She smiled, looking from Mike to Annie and back again. "You're on holiday here?"

"On a ship called *Oriana*," Annie answered. "They pamper us all day long, but we escaped for an hour."

"So did I," Roman said.

Mike's heart gave an involuntary spasm. "You mean . . . ?"

"I'm crew," Roman interrupted him. Mike, for once, seemed almost incapable of coherent speech. "I'm one of your entertainers," Roman went on. "You mean you haven't heard me sing?" She pretended to be offended.

"My God, no," Mike said.

"If he had, my dear," Annie said, "he wouldn't be here with me. He'd be outside your stage door."

Roman laughed. "The Pacific Lounge, Mike, on the Promenade Deck. I'm there almost every night, and tonight you can catch me at nine-thirty and eleven o'clock. You can applaud, hurl flowers or both."

Mike was flustered. "If only I could. Oh, dear . . ."

"Of course you can!" said Annie. "He was going to suffer tonight," she explained to Roman, "and eat tepid octopus with me, but he didn't really want to. He'll be much happier with roast beef on board. He's a traditional Englishman." She looked at the two and felt a pang of jealousy. Wild horses wouldn't keep them apart. Plainly it had been love at first sight, or at least lust which was usually where love had its origins. She sighed, knowing this rare, heady excitement would never be hers again. "Never mind," she said aloud.

"What?" Mike asked, immediately concerned.

"Nothing, my dear, nothing. I shall be fine. Maybe you're right. Maybe tonight I should talk to Chrissie. So how did you two meet?" she asked as they walked toward the harbour.

Ahead of them, framed by the white houses and the glittering blue sea, *Oriana* waited for her passengers. The ship looked beautiful; a great white pleasure craft lording the seas where Homer's heroes had sailed to war, where once the quinqueremes had dipped their oars and where Cleopatra's gilded barge had come to fetch Mark Anthony and take him to her bed beside the Nile. Annie sighed. Oh, to be young again, she thought, oh to be young.

The sun was setting as the great ship sailed north around Paros toward the neighbouring island of Naxos where Dionysus the god of wine had fallen in love with the mortal Ariadne, Princess of Crete. "Did goddesses fall in love with mortal men?" Dr Horatio Patel asked Hilary Brown. Dr Patel had been leafing through a guide book in Hilary Brown's cabin where he had come to deliver a sedative to Rosamund Westcott.

"I'm sure they did," Hilary said briskly. "No point in being a goddess if you can't take your pick of the earthly talent. She's sleeping." She added the last two words after peering around the curtain of the stateroom to look at her friend.

"Good." Dr Patel dropped the guide book back on the coffee table. "I shall call tomorrow morning?"

"Please do," Hilary said. The eminent psychologist and ex-head girl of Lady Harriet's College for Young Ladies had taken charge of her old school friend Rosamund whose husband, Patrick, had now been missing for twenty-four hours. The police in Crete, *Oriana*'s last port of call, had been alerted, but there had been no news yet. Patrick had simply disappeared, leaving behind a corpse in an empty cabin. Though of course, Hilary assured herself, Patrick could not have done it. Patrick did not have the guts to stab someone in the chest . . . in the back, maybe. "Won't you have something to drink?" she asked Dr Patel.

"I'd like that, thank you."

"Off duty, are you?" Hilary Brown did not wait for an answer, but stooped to open the refrigerator. "I've got vodka here, gin, tonic and club soda. There's some sherry somewhere."

"A gin and tonic would be wonderful, thank you. And yes, I'm off duty till tomorrow morning. Someone else is catering to the sunburns and upset stomachs." Dr Patel stood at the door leading to Hilary's balcony and stared at the steep, dark-clad slopes of Paros's central peak. "Thank you." He turned as Hilary Brown gave him the drink. "Cheers."

Hilary turned off the television set. "It seems to soothe Rosamund," she explained. "Can't stand it myself. I wish television had never been invented. Shall we go onto the balcony?"

"You must do well out of television," Dr Patel said as he followed Hilary onto the private balcony. "I've seen you on the box often enough."

Hilary smiled and shrugged. "Television is for appearing on, not for watching." She raised her glass of sherry, sipped, then glanced back toward the cabin where her friend was sleeping. "Poor Rosamund. Married to the wrong man all her life and now agonizing because the silly bastard has gone missing. She started out saying she didn't care if he disappeared forever, but I didn't think it would last. Rosamund doesn't like loose ends, never has done, they make her jittery. If Patrick is going to go she will want to see him in a box and be able to organize a nice little funeral for all his Cambridge cronies to attend. She can't bear the thought of not knowing what has happened to him. I suppose that apart from anything else she needs to be sure he won't turn up again." Hilary gave a short bark of a laugh. "Do you think he fell overboard?"

"That never seems to happen," Dr Patel said.

"A good way to go, I sometimes think." Hilary gestured to Dr Patel to sit on one of the cushioned chairs. "A momentary discomfort because of the breathing reflex, then all rather calm."

"Was Professor Westcott suicidal?" Dr Patel asked.

"Heavens, no. He's one of the most self-satisfied beasts I know," Hilary said as she sat herself down opposite the doctor. "Complacent and smug and not very useful. Like a big spoiled dog."

"A clever man, surely?"

"Because he's a professor?" Hilary laughed. "The academic profession, my dear Doctor, is filled with timid creatures who've never dared step outside the schoolroom. They retired from life before it ever began! Patrick's like that, though God knows he must have made some money from somewhere. Private inheritance, I suppose. Not that it's any of my business."

"Other people's business is usually more intriguing than our own," Dr Patel responded mildly.

The first stars were shining above Naxos, tiny pinpricks of brightness in a sweep of velvet dark. The sea was rippled by the setting sun so that the ship left a great swathe of tumbling liquid light in its wake. "You should know that," Dr Patel went on. "Other people's business is your business."

"You sound resentful," Hilary said.

"No, in fact I envy you."

"Why?"

He gave a ghost of a smile. "I suppose," he said, "because you seem so in control of life. Most people live in incipient chaos, prey to every emotion. They come to my surgery and want Valium, sleeping tablets, whatever, always something to dampen down the fires of life. No one ever comes and asks me for an elixir to make life brighter or more exciting." He waved a slim hand at the island silhouetted against the star-pricked evening sky. "The land of heroes, Dr Brown, who didn't need chemicals to hide from life."

"Rubbish," Hilary said. "The heroes all drank like fishes. Ambrosia was probably neat whisky with a dash of rubbing alcohol."

Dr Patel would not be deflected from his thesis. "I still say most people don't want to be heroes. They crave the ordinary and the safe, and they write to you when life goes wrong and pushes them out of their emotional depth, and you are so very good at giving sensible answers. I envy you that."

Hilary Brown smiled at the compliment. "Are you saying you don't give sensible answers in your surgery?"

Dr Patel returned the smile. "I have to look into their eyes while I give it."

Hilary was silent for a few heartbeats. "You're accusing me of being like Patrick," she said. "Of being disengaged from life."

"Am I? I didn't mean to. I apologize."

"No," Hilary said, brushing aside the apology as she stared at the glimmer of lights waiting ashore. "No," she said again, thinking of her impeccably tidy life and wondering why Horatio Patel had suddenly made her feel the sterility of it all. Or maybe, she thought, it was the ship that had done it; the exquisitely privileged, beautiful, comfortable ship that could take a person temporarily away from the mundane world and so give them a chance to reflect on life. "How very dangerous," she said aloud.

"What is?"

"*Oriana*, Doctor. It could change people's lives."

"Is that a bad thing?"

"I don't know," she said. " I don't know."

The ship gave a mournful hoot on its siren. Lights were bright and welcoming ashore while high overhead, above the island where Dionysus had loved his mortal girl, a shooting star whipped light across the sky like fire from heaven.

Professor Patrick Westcott woke in a wide bed. It was nighttime and a bare light bulb burned on a bedside table. A fan beat monotonously above his head which was splitting with the most excruciating headache. Like one of Mummy's migraines must have been, he thought. Poor Mummy. He tried to sit up and the pain slithered down to his gullet, making him want to retch.

"There's a bucket beside the bed, Professor."

"Oh, Jesus!" Professor Westcott retched dryly into the filthy bucket. Everything was filthy in the room. A cockroach scuttled away from the bucket. The bedsheet was grimy, the room smelt of damp decay. "Who the hell are you?" he asked when he had recovered.

The man sitting facing the foot of the bed was middle-aged and bald. His face was plump and had a clever, world-weary look like someone who has seen and suffered much. "My name," he said, then paused, "is Nicholas." His tone suggested he had plucked the name out of thin air. "You don't remember meeting me last night?"

All Patrick remembered was a message coming to his cabin where he had been working on his lecture notes. His wife had fallen in Elounda, the message said, nothing too serious, but a taxi was waiting to take Professor Westcott to the clinic where a cut on Rosamund's head was being stitched. Except there had been no clinic, and when Patrick climbed out of the taxi in some horrid back street in Iraklion a man had hit him. He remembered thinking he was being mugged, and how very unpleasant that was and also how very typical of foreigners, and now he was here, in a large but filthy bed with a plump man called Nicholas smiling at him. "Where's my wife?" Patrick demanded. "Oh, my God!" Patrick had suddenly realized he was stark, pink, plump and shrinkingly naked. He had never been overly fond of his own body, now he felt positively ashamed of it as he snatched the dirty sheet up to his waist. There was a throbbing swelling on the side of his head. "I demand to know . . ." he began.

"Quiet," Nicholas said in a soothing voice. "You are in Iraklion, Professor, and your ship is in Naxos. You can easily reach Naxos before the ship leaves in the morning. Your clothes are in the cupboard," he gestured towards a broken wardrobe, "and I'm sure it will not be beyond your wit to invent a tale for your wife's consumption. Too much to drink ashore? The heat, the unfamiliar liquor, the excitement? The ship leaving before you recovered?"

"You're drivelling, man," Patrick said, then winced because of the pain in his head. "I demand to be given a telephone now."

"Of course," Nicholas said, but instead of producing a telephone he threw a packet of photographs onto the bed. "They're not the best pictures I've ever taken, Professor, but they'll suffice, don't you think? We drugged you, of course, so you're not co-operating with your partner, but I doubt the newspapers will know that."

Patrick stared aghast at the photographs that showed his horrid body in the passionate embrace of a small, lithe, suntanned boy who looked scarcely a day over fourteen. What was so awful, so terrible, so completely shaming was that Patrick felt an immediate and overwhelming lust for the boy in the pictures. That lust was so untimely and unexpected that he wanted to weep. "You can keep the pictures, Professor," Nicholas went on. "We, of course, have the negatives. Spiridos is a beautiful child, is he not? What is the proper word? Pederasty?" Nicholas smiled. He spoke perfect English, but with a trace of a foreign accent. "We could have used a girl, of course, but somehow, I don't know why, we always thought you preferred boys."

Patrick sat up in bed and tried to muster what tiny scraps of dignity he could find. "What do you want?"

Nicholas shook his head sadly, as though Patrick was being a particularly obtuse and difficult pupil. "You know what we want, Professor. We asked you for it a year ago."

Patrick leaned back on the bedhead and closed his eyes. He had one secret in his life, one terrible, awful, huge secret, but he had never thought of that secret as something dirty like this nasty back room with its peeling blue paint and its creaking iron-framed bed. He had thought the secret was something rather noble and exciting, but also something so far in his past that it would never catch up with him.

For Patrick Westcott, erstwhile Mallalieu Professor of Byzantine Studies at the University of Cambridge, had been a recruiter for the KGB. If they ever found out the newspapers would call him a spy and a traitor, though whenever Patrick thought about it these days, which was not often, he preferred to think that he had merely been a passionate crusader for justice. But the world would not see it that way; they would just complete the list: Philby, MacLean, Burgess, Blunt . . . and the newspapers always claimed there was a 'fifth man' and always suspected that the 'fifth man' was a Cambridge don, but no one had ever pointed a finger at Patrick Westcott pottering in his Byzantine world with his stock liberal attitudes and his plump wife busy at her tapestry classes. Or no one had pointed a finger until a year ago when Patrick had been asked to contribute, that had been their word, contribute, a hundred thousand pounds toward the retirement fund of some KGB thugs. Patrick had dismissed the request and had almost forgotten about it.

"We paid you a lot of money once," the man who called himself Nicholas said.

"And I earned it!" Patrick snapped.

"How could you have earned it? We lost!" Nicholas said. He stood and walked to the shuttered window and opened it a crack. He lit a cigarette, then turned back. "The filthy imperialists won, Professor. The workers' paradise is now a slum of pizza cafés and hamburger stands. The brave new world is just a shadow of the old one after all." Nicholas drew on his cigarette. "What did your hero St John Chrysostom say? That wealth doesn't belong to the wealthy, but is only held in trust for all mankind. Wasn't that why the Empress Eudoxia hated him so much? He was a proto-communist, but you're a real communist, Professor, and your wealth has been held in trust too long. Some of us need it. We have been abandoned by our country, so now we are collecting debts from those who took from our country in the past."

"But I earned it!" Patrick protested feebly.

Nicholas leaned over the foot of the bed and snatched the sheet away from Patrick's body. "You earned nothing! You were a fellow traveller, you played at being a radical, nothing more! Some of us risked our lives, Professor, and now we are thrown out of the security service like garbage! No one wants to touch us. No one wants to help us. We are given a pension that won't buy warmth in winter or shade in summer, yet we fought and we died and we struggled for the communist cause and now we've lost. We are on the scrap heap of history, isn't that what they say? Yet some people, like you, Professor, hardly fought at all and lost nothing. You just became rich out of the workers' struggle. You are a wealthy man, Professor, and this little demonstration," Nicholas scornfully flicked one of the photographs, "is to show you that though we are not wealthy, we are not helpless either. You didn't bring a cheque book with you, which is a pity, but before your capitalist cruise ends, Professor, we shall come to you." He drew on the cigarette. "Two hundred thousand pounds for now."

"No!" Patrick protested.

Nicholas laughed. "You're free to go, Professor. There are hotels not far away. You can doubtless use your credit card to fly to Naxos in the morning. Or perhaps you'd prefer to go home? But we'll find you, and find you soon, and if you do not give us money?" Nicholas shrugged, then laughed. "Your choice, Professor, your choice. Good day."

Patrick heard the footsteps go down the stairs, then the crash as an outside door closed. He wanted to weep. He picked up one of the photographs and looked at the slim lovely boy and suddenly, unstoppably, did so.

Chrissie Young stirred her Kir Royale with a swizzle stick, then pushed black hair out of her eyes and gave Rupert Revell a speculative look. She liked Rupert more and more. He had a sophistication that she envied. He had travelled the world, been an actor and knew what drinks to order. He was so different from her family in Bedford with their cheese-paring economies and their cloying admiration for her elder brother Mike and his lorry business. The insinuation was always that Chrissie should get herself a job, an education, a husband, a career, a family, a future, whereas Rupert Revell seemed to understand that not everyone was supposed to follow the dull roads of duty. Some people, he had told her that afternoon, were born corsairs.

Now they were sitting in the Crow's Nest, at one of the tables hard by the forward windows that offered a marvellous view across the harbour toward Naxos's floodlit castle and cathedral. To other passengers the couple looked almost as dazzling as the view itself, for Rupert's golden good looks were effortlessly matched by Chrissie's careless dark beauty, illuminated by his company. They looked magnificent together.

"That's the sort of boat we should be on," Rupert said, pointing toward a private yacht that was sliding in a blaze of cabin lights out into the dark evening sea.

"Why aren't we?"

"A lack of nerve, maybe?" Rupert said.

"Go on," Chrissie said.

Rupert lit a cigarette, then pushed the packet to Chrissie. "People are frightened of the consequences of their actions, when they should be looking at the rewards."

"Go on," she said.

"People are scared of being caught," Rupert said.

"Go on."

"Morality," Rupert said, enjoying this chance to play a worldly man to a beautiful young woman, "is the fancy label that dull people attach to timidity."

"Go on," Chrissie said.

"Most criminals," Rupert said, then gave a slight shrug as though to apologize for introducing the word, "are low rent. They're fools. They're uneducated, unimaginative and unpleasant. Apply some wit and intelligence to a crime and what could we not achieve?"

"One of those?" Chrissie asked, nodding toward the yacht that was now silhouetted in the harbour entrance.

"One of those each," Rupert said. He was amazed to meet someone who so perfectly matched himself. Chrissie was as dependent on her brother as Rupert was on his sister, and Mike Young sounded just as virtuous, hard-working and boring as Julia. Chrissie had an innate sense of life's unfairness that matched Rupert's own, and she revealed a ruthlessness Rupert would like to think matched his own. They'd been inseparable from the moment they met, and now, step by step, aided by alcohol, they goaded each other toward the dark centres of their own hearts. "That's him," Rupert said, nodding towards Simon Daviot who had come into the bar with his two daughters, Charlotte and Sophie, and was now settling at a table near the piano. Daviot was in smart but casual dress, whilst the children looked as if they would much rather be somewhere else.

"You're sure that's him?" Chrissie asked.

Rupert nodded. He had pestered Julia into revealing which of the passengers had been her lover and now he shared that secret with Chrissie. "Simon Daviot, Member of Parliament for West Somerfield."

Chrissie sipped her drink. "He wouldn't like the *Sun* to be told about your sister?"

"No, I should think not," Rupert said.

"And your sister wouldn't like it," Chrissie said.

"No, certainly not."

She smiled at Rupert. When Chrissie smiled all the sullenness went from her face to be replaced by a radiant beauty that would have broken the heart of a saint. "And my problem," she said, "is a mean cow of an aunt who we are going to have supper with." Chrissie had virtually been ordered by Mike to accompany Annie, and all because he wanted to listen to some scrubby little lounge singer. Chrissie had grudgingly agreed, but insisted that Annie treated Rupert to dinner as well. "And don't be surprised if my aunt flirts with you," Chrissie went on. "She's as ancient as Stonehenge, but insists on dressing like a seventeen year old. It's so embarrassing."

"But she's wealthy?"

Chrissie nodded. "Huge house, widow, no children. She writes these sickly children's stories, all about cute little bunnies and wily old foxes. They sell by the ton. They even make them into television cartoons."

Rupert smiled. "We could be busy these next few days."

Chrissie smiled again. "We're corsairs, you and I." Then she leaned across the table to kiss Rupert. He met her halfway. The kiss lingered and other passengers smiled to see such young and perfect love. That was, after all, what a cruise was all about.

Oriana's restaurants were full that evening, her casino was busy and her theatre was stirring to life as the stage crew set up for the opening act of Guys and Dolls. Jasmine and Lisa put on make-up in their shared cabin, good humouredly squabbling over lip gloss and eye-liner, and wondering what men would light up their lives tonight. Couples danced in the Pacific Lounge, others strolled the smooth, wooden decks, some went to the lavish wide-screen cinema while a few die-hards still worked out in the health club or swam their laps in one of the ship's three swimming pools. Hilary Brown and Horatio Patel agreed to dine together, while Adrian Clarke pored over the passenger list in his makeshift office. Sandra Van Horn went to the beauty shop for a late makeover and wondered, as she sat beneath the beautician's lights, just why she went to all this trouble when there was no lover to escort her into the elegant Oriental Restaurant. In the Pacific Lounge Roman Brindle sang as she had never sung before, though Mike Young would not have cared if she could not sing at all. Both of them were trembling on the delicious edge of love because for them, as for so many others, *Oriana* had worked her magic. From afar the lustrous ship looked like a palace of floating light and all her eleven passenger decks were filled with an air of joy and expectation.

Ashore, where she was waiting in the warm Aegean night for Chrissie and her handsome escort, Annie Young shivered.

chapter SEVEN

Brenda Daviot stood at the very top of the four-deck atrium and looked across at the scattering of people in the Tiffany Bar. She was slightly out of breath, partly because of climbing the stairs all the way up beside the waterfall – a waterfall . . . on a ship, she thought in amazement every time she saw it – and partly because she was in more than a small flutter due to her rising apprehension. It was one thing to sit in the security of the stateroom and declare that if Simon declined to have a drink with her, she would jolly well have a drink alone, and quite another, standing here in the yellow frock the girls said made her look like a giant Easter chicken, to actually do it.

Simon was in a mood about something. He insisted it had nothing to do with being questioned about that poor girl being murdered, and rather implied, instead, that it was Brenda's fault.

"Join in, can't you?" he'd said crossly, pulling on his trousers.

She had said nothing. She had stared at his legs and had wondered, for a second, if his mistress had also noticed that they were too thin. In a few years, they'd be elderly legs, not at all the kind of legs a real Lothario needed.

"Don't sulk," Simon said.

Brenda turned back to her dressing table mirror. It was in just the right place, as was everything in the stateroom. Brenda never stopped marvelling at the ingenuity of it all. She looked, without any affection, at her unmade-up face.

"It's difficult," she said. "We've only been here a few days and there's so many people. And the murder –"

"Do not mention the murder," Simon commanded. He was buttoning up the cuffs of a blue linen shirt.

Brenda thought of last night, when he had, with a sigh of duty, flung himself across her. He'd done the same every night of the cruise so far in order, she supposed, to satisfy himself, purely technically, that this was a second honeymoon. She had lain there, as she had lain now for too many years, waiting for him to finish, staring into the darkness and wondering what it would feel like to be so excited yourself that you wanted to devour your lover. Once or twice she had smelt other women on him. When Simon finished, he put the light on and looked at her for a moment with an odd expression, as if he was waiting for her to say thank you. Last night, looking back at his entirely insensitive face, Brenda had resolved that when he threw himself on her the next time, she would throw him off again. She was prepared to pay quite a price for the status and security of being his wife, but not, she felt, in this way. The hypocrisy of it psychologically and the nastiness of it physically were too much.

She had woken feeling almost cheerful. It was an unspeakable relief. The cruise was proving such a trial, what with Simon being so phoney and so selfish and the girls, encouraged by him, behaving so badly. If they'd only been a little older, Brenda thought, old enough to have had their own hearts bruised, they might have had some sympathy for her. But they seemed to have none and, on top of that, appeared intent upon behaving in an abandoned, philistine, almost trashy way that was very hard to bear. And Simon wouldn't reprimand them, wouldn't support her in her anxious shame about them.

"At least," he said with some edge, "they're joining in."

She supposed they were, if joining in was to be defined by almost casting themselves in front of every crew member and Greek waiter in sight. Charlotte had even tried to flirt with the guide at Knossos, a deeply serious young man who had spoken passionately to them about the Minoans. He had laid his hand on a little stone throne and said in a voice that was full of awe –

"The throne of Ariadne."

The way he said it had made Brenda shiver for a moment, as if all the ghosts of the Cretan past were shimmering about them in the hot blue air, Ariadne and the Priest King and the graceful boys who leaped over the bulls. But Charlotte was awful, simply awful. She had cast herself down on the little throne, spreading her legs in her cut-off denim shorts and giggling up at the young guide. Brenda had seized her arm.

"Charlotte!"

The guide had simply said, with a kind, reproving courtesy, "I am afraid it is forbidden to sit there, madam."

Simon had refused to be horrified. He had said it was simply high spirits and he wished other people would show a few more of them. Brenda had been very cast down as she had been by everything that had happened for ages until, for some reason, that small midnight resolve not to allow Simon to have sex with her just for form's sake. Until he could tell the difference between having sex and making love, Brenda told herself, he could go without. It was astonishing that such a resolve could make her feel so much better, but it did. So much better, in fact, that when Simon declared that he and the girls were going to drink together in the Crow's Nest without her, thank you, Brenda had replied to her own amazement, "Fine. I'll drink somewhere else."

Simon had snorted. He had added a cravat to the blue linen shirt, immediately ageing him by ten years and said, with weighty sarcasm, "That'll be the day, when you show even a glimmer of initiative."

She thought now that the yellow dress had been a mistake. Her black one would have been better; even if the cut wasn't as good, it was less conspicuous. She hovered, plucking at a nearby arrangement of plants, wondering what sort of drink she would ask for, what words she would use.

"Deep breath," Brenda said quietly to herself. "One, two, three –"

Nothing happened. She straightened up and pulled her tummy in. Women of forty-two in the Western world in the 1990s were both entitled to drink alone and should be accomplished at it. Head up, eyes ahead, walk straight through to the end of the bar, find a table without hesitating, sit at it, summon a waiter. Off you go.

It seemed a long way. It also seemed that a lot of people, those comfortably coupled people who appeared to fill the ship, had run out of anything to say to one another and therefore had all the time in the world to watch a woman who should have been a size twelve, in a too-bright size sixteen yellow dress, walk past them with the mechanical step of a wind-up toy soldier. She made it bravely to the end of the bar. There wasn't an empty table. There were two people at every one, and at the last one, a man alone, a dark man in spectacles, with slightly drooping shoulders. He looked, Brenda thought, very much as she often felt. She stopped marching and peered at him. It was the ship's doctor, Dr Patel.

Brenda summoned up every reserve of courage she had and said, in a high voice she didn't recognize as her own, "Dr Patel?"

Horatio Patel looked up. His face, she saw, was full of sorrow, which he removed with professional politeness when he saw her. He stood up. "Madam."

"I'm . . . I'm Brenda Daviot," Brenda said. Her hands fluttered about her, as if to indicate her confusion.

He looked at her gravely. "How may I help you? Are you ill?"

"No," Brenda said, "not in the least."

"Then –"

"If I'm not interrupting you," Brenda said in a rush, "I'd be so grateful if I could sit at your table. You see, there isn't an empty one . . ."

Horatio Patel pulled a second chair away from the table. "I should be delighted."

"But I expect you are waiting for someone . . ."

"Yes," he said, and then untruthfully, "but I would rather not wait alone. May I get you a drink?"

"Oh no!" Brenda said, scrabbling for her bag. "Oh no! You mustn't! I mean you really shouldn't pay for me! Otherwise . . ."

"Otherwise what?"

Brenda said impulsively, "Otherwise you'll think I interrupted you for more than just somewhere to sit."

Horatio Patel looked at her more carefully. She was, poor woman, the wife of that dreadful MP, he knew that, and the mother of two of the kind of loud-mouthed confident English girls he hoped his boys would never marry. But she had a sweet face, an anxious, pleading face, and a pretty colouring quite swamped by that terrible dress, the colour of cheap butter.

"I shall buy you," he said, "a glass of champagne."

"No!" she said, horrified.

"Yes," he said firmly. "I prescribe it often. As a tonic. Wouldn't you like a tonic?"

She nodded vigorously. "But I can't let you pay . . ."

"This time you can. Another time, you shall pay for me."

He amazed himself. Why on earth had he said that? He, the least flirtatious of men. Beware of pity, he said to himself sternly, beware of pity.

Brenda's face was illuminated. "Oh!" she said, and then, "how sweet of you!"

When he had brought her the drink and the refill for his own tomato juice, she seemed prepared, almost eager, to talk. She wanted to know more about Olivia Harman. Horatio Patel shook his head.

"We can say no more, I'm afraid. Not until the people from Scotland Yard arrive. All I can tell you is that the ship is quite safe now. I can absolutely assure you of that."

Brenda said, a little recklessly, "I don't think I'm very interested in safety . . ."

"No?"

"No," she said. "There seems to be such a high price to pay for it."

He glanced at her. “In what way?”

Brenda took a large swallow of her champagne, rather than a decorous sip. “A woman like me, an unfashionable sort of wife and mother woman, might seem to have security, enough food and clothes and things, but because of that outward security we’re not expected to ask for the other kind.” She stopped. “I shouldn’t be drinking this.”

“What other kind?” Horatio asked.

“I’m talking terribly out of turn,” Brenda said. “I hardly know you.”

He leaned across the table. He said, astonishing himself, “You mean love?”

She nodded vigorously.

He said gently, “Finish your champagne. My guest will be here in five minutes. But we’ll talk about this another time, shall we?”

She nodded again. “I’d love to. Have I behaved badly?”

“No,” he said, “only honestly.”

She drained her glass and stood up. “Doctors must get so sick of people unburdening themselves –”

He rose, too. “We wouldn’t become doctors, you know, if we didn’t quite like people. We’d be engineers instead.”

She smiled at him. “Thank you, Dr Patel.”

“Horatio.”

She said delightedly, “Oh, how funny!”

“My father didn’t think so. He had a passion for Lord Nelson. Our house in Kampala was full of books on eighteenth-century naval history. My sister was called Emma and the family dog was Victory.”

Brenda held her hand out. “Goodbye.”

He bowed slightly over it and then watched her walk, not very gracefully, among the tables back to the staircase and disappear down behind the waterfall. She had hardly vanished from sight when he became aware that Hilary Brown, immaculate in white linen with turquoise and silver necklace and bracelets, was standing beside him and wearing an expression very like the one his mother had worn when he had confessed to her, soon after their hurried and alarming arrival in England, that he had a crush on an English girl at school.

"And who," Hilary Brown demanded, "was that?"

Rupert Revell lay alone on his bed in the double cabin he shared with Julia and cleaned his nails with a toothpick. He was naked, except for a bath towel, and had spent the last five minutes examining himself in the mirror because he thought he could detect the very faintest curve of flesh above his waist – which definitely wasn't there last week – and two new lines at the sides of his eyes which didn't vanish, as they used to, when he stopped smiling. He had also hunted about above his ears for a grey hair or two, and although he hadn't found any, he had come across several that looked as if they were about to give in. It was tremendously depressing. It added to Rupert's general feeling that having been brought along on this cruise to fulfil Julia's mad purpose, which she had now abandoned in favour of this Adrian Clarke bloke who looked to Rupert more like a cardboard cut-out detective than you would have believed possible, he had now been dumped. He had tried to do what she wanted. He'd tried to play this idiotic married game but she wouldn't play with him and then she got furious with him for drinking too much and was full of aunty-ish warnings about Chrissie Young who she said would prove to be nothing but trouble.

"I like that," Rupert had said. "I like trouble."

It was true. He did. At least, he liked it as long as it didn't really touch him, as long as it stayed just a bit of a buzz, a turn-on. He had thought Chrissie was a real turn-on, all smoulder and simmering resentment, until she had erupted last night, on the way back to the ship, and accused him of flirting with her aunt. Rupert had been amazed. Of course he had flirted with her aunt! He thought he was supposed to.

She was a pretty weird sort of aunt. Rupert had started the evening thinking he couldn't stand watching an elderly woman in all those 'summer of love' clothes, playing the amateur detective with her wretched notebook. Chrissie said sourly that her brother Mike adored this aunt, really adored her, which she, Chrissie, thought was creepy. Rupert did, too, at first, but then something peculiar had begun to happen as the meal wore on, something that had nothing to do with all those awful tentacle things they were eating, nor the paint-stripper wine, but seemed more and more to have everything to do with Annie Young's personality. She was fun. She was, in fact, far more fun than Chrissie and once, when she leaned forward to pour more wine and Rupert prepared to avert his gaze as he always did from the possible horror of the sight of any cleavage over the age of thirty, he saw that she had smooth skin and a perfectly passable bosom. Rupert had choked on his retsina.

I must be out of my mind, he told himself, I must be. Here I am, actually fancying someone old enough to be my mother. He felt his forehead, furtively. It was quite cool. He looked at Chrissie. She was glaring at him and she appeared, only a night after she had looked so desirable, about as fanciable as a dustbin.

He'd then gone a bit far. He had openly flirted with Annie. He'd trapped her foot between his under the table and she had let at least a minute go by before she pulled hers away again. He'd tried to hold both hers and Chrissie's hands as they walked back along the waterfront to the ship, but Chrissie had snatched hers away, so he had interlaced his fingers with Annie's and kept them there.

Chrissie had followed him to his cabin and screamed at him. He had tried to lock her out but she made so much noise outside that he had to let her in and listen to a screeched catalogue of his vices. He had said, once or twice, in injured innocence, "But you said she'd flirt with me! You told me not to be surprised."

Chrissie had yelled at him, "I didn't think you'd bloody well flirt back, you repulsive little gigolo!"

When she finally went, he made his way stealthily up to B Deck and quickly checked where Annie's cabin was. He hadn't quite the nerve – not quite – to knock on the door and ask her for a nightcap.

But the whole episode set him thinking. If Julia lost interest in her programme of revenge and ceased to feel that he, Rupert, was anything more to her than an expensive nuisance, he'd better start looking out for himself a bit. He remembered mooning about Julia's flat and daydreaming about this personable, sweet-natured older woman who'd turn to him with such gratitude and generosity, overcome by his charm and youth. Well, perhaps he'd found her. Perhaps Annie Young, rich, alone, and plainly susceptible both to young men and to the possibility of her own continued attractiveness, would be a prey worth stalking.

Rupert sat up and ruffled his hair. He looked into the mirror again. Women of over fifty couldn't care less, he was sure, about slightly softened waistlines or three threatened grey hairs. He got off the bed and stretched. Then he dropped the towel and looked at himself, front, side and back, over his shoulder. Pretty good really. He thought fleetingly of Chrissie. She could spit like a wild cat, but she couldn't do him any harm. She'd got nothing on him, had she, to tell the *Sun*? Humming, Rupert practised a few nonchalant pelvic thrusts and went to find his white jeans.

Jazzy and Lisa lay on their twin beds and groaned. It was too much lunch again, after too much breakfast and a doughnut around eleven-thirty. Jazzy had said that if she couldn't have a bloke, she was bloody well going to have a doughnut.

"Christ," she said, "the talent round here makes you weep! Nancy boys or old geezers who make my dad look a boy."

Lisa had painted her toe-nails frosted orange. She examined them now.

"There's the Greeks –"

Jazzy pulled a face.

"Another day like this and it'll come to that."

She turned over onto her side and opened the bedside cupboard between them. A bottle of Bacardi rolled out.

"Wanna get slaughtered?"

"Nope," Lisa said. She closed her eyes and dreamed of feeling thin and energetic, not fat and stuffed and bored.

"What're we gonna do then?"

"I dunno."

"Want to go on shore?"

"Not much."

Jazzy poked the rum bottle and it rolled quietly away and came to rest in the pile of multi-coloured Lycra they'd been meaning to take to the ship's washing machines for days.

Jazzy could see her leopard print leggings and Lisa's neon pink mini, and her Madonna bra-top, all black and covered in zips, that Den said was dead common. If Den felt that, it made her like the bra-top a lot. She said, "I could do with a furry chest round here."

Lisa sighed.

"I'm too full to think of sex."

"Come up on deck," Jazzy said.

"Can't be fagged."

Jazzy sat up and yanked her white crop-top down. She fished about on the floor with her feet for her stilettos.

"Come on."

"No –"

Jazzy leaned over and gave Lisa a sharp dig in the soft flesh above the waistband of her shorts. Then she stood up.

"Give over!"

"Get up, you load of old blubber. Get up and come on deck with me."

"Jazz –"

"I didn't ask you to come with me just to lie about all day being such a bleeding misery guts."

Lisa sat up very slowly and looked down at the roll of flesh which now lay snugly between the bottom of her top and the top of her shorts.

"It was that Black Forest Gateau –"

"You didn't need to eat two slices. Fat pig."

Jazzy reached down, seized Lisa's hands and yanked her to her feet.

"Put your shades on. You look awful."

"You too, sweetie pie."

They tottered out into the air-conditioned corridor of F Deck and made their way unsteadily towards the reception area. One of the receptionists, slim and bright-eyed who no doubt lived on a diet of lettuce leaves and mineral water, greeted them brightly.

"Good afternoon, ladies. Have you everything you want? We shall be off in an hour. Istanbul next. Shall I book you on a tour for the Black Sea?"

They stared at her.

"Not bloody likely," Lisa said.

She smiled back, undaunted.

"Just a spot of sunbathing then –"

They turned away from her and toiled up two flights of stairs to the Promenade Deck.

"Jesus," Jazzy said, "Istanbul! Did you know we were going to Istanbul?"

"I didn't come for Istanbul," Lisa said. "I didn't come for any old screwball places. I came for the nosh and the flesh and I've seen too much of one and not a bloody whisker of the other."

They stumbled grumpily along the Promenade Deck to the point where they overlooked the gangway – a bit of a grand staircase Jazzy had said – which ran down to the waterfront. There were hawkers at the foot of it, hawkers of all the usual Greek tat that you didn't want here, let alone at home on a wet Monday.

Jazzy clutched Lisa's arm.

"Look –"

"Where?"

"There," Jazzy said, "coming towards the ship! Oh look –"

In the ramshackle, colourful crowd down on the edge of the port, was a small compact phalanx of men. There were perhaps five of them, and they walked a bit like soldiers, very purposefully, except they were in civvies rather than uniform. They were making unquestionably for the ship, not looking to the right or to the left, taking no notice of the embroidered tablecloths and woven bags being flapped in their faces.

Lisa stood up straighter. "Well," she said, "what do you reckon?"

Jazzy had already fastened her gaze on one of the men at the back of the little squad, biggish and blond. She took off her shades to see him better. She said softly, "Scotland Yard."

"Cripes. The fuzz."

"Posh fuzz," Jazzy said. "I'd recognize them anywhere."

The five men began to mount the gangway.

"Fuzz or no fuzz," Lisa said. "You know what I think?"

"What?"

"Gorgeous," Lisa said.

Sandra Van Horn sat upright under an umbrella on the pool deck with The Blue Guide to Turkey open in front of her, and a pot of lapsang souchong tea. She believed in fresh air, but not in sunlight, so she wore a long Italian silk robe she had bought in Bergdorf Goodman, a matching turban and DKNY sunglasses.

Her eyes were on the book, but not her mind. Her mind was not in any way as composed as her upright posture behind the teapot might suggest, and she was not in the least sure what she should do to calm it. She had considered confiding in Warren, but Warren had been, for some reason, determined to go to Professor Westcott's lecture. There was a lot of whispering about Professor Westcott. He had reappeared in a shocking state, bruised and ill-looking and it was plain he'd been in some kind of trouble. His wife, Rosamund – just the sort of woman, Sandra thought, to be avoided on a ship – had put up a statement on the lecture notice board saying that Professor Westcott had been involved in a little accident in Iraklion, but it would not prevent him from giving lectures as usual. An accident with a bottle, no doubt. Or several bottles. What a way for an academic to behave! Especially on a cruise where everything was so public. It was extraordinary of Warren, usually so fastidious, to want to show support to an Englishman, however scholarly, who dressed like a rummage sale and couldn't hold his liquor.

Sandra felt let down. She needed Warren this afternoon, needed to have him reassuringly beside her, so that she could tell him what was on her mind. The thing was, she couldn't be certain, but she felt sure that someone, who was not one of the ship's crew, had gone through her suite quite thoroughly in her absence. Everything had been moved just slightly – magazines placed the other side of the oval glass-topped coffee table from where she had left them; a pile of letters turned upside down. Neatly, but upside down.

Sandra picked up her cup, noticing that her hand wasn't perfectly steady. She'd tried not to think about the murder. "If you live in New York," she had told someone when they tried to raise the subject with her, "you either don't think about it or you think about it all the time, and go crazy." So she had deliberately not asked any questions, had moved on her smooth passage between the beauty salon and the library and the necessary pool exercise and the Oriental Restaurant, declining to join in any of the conversations about the murder. But the incident in her cabin had unnerved her.

Warren had not gone to Patrick Westcott's lecture because he was the least interested in the Emperor Constantine.

Modern colossi appealed to him, kings of industry and heads of state, but not the greats of the past. They'd had their day, in Warren's view. It was the future that mattered. But something had drawn him to Patrick Westcott, something he recognized as clearly as recognizing one's own native language spoken in a foreign place. When he had seen Patrick Westcott come back on board in that terrible physical state with its air of shamed elation underneath, Warren had known at once what the professor had been up to. After all, he said to himself, adjusting his cuffs in the sleeves of his English blazer, it takes one to know one.

He'd liked a bit of rough in his own time. For a year, in fact, in the seventies, he'd kept an apartment in San Francisco largely for the sake of the bath houses. He'd been thrilled and terrified, and for that year he'd been kind of addicted too. But the addiction had abruptly died out of him when his New York doctor told him about AIDS. Back in 1976, nobody had heard of AIDS. But now it panicked him, it panicked him clean out of the pleasures that San Francisco still had to offer. He sold the apartment and became virtually celibate, insisting that his astonished dentist – who couldn't, then, think what the fuss was about – wear gloves. Almost twenty years of celibacy had now gone by, a third of his life. He'd never quite got used to it, but he'd never got rid of the panic about AIDS either. Underneath the American shirts and the English suits, Warren was still mesmerized by the spectre of the disease, and morbidly fascinated by those who risked getting it. It had come to be a kind of voyeuristic thrill, and it caused him, this last afternoon in Naxos harbour, to be sitting in the Chaplin Cinema, listening – or pretending to listen – to Patrick Westcott talking, not altogether steadily, about the Emperor Constantine.

Warren studied him. He had a bruise on his face, and when he lifted his right arm he winced, as if it hurt him. His clothes were clean, but bore no relation in shape to the body underneath. Perhaps that dreadful wife bought them. Warren had a shuddering sympathy for closet gays who married. They always seemed to end up with the worst kind of women, the overtly homemaking kind who were emotional tyrants underneath. Now, not all women were like that. Some were wonderful, just wonderful women like Sandi. Warren adored Sandi. At least, he adored her elegance and her wealth and her poise even if, like all other women, her body was impossible. He looked up at the little stage. Poor Professor Westcott, poor tormented guy, doomed to spend every night beside a body that – Warren swallowed and shot his cuffs again. Better not to think of that.

The lecture ended with Constantine's conversion to Christianity. The seven or eight other listeners melted quickly away and left Warren alone, looking at the sad, disorganized figure of Patrick Westcott, shuffling his papers, and fighting down his thrilling secret. Something in Warren stirred, something that, if he had been a compassionate man, he would have called the sympathy of the fellow traveller. He stood up, and made his way to the stage.

"Professor Westcott?"

Patrick looked up, an uncertain smile on his face.

"I sure enjoyed that, Professor."

"Oh. Oh . . . good. I'm so glad. I'm afraid I've delivered lectures better . . ."

"Professor –"

"Yes?" Patrick said.

Warren leaned forward and put his hands on the lectern where Patrick's notes had rested. He couldn't for the life of him think why he was doing this, but doing it he seemed inexorably to be.

"Professor. Professor, would I be right in surmising you are in need of some kind of help?"

Chrissie Young drank too much vodka that night. She sat on the edge of the dance floor at the Harlequin's disco, refusing to dance and drinking steadily. Annie had asked her to join Rupert and herself for a drink in the Crow's Nest, but Chrissie had refused, quite rudely.

"Don't let me spoil your fun," she said.

Annie had looked at her. She was wearing a long skirt Chrissie would swear had a split in it, a long split, to the thigh.

"Don't worry," Annie said, smiling sweetly. "You won't."

Chrissie had looked at her murderously. Annie hadn't seemed to notice. She was wearing long silver earrings as well as the long skirt and a long tunic thing, too, with a wide neckline. She looked bloody daft, Chrissie decided furiously, old and stupid and daft. She picked up the very large vodka she'd ordered and drank from it defiantly, her glowering eyes fixed on her aunt. Annie's eyes registered nothing, and then she went out of the cabin leaving Chrissie alone.

Solitary drinking wasn't much fun. After a while, Chrissie decided to go down to the disco and sulk and drink in public. Several men asked her to dance and she refused them all. She sat and watched the dancers instead and thought how moronic they looked and how bitterly unjust her life was and always had been. And how, whenever she thought she just might be getting something of her own – like Rupert – it got bloody taken off her again. It happened every time, always had – something for Mike, nothing for

Chrissie. Even Annie, turning against her now, betraying her, making a fool of herself and betraying Chrissie into the bargain.

She picked up her glass and looked at the mess of melted ice and collapsed lemon slices in the bottom. She wouldn't stand for it, not any longer. Why should she? Why should she just hang about on the edges of life while all the lucky people chucked shit at her? Why shouldn't she have some shit to chuck for once? Why shouldn't she get even for some of the things she'd had to bear? Why shouldn't bloody Rupert and bloody Annie have to pay for some of the injuries they'd done her? Why not? Why fucking not?

She put her glass down and stood up. She was going to feel awful in the morning, so she'd better do it now, better do it woozy than hung over. Anyway, when she was woozy her courage was up and she could tell the story the way she wanted to tell it. She planned to tell them that Julia Grant's brother had asked her – the anonymous caller – to confirm that his sister had had an affair with the MP, Simon Daviot, and was now embarking on another on a cruise ship where there'd been a murder the shipping line was trying to cover up. And that she, the anonymous caller, could vouch for the fact that Rupert Grant, who called himself Revell to sound sexier, was screwing a woman old enough to be his mother and that one of the singers on the ship was about to have it off with a passenger. That should do it. That should create a nice double page spread. 'Ship of Scandal' maybe, or 'Vice Cruise'. Holding the gleaming walls for support and her head high to show the vodka had had no effect on her whatsoever, Chrissie Young made her way, with difficulty, back to her cabin and the note she had already made of the telephone number for the news editor of the *Sun*.

chapter EIGHT

Rosamund Westcott signed on for the 'City highlights and Topkapi palace' tour in Istanbul. Not because she gave a damn about antiquities or the history of the city in any of its reincarnations, nor because she cared for the cast of characters that made Istanbul what it is today. In fact, she was quite fed up with the Empress Eudoxia, St John Chrysostum, Theophilus, Arcadius and the rest of that lot. Patrick never shut up about them. She knew more about them than she did about her neighbours in Cambridge, and she was sure there was a juicy tale to be told behind each and every door on the street. The reason she signed on was to get away from the ship and, most particularly, from Patrick, who was being annoyingly secretive and insistent on keeping a low profile as far as the rest of the passengers were concerned. She wanted to be on her own for a while, to get away from everything and everybody.

However bored she may have been by the prospects of an historic ramble, she did have to admit that the skyline, with its brilliant, gleaming domes and minarets, was irresistible, and she rather liked the idea of sitting on a bus, not talking for a change and not paying the slightest bit of attention to the poor tour guide doing his best to impress with information about the magnificent Hagia Sophia, the Sultans Beyazid, Ahmed and Sulaymon and the spectacular Bosphorus Bridge. She had learned years ago she did her clearest thinking when Patrick was going on and on and on about some significant moment that changed the course of history or some person, dead for centuries, who merited a dozen books being written about them, so she hoped the bus trip, with the barrage of names and dates and facts and figures, would help her out of the conundrum she felt she was in and put things in proper order.

The first time it happened, she remembered, that is the first time she completely tuned out from what Patrick was saying, still smiling and nodding as though she was hanging on his every word, was two years after they were married. She hadn't the slightest recollection of what Patrick was talking about but she distinctly remembered where it happened and what was going through her mind. They had gone to Henley-On-Thames to visit her grandmother on one of the few weekends Patrick had managed to tear himself away from his beloved students. Gran, always acerbic and unpleasant, had the rather bucolic habit of saving crusts and bits of bread for visitors to take to the river to feed the swans and ducks. Something Gran wouldn't do herself even if her life depended on it but obviously something she thought appealed to the rest of the family. Or was it a way to get them out of the house for a while? Rosamund hated the swans and ducks. They were filthy, and when she was a child, a vicious cob had nipped her ankle and she was certain she was going to have a hideous death from rabies, but rather than risk Gran's ire she took the bread bits to the river and threw them as hard as she could at the beasts hoping by some twist of fate she might drown one or two. Until that day, Rosamund had made it a point to pay rapt attention to Patrick but while they were escaping an icy downpour, squeezed into a table with Canadian tourists and enjoying a coffee at the Angel On the Bridge, she turned him off as easily as one turns off a tiresome television show.

What was going through her mind now was their sex life. Just two years married and it was almost non-existent. Patrick was the only man she had ever slept with so she had nothing by way of comparison but she had come to the conclusion that sex was definitely much ado about nothing at all. And there had been so much talk about it at school! The chorus of sighs of anxious virgins was positively deafening at Lady Harriet's. She remembered talking into the wee hours of the morning with Hilary about the fire and music they expected to accompany their first sexual experience but when she married Patrick and they finally did it, not only was there no fire and not so much as a tuning fork, the whole thing, for Rosamund at least, was rather like going to the dentist. She shuddered at her own simile, but it was just another cavity being filled. Without the benefit of a local anaesthetic. She was certain Patrick was as disenchanted as she was because he attended to sex exactly as he attended to the car – every six months or so, whether it needed it or not. But why on earth was she sitting on a bus in Istanbul dragging up all this rubbish? She really must talk more to Hilary, she thought.

Her mind wandered a bit, looking at the people on the streets hurrying to wherever it was they were going and whatever it was they were doing. All different nationalities, all different colours and different appetites. Were their lives in the same hopeless muddle as hers? Perhaps Patrick wasn't the man she was meant to marry. She'd certainly been down that road a few hundred times. He was handsome, always had been, but during the courtship, which was passionless, she was too busy planning what a perfect wife and mother she'd be to ever really question her attraction to him. Then, after they married, she discovered she wasn't attracted to him in the least. Especially when she saw him naked. Poor dear, he was as pink as a piglet. But then all men look ridiculous naked.

No, she thought, that's not true. There was young Mr Angelo Commisso, who repaired the brickwork in the garden one sweltering week in midsummer so many years ago. Patrick was absolutely no good in the garden, nor did he like the sun. Mr Commisso worked in very short shorts, long before short shorts became fashionable, and Rosamund found herself going into the garden on the slightest pretext to look at all those well defined muscles working so beautifully under his remarkably smooth-looking dark skin. And when he bent over, she couldn't take her eyes off his behind. She never saw him completely naked but until then she had no idea she had such a vivid imagination. He became her fantasy lover whenever Patrick engaged her in their semi-annual madness. Heavens, when she looked back, it was a wonder to her that she and Patrick had managed to produce Camilla and Giles. She spent the first twenty-five years of her marriage thinking about what she was missing and then decided it was best to put it away and enjoy what everyone, including herself, perceived to be her wonderful, wonderful life.

And here she was, bouncing along through the narrow streets of Istanbul, at the unmentionable age of sixty whatever and her head was full of what she feared she would never have. What the hell was an orgasm, anyway? All the chat shows, all the women's magazines and Sunday supplements were full of talk about the damn thing. She was absolutely certain she'd go to her grave wondering what they were all talking about. Life was quite bizarre. What was the likelihood of a person, if they lived to be two hundred and fifty, finding a murder victim at sea in their very own stateroom, for heaven's sake? And yet it had happened to her! If she was to be allotted only one momentous surprise in her life she would have much preferred an orgasm.

When they arrived at the Topkapi palace she decided to stay in the bus, have it all to herself, and even though it was quite uncharacteristic, to wallow in her musings. She begged off joining the group by saying she was feeling slightly ill.

"Can I get you something?" asked Annie, when she overheard Rosamund talking to the tour guide.

"Oh, thank you, no, dear." Rosamund had seen Annie jotting things down in her notebook and what with the long braid and gypsy skirts and ethnic jewellery, surmised she was a fiction writer. "It's very kind of you to offer but I'm sure I'll be feeling quite all right in no time at all. I'll just rest here."

"You're sure?" Annie had such a lovely smile, thought Rosamund, and such clear unlined skin. Two things she didn't trust in an ageing woman.

"Yes, thank you."

She seemed to be taking the tour with that dashing young man whom Rosamund had thought was married to Julia Grant, the friend of Chief Superintendent Clarke. The unfortunate murdered girl had looked so much like Julia Grant, it was uncanny. It was also very confusing. Not to mention, frightening. People like Rosamund, nice people, that is, simply didn't get involved in murder cases. It was all too dreadful. When Annie was getting off the bus, Rosamund noticed what a good figure she had. She must be at least fifty, she thought. How in the world does she do it?

And there was that American woman as well, Sandra Van Horn, so elegant and immaculate. Lord alone knew how she managed to keep herself looking so wonderful? It couldn't just be a question of money, could it? There must be some secret to it that Rosamund had never been privy to. After all, she and Patrick had always had enough money, although getting it out of him was like getting blood out of a stone. That MP must have plenty of money too, but his wife had the same worn-down look that Rosamund had come to imagine she had. Was it because they were both married to people who didn't care for them? Tears sprang involuntarily to her eyes and she jumped to her feet, bustling out of the bus after the others. The one thing she didn't want to do was delve any further into the truth; she wanted to win back the jaunty certainties that had been serving her so well for the last thirty or more years.

"I know I must look awful," said Julia Grant, "but I haven't been able to sleep. And I'm smoking again. Damn it! I was doing so well."

"What you need to do is pamper yourself. Have a massage, do your nails, all those things women indulge in to remind themselves that they're women." Adrian Clarke smiled, trying to lighten the tone of the lunch. "I'm quoting my wife. She used that as an excuse to get anything she wanted. She was always 'reminding herself she was a woman'." He laughed. "Actually, she made me feel rather guilty when she said that. I thought it was my job to remind her that she was a woman. But," he sighed, "the police don't have all that much free time . . ." He stopped himself mid-sentence. "Seriously though, you must try to relax." He was glad he had taken time to lunch with Julia and forget about the murder investigation, which seemed to be going nowhere fast.

"I know I must," she said and looked away.

"Maybe you'd like to see Guys and Dolls. I saw a revival years ago and thought it was quite good. Did you ever read any of the Damon Runyon stories?"

"I don't think so."

Julia wasn't the least bit interested in talking about Damon Runyon and Adrian was very aware of it. He knew what was troubling her so deeply. He had seen it so many times with suspects and witnesses. The averted eyes, the body language, the slightly misplaced voice. She had something she wanted to say but she didn't know how. He also knew there was some connection between Simon Daviot and Julia. It was just too much of a coincidence that Daviot was seen arguing with a woman he called Julia and the murder victim, the same woman, looking so like Julia. He also felt certain, trusting his instincts that had rarely let him down, that Julia Grant had nothing to do with the murder. And that confused him. Why, if she was innocent of any connection with the actual murder, would she be reluctant to tell whatever it was that was on her mind? Especially to Adrian? He had thought they got on quite well. Certainly well enough for her to trust him. The only conclusion he could logically come to was that she was protecting someone – Simon Daviot? But he seemed to have an alibi. Her brother, perhaps?

"Istanbul looks gorgeous," said Julia, trying to change the subject, knowing that Adrian was scrutinizing her. "I wish I felt more like being a tourist. Although I've never been very good at it. I think I like people so much more than places. Are you a people person or a place person?" she asked, making only the briefest eye contact. "I'm most definitely a people person." She realized she was blathering on and she could feel her cheeks redden. "I wish smoking was permitted here."

Adrian reached across the table and took her hand. "I'm a very good listener, you know."

"Yes, well, you would be, wouldn't you? That was your job, for God's sake." She was flippant and she was sorry the minute the words were out of her mouth. "I apologize. That was uncalled for."

"You'll feel so much better once you've gotten things off your chest. Am I sounding too much like Hilary Brown? She's on this ship, you know. I've seen her."

"Yes, I know," she laughed. "No, you're being very kind."

"You will feel better. Take my word for it."

"Oh, Christ," she sighed. "I don't know what to do." She looked around her for a moment and then, having made a decision, she looked at Adrian directly and steadily for the first time since they sat down. "It's about Simon Daviot."

"Oh yes," Adrian waited with bated breath for what was to come.

"Until very recently . . ." and her voice trailed off.

"Yes?"

"Well," she took a very deep breath, "I was his mistress." With those utterly impossible four words out of her mouth she felt she could say anything and she started telling Adrian the whole story.

Warren chose a table beside the Riviera Pool outside the Conservatory for his luncheon with Patrick Westcott. The atmosphere was casual, bright and airy and he thought it was the perfect place for Patrick to unburden himself if he felt so inclined. He had invited him to lunch because the man was obviously in pain and Warren suspected it was much more than his being gay and closeted and married. Gracious, if that was reason enough to cause severe anxiety, half the men in New York and London would be hooked on Valium. Warren had decided not to push the issue. He wasn't there to pry, merely to be a friend if Patrick needed one and by the look of things, bruises included, he most certainly did. Warren suspected a tangle with rough trade but if Patrick Westcott wanted to stay in the closet that was his business and Warren wouldn't think of forcing him out. He thought of himself as being very sensitive to people in Patrick's situation when actually it was more curiosity than sensitivity. To begin with, Warren wasn't at all interested in him sexually, so there would be no game playing. Patrick wasn't his type by a long shot. But he thought it would be nice to have one of his own, so to speak, to have the occasional drink with. He was absolutely devoted to Sandi but he needed a break from her every so often. Poor angel. She was being so needy and seemed to depend on him for everything. In fact, from Warren's viewpoint, she could barely function without him. But he never had an opportunity to meet anyone on his own when he was with her all the time. This cruise she had been behaving particularly strangely, snapping at him quite unkindly on a number of occasions and constantly staring at passing men, which he found very humiliating. In the past he had always admired her self-composure, her ability to give the impression that she didn't need anyone or anything except her art collection, but on this cruise she was jumpy and unpredictable and he was beginning to find it all rather tedious.

Patrick, Warren decided, would be a perfect alternative drinking buddy. Most of the other gay men on board were either paired off and in love or hustling, and he wasn't at all interested in that. He hadn't been celibate for so many years only to catch something dreadful from a hustler. And pay for it, to boot! No thank you, he thought, slightly rearranging the flowers on the table. Patrick was non-threatening and obviously bright, undoubtedly stuffy but Warren was sure once he chiselled through the icy English exterior, he'd find a pretty nice guy. Troubled, certainly, but nice.

He ordered a dry martini while he waited and perused his shipmates as they devoured their sandwiches and poked around in their salads as if they were on an archaeological dig.

He noticed Chief Superintendent Adrian Clarke sitting at a table with Julia Grant, obviously caught up in an intense conversation. Now there, he thought, was a man he could be interested in. So naturally graceful and at ease with himself and so self-assured. Self-assurance was such an attractive attribute in a man. And he was handsome, too. But he was clearly a breeder. What a waste. The Grant woman was nice looking. He could see why a man might be interested in her. She had style and a certain working girl sort of class. She looked like a woman who could take care of herself . . . most of the time. At the moment, however, it was clear that she was anxious about something and Adrian Clarke was very interested in whatever she was saying. Oh, thought Warren, to be a fly in the salad dressing.

"Sorry I'm late."

Warren hadn't heard Patrick Westcott come up to the table. He was as rumpled as ever, poor man. "You're not," he smiled, "I was early. What'll you have to drink?"

"Gin and tonic, please." He sat down and Warren could feel his discomfort emanating from across the table. An eager young waiter was there instantly and Warren ordered the gin and tonic, and noticed Patrick's automatic and quick assessment of the young man as he left the table.

"I take it you're not going ashore," said Warren.

"No. I've done Istanbul many times."

"Have you?" Warren raised his eyebrow ever so slightly; but the silly double entendre went completely over Patrick's head.

"Oh yes, many, many times when I was doing research for my book on Constantine." And he was off and running, all about Constantine's hallucinatory visions and his conversion to Christianity and his persecution of the pagans in the name of Christianity and the possibility of his having murdered his wife and son. It was the capsule version of his lecture on Constantine and people seemed to like it when he was in a one-on-one situation. After all, it was what he was paid to do. And it was also a diversionary tactic. He knew nothing about this obviously wealthy American and he wasn't very good with strangers under the best of circumstances, especially American strangers. They were usually so tiresome. He had accepted the luncheon invitation because he didn't wish to appear rude. Warren had offered to help, after all, but now he was feeling quite awkward and out of place and he wished he hadn't come.

"How interesting," said Warren, trying to think of something, anything, to say about Constantine. "I find Constantine so . . ." he couldn't think of a word, "constant." He laughed. "Where in the world did that come from? You may use that if you like in one of your lectures."

"I don't think so," said Patrick without the slightest trace of humour. The waiter delivered the gin and tonic and this time, both Warren and Patrick watched admiringly as he walked away from the table.

"Look, Patrick . . . May I call you Patrick?"

"Please do," there was a slight pause, "Warren," he said stiffly. It was an effort on his part to seem casual and friendly.

"I want you to know, right from the start, that you can relax with me. We have quite a bit in common, if you know what I mean."

"Are you a Byzantinist, also?" asked Patrick, quite surprised that Warren would be interested in anything more than a good drink and the stock market reports.

"Lord, no. That's not what I meant." He leaned across the table, checked to see if anyone was listening to their conversation and said confidentially, "I'm a friend of Dorothy." He smiled, thinking the very old password gays used to identify each other would relax Patrick.

"Dorothy who?" asked Patrick in the same confidential tone, wondering why Warren's being a friend of this Dorothy person was mentioned in such hushed tones.

"You know what I mean."

"I'm afraid I don't know what you're talking about."

"Dorothy! Dorothy!" Surely Patrick, whom Warren supposed had been sneaking around for years, knew about Dorothy!

"I don't know anyone named Dorothy. At least I don't think I do. My wife's so much better at remembering names. Am I supposed to know this Dorothy?"

"What I'm trying to say is," he whispered again, "I'm family." Having said that, Warren, the great clarifier, nodded his head, certain Patrick would understand completely.

Patrick was thoroughly confused. "Really? Family? How extraordinary. On my side or Rosamund's?"

Warren was annoyed and wanted to tell Patrick he was an idiot but instead, with great patience and secrecy he said, "I am not a member of your family, Patrick. Look, I know you're in some kind of trouble and I just want you to know I'm the same as you. Do you understand what I'm saying?"

"The same as me?" Patrick was trying to make sense of this impossible conversation.

"The same as you."

"Oh," said Patrick, shocked. "I see. The same as me."

Finally, thought Warren. "Yes, the same as you."

Patrick leaned forward and the two of them were almost nose to nose. "You're KGB?" he whispered.

Absolutely nothing registered on Warren's face for a full ten seconds. "KGB! What the hell are you talking about?"

"You said you were KGB."

"I did not say I was KGB!"

"You did. You said you were the same as me."

"You're KGB? I didn't think there was a KGB anymore."

"There isn't. But I was a recruiter for the KGB. Isn't that what you were talking about?"

"No, I'm not KGB nor was I ever KGB, for God's sake." He said it with the revulsion most Americans, especially rich ones, felt for anything that smacked of communism. "I'm not KGB. I'm just queer."

"You're what?" Patrick was absolutely stunned.

"Queer. Aren't you?"

Patrick pushed his chair away from the table. "If you don't mind, I must be going now." He stood up.

"Sit down, for God's sake," said Warren. "If there's one thing I cannot abide it's high dudgeon. It's like something out of an old Barbara Stanwyck movie."

"What makes you think you can presume –" started Patrick.

"Please sit down. People will think we're having a lover's quarrel."

Patrick sat immediately. Anything to avoid drawing attention to himself. Good God, he thought, what have I got myself into with this improbable man. But at the same time he realized that this was quite possibly the one person on the ship with whom he could discuss his problem. He didn't think, after what Warren had blurted out, that he'd be judgemental. How on earth could he be? Patrick might even be able to bring himself to show the compromising photos to Warren. In fact, Warren might even help Patrick arrive at some solution. If there was one, of course. He didn't want to part with two hundred thousand pounds, that was certain, and Warren would most assuredly understand his position.

"So," said Warren. "The KGB? Really? How fascinating! Why were so many homosexual Brits involved with Russia? What the hell do the Russians have that the rest of us don't know about?" He moved the flower arrangement to the side so he could lean in even closer to Patrick. "Drink up and tell all, please."

"Photos! Isn't the story enough?" Chrissie listened for a moment. She had tried to call the night before but couldn't get through to the *Sun*. "Never mind what my name is. Yes. Yes, I told you, Simon Daviot, his wife and his mistress. Yes, all on board. And a gigolo named Rupert Revell . . . or Grant. He's an actor. And an old lady. A crazy old lady. And don't forget the murder! For Christ's sake what more do you want? Look, I've told you all this already. OK, OK, I'll get the bloody photos." She slammed down the receiver. Nothing is easy, she thought, going to the bathroom and ripping the top off a bottle of aspirin. She had a killer of a headache. Why wasn't she talking to an editor at the *Sun*? Why only a bloody assistant editor? The aspirin stuck in her throat for a moment and she choked before managing to swallow. "I don't think I packed the damn camera. I didn't want to come on this stupid cruise in the first place. No way did I want photos to remind me of it." She was mumbling to herself as she tore open the drawers and went through her luggage. There was no camera. Her brother Mike must have a camera. He was stupidly sentimental enough to want to record every boring minute. She called his cabin.

"Hello?" He was as cheerful as ever.

"Do you have a camera?"

"And a good day to you, too."

"Shut up Mike. Do you have a camera?"

"Yes. You know I have a camera."

"I want to use it. Today."

"Well, since you asked so nicely . . ."

"Just give me the camera."

"On second thoughts, you can't."

"Why not?"

"Aunt Annie has it. She went ashore on the Topkapi tour."

"And you didn't go with her! Couldn't tear yourself away from your little bimbette of a cabaret singer?"

"There's that, of course," Mike knew it infuriated Chrissie if he didn't let her get under his skin, "but the truth is, Annie didn't invite me along. I do believe she had a date."

Rupert and Annie, thought Chrissie. It was absolutely revolting. "Careful, brother, the old bitch will cut you out of her will too."

"Chrissie, she'll change her mind. You know it's only a matter of time until she does. Meanwhile, you might try being a bit more pleasant."

"When will she be back?"

"I don't know. I expect it's an all-day tour."

"Damn it!"

"Why do you need a camera all of a sudden?"

"To record all these magic moments, why do you think? Never mind." She hung up. She'd buy a damn camera if she had to. After splashing water on her face and brushing her hair, she threw on a sun-dress and left her cabin. There was a young couple, clearly in love and hanging all over one another waiting for the lift. Why don't they just stay in their cabin and screw until they're blue, she thought, instead of making fools of themselves in public. She gave them a dirty look when they entered the lift but they were so wrapped up in one another they didn't even know she existed. She decided to get a little fresh air before shopping for the camera and went out on deck. "Oh my God," she said, shielding her eyes against the brilliant sun, "a person could go blind." It was so bright she had to close her eyes and quite accidentally walked into two young women leaning over the rail.

"Here, now, look where you're going," said Jazzy. "You stepped right on my foot."

"Well, keep your big feet out of the way."

"Big feet!"

"Excuse us for living," said Lisa.

"Get out of my way." Chrissie moved along the deck.

"Who do you think you are? Princess Di?" Lisa called after her.

"Stuff it," shouted Chrissie, without looking back.

"She's a bitch, that one," said Jazzy. "I've seen her before. Rude, that's what she is. You should have heard the way she talked to one of the waiters. Like she was bleeding royalty."

"No class, that's what I say. You can always tell by the way they treat the hired help."

"Isn't that the truth," agreed Jazzy.

"Some people." They hung over the rail again. "Look at Istanbul, will you?"

"I am. Doesn't look much like home, does it."

"It's not supposed to. It's Istanbul. It's Turkey."

"Well, I know that much. I'm not retarded, you know." Jazzy poked at Lisa. "What do you want to do now?" she asked, looking at her stomped foot to assess the damage.

"I don't want to eat. I know that much."

"Oh, please don't mention food. I've had enough to last me till Christmas."

They walked along watching the activity in the harbour. "I've a good mind to do something important today."

"Important? Like what?"

"I dunno. Actually, my horoscope said I should do something to improve myself."

"Read a book or something like that?"

"Not bloody likely."

"We could go to the Oasis and exercise," said Lisa, trying to be constructive. "You could stand to lose an inch of that pinch, Jazzy."

"Me! You cow. Your behind is as big as a bloody barn!"

"Thank you very much. I was only trying to help. You said you wanted to improve yourself."

"Yes, but I was thinking more along the lines of a new hair colour."

"Oh, that's good. Maybe I will, too. Come on, let's see if they're all booked up in the salon." They hurried along the deck trying to decide on a colour when suddenly Jazzy stopped.

"What's that?" She pointed at something lying at the foot of a staircase.

"What's what?" asked Lisa.

"That. It looks like a man."

"Blimey, I think it is."

"Probably a drunk."

"Let's get out of here." Lisa grabbed Jazzy's hand and started to pull her in the opposite direction.

"What if it isn't a drunk? What if he's fallen and hurt himself? We can't just walk away."

"Well, someone will come along and find him. Why's it have to be us? Come on, let's go. I hate accidents. They make me sick."

"Stop being such a twit. We can't just leave him lying here. Come on."

Jazzy went up to the man but Lisa stayed her distance. He was lying with his face turned away from Jazzy. "There's blood," she said.

"Oh, God, I hate this." Lisa was dancing back and forth, afraid to really look at the man. "The only guy we find at our feet and he's lying in a pool of blood. Where the hell is everybody? Why do we have to be the ones to find him?"

"Half the ship went ashore."

"Bloody Istanbul. I wish we had gone, too. But, no, you didn't want to."

"Oh, shut up." Jazzy stepped over the man and bent down to get a look at his face.

"You won't know him. There are a million people on this ship."

"It's the MP. That Daviot bloke! I've seen him talking to girls in the Lord's Tavern."

"What's he doing lying there?"

"How the hell do I know? Don't ask such stupid questions."

"Oh, shit!" squealed Lisa. "Another murder. Is he dead?"

"Do I look like a bleeding coroner? How do I know?"

"I don't like this. I really don't."

"You stay here. I'll run and get some help." Jazzy started off.

"Wait," screamed Lisa. "Don't leave me here. I'll go with you."

"What the hell are you afraid of? Stay here in case he comes to."

"What if he's dead?"

"Well, then, he won't be going anywhere will he? This could be our chance to meet those coppers, the ones we saw coming on board. How do I look?" and she ran off.

"Where is everybody? This is bloody weird, that's what this is. Oh, I have to go. I'll pee in my knickers if I stay here. Please don't be dead, Mister."

An elderly couple came by and stopped to look at Daviot. "What happened?" asked the man.

"Dunno. My friend went to get help."

"He must have fallen, poor man. I'm always very careful with stairs." The old woman was looking at Daviot's face.

Several other people arrived and circled around Daviot and Lisa felt much better. The responsibility of looking after him, dead or alive, was no longer hers.

chapter NINE

Simon Daviot lay on his bed and passed a hand tenderly over the wound to his right temple. Even beneath the plaster the ship's nurse from the Medical Centre had so efficiently applied, it still throbbed. He groaned and opened his eyes, staring disconsolately at the ceiling. It was the mortification of it all, that's what hurt most. Missing his footing on the stairs like that; they would all think he was drunk. All those leering faces . . . He could just see the latest tabloid headline: TORY MP FOUND DRUNK ON *ORIANA*. It would send half his bloody constituents into their nudge-nudge, wink-wink mode, sniggering, "So who's this *Oriana*, then, that Simple Simon's been found on top of?" God, how he hated that nickname. He groaned aloud. More Tory sleaze to add to the gaiety of life. The papers would love it.

Whatever had possessed him to come on this damned cruise in the first place? It wasn't as if Brenda even appreciated the gesture. Precious constituency time he had given up to treat her like this and was she grateful? Not a bit of it.

And where was she now, eh? Where was she when he needed her? It was ages since he'd last seen her talking by the Crystal Pool to that awful American Van Horn woman. Brenda had been smiling at her in awe. Sandra Van Horn impressed her, he could tell. Someone had told them shortly after their arrival on board that the bitch had pots of money and went around Europe buying up Old Masters.

But to hell with Old Masters, it was Old Mistresses that concerned him most right now. He had honestly thought he'd had a heart attack when he walked round the corner and nearly went smack into her. She had looked like a startled rabbit and just as Simon had been about to let rip he had noticed the bloody policeman with her. The two of them had looked very pally and Simon had felt nauseous with jealousy. The feeling had taken him completely by surprise. He had had no idea he cared so much for her. Utterly unable to think how to react or what to say, he had walked off in a daze. He could remember his foot shooting out from under him on a step a few minutes later, but that was the last thing before waking up to find a crowd of faces staring down at him. How could Julia do this to him? How dare she follow him to sea like this, then flaunt herself in front of him with that awful Geordie bloke? And who the hell did that Ancient Mariner on a police pension think he was, going round like Hercule Poirot on a bad day accusing innocent people of murdering that Harman girl? Did nobody tell him he was supposed to be retired and had absolutely no jurisdiction out here? He just didn't buy that crap about being given a free hand by New Scotland Yard at all.

Sighing deeply at the awfulness of it all, he sat up slowly and swung his legs over the edge of the bed, taking care not to move too abruptly and make the pounding in his skull any worse.

Those painkillers the nurse had given him were wearing off and his head was throbbing fit to burst. Where the hell did Brenda keep the paracetemol? He glanced in the direction of the dressing table. At the bottom of her spare toilet bag most probably. She had just about every damned thing but the kitchen sink in there. She would insist on lugging spares of all her essentials with them, just in case she ran out of any of her favourite lotions or potions whilst abroad. She always carried enough first aid items to cope with a third world war into the bargain. But little did he imagine, he mused ruefully, that he would have such dire recourse to that rosebud-covered monstrosity of a toilet bag as he did right now.

His wife had allotted herself the bottom drawer of the dressing table and Simon groaned as he walked over, a trifle unsteadily, and bent to pull it open in search of the tablets.

The drawer was full of spare sets of Marks and Spencer undies bought specially for the voyage which he cast aside impatiently as he searched for the bag.

"Got it!" There was no mistaking the lurid pink rosebuds.

But wait. Something was jamming it. A green plastic bag was wedged between it and their travelling iron. Irritably Simon tugged at the offending object until it came loose. What on earth had Brenda stashed away in that?

Curious, he opened the plastic bag and looked in.

"Christ Almighty!"

He almost dropped the thing in shock.

"Oh no! Oh no! Oh no . . ." he repeated, over and over again, completely lost for words as his whole career flashed before his eyes like that of a drowning man.

He stared down into the bag and backed unsteadily over to a nearby chair, and sat down heavily. A thin film of sweat appeared on his brow and upper lip as his heart began to pound. He started to shake his head as if to negate the evidence of his own eyes. Inside the bag lay a bloodied knife. Even in his state of shock he was aware he must not touch the thing, but the mere sight of it made him want to throw up.

He was sweating profusely now as he closed the bag. Pictures were dancing through his mind. Terrible pictures of Brenda and that young woman. He could see it all: the confrontation, the recriminations. Brenda screaming, "Harlot! How dare you sleep with my husband and follow us on holiday!" And the young woman looking askance at the mad woman in front of her and protesting she hadn't a clue what she was shouting about.

He glanced at a framed photo taken of the two of them on their honeymoon. It was always brought on holiday with them. Pert and pretty with a fashionable long bob and flares, she had been a partner to be proud of then. Poor, sad, distraught Brenda. All the angst about his affair, all the misery and rejection, she had hidden it so well, repressing it until it finally broke through in an orgy of violence and anger.

He leant back on the chair, threw back his head and closed his eyes. Drawing a deep breath, he tried to blot out the vision of his wife attacking that poor unsuspecting young woman in a frenzy of frustration and jealousy he could barely comprehend.

He was so sure he had played his cards right and kept the affair with Julia well and truly under wraps. He had been so discreet, always passing his mistress off as a colleague if ever the paths of the two females in his life had happened to cross. But women have a way of knowing things. Feminine intuition they called it. All this time she must have known, must have been going through agonies whilst trying to pretend everything in the marital garden was still rosy. How she must have suffered in silence to end up doing something like that. God, he had been such a cad!

For the first time in their entire marriage Simon found himself looking at the relationship from his wife's point of view. And, to add to the awfulness of it all, he did not like what he saw one little bit. Reaching into a drawer he took out a packet of slim panatellas and lit one from the lighter on the dressing table, slipping the packet into his jacket pocket.

He drew the smoke deeply into his lungs and let it out slowly. That was better . . . he could almost feel his heart-beat begin to steady. All right, so he had been unfaithful, but it wasn't the end of the world. Didn't all those surveys in women's magazines reckon most men cheated on their wives at some time in their lives? Certainly in his profession it was hard not to resist the temptations – all those doe-eyed young researchers with no bras and sweaters so tight sometimes he could hardly breathe as he watched them sashaying in and out of the office and up and down the corridors.

But if he had been a bit of a gay dog at times, as far as women were concerned, he had been damned sure not to mess on his own doorstep unless it was just the briefest of meaningless flings, like the girl whose cabin he had gone to the night of the murder. He closed his eyes in horror as he realized that he had admitted to the policeman that he had been with another woman that evening in order to give himself an alibi. If they found out Brenda was the killer his whereabouts would be bound to come out. What a field day for the press! An MP in bed with another woman while his wife murdered some innocent person, mistaking her for his mistress who was also on the same ship. He'd never seen the girl again since that night, he wasn't even sure now what she looked like, she had just been in the bar at the right moment. Once this came out, however, and the tabloids started waving their cheque books about, he was pretty confident that she would remember him with absolute clarity, and what she didn't remember she would make up. A loud moan involuntarily escaped him. Up until now he had always been so careful not to get involved with anyone who might compromise him. Too many other honourable members had been caught with their pants down recently. There had been no sexy little pieces from the House of Commons secretariat for him, well not many anyway. How bloody stupid and unforgivable of Julia to sign up for the same cruise. And how bloody unfortunate for that other poor girl that she happened to look so like the revengeful Ms Grant. If Olivia Harman had been a different shape or had had a different hair colour she would be alive and kicking right now and enjoying the trip ashore with the rest of the passengers.

The panatella seemed to be making him feel even more lightheaded so, stubbing it out in a nearby ashtray, he got to his feet and stared at the green plastic bag in his left hand. For Brenda to have been driven to do such a thing she must have suspected long since that Julia was far more than a colleague, and it must have come as a great shock to her to find his mistress on the cruise. Simon found himself nodding his head as it all began to make sense. If he himself had had the odd occasion when he mistook Olivia for Julia, it was not surprising that his wife should have had the same problem. It was perfectly natural that Brenda would have assumed his affair was with Olivia whom she had then accidentally killed in a fit of rage and desperation when the confrontation went so sadly wrong.

Yes . . . yes, that was it. But it wasn't murder. It was an accident. He felt a surge of relief at the realization. But what the hell did he do now? Accident or not, due process would have to be gone through and there was no way on earth he could allow his wife to be caught. And right now he had no wish to confront her with the awful truth. Poor Brenda obviously had to be going through some sort of mental and emotional crisis and would need help – real medical help – that he would see she got just as soon as they returned home. He had read about women going off their heads and doing crazy things at this time in their lives. Some even used the menopause in court as a defence for murder these days. The thought comforted him. If the worst came to the worst and poor Brenda was actually accused of killing that girl, then that is what would happen, and, if found guilty, she would probably get discharged on the proviso she received medical help. An accident whilst the balance of her mind was disturbed. It certainly didn't sound as bad as murder. But his political career would still be in ruins. He could almost see his chances of a cabinet post flying out of the window right now.

He needed a drink, he decided. A scotch, preferably a double, to calm his nerves and help him think rationally.

The Tiffany Bar at the top of the four-deck atrium was almost empty when he walked in. One or two people he vaguely recognized were dotted around the place but most of the passengers seemed to have taken the opportunity of going ashore. Istanbul still held a certain magic, even these days, it seemed.

He walked across to the bar, acutely conscious of the plaster gracing his right temple and of the tightly rolled up plastic bag containing the knife in the inside pocket of his linen jacket. He had decided he could not leave the weapon in their cabin in case that moron Clarke persuaded the captain to have it searched. The safest thing to do was to take it with him and, once fortified by a scotch or two, he could decide as to the best way of disposing of it.

He was halfway through his second drink when SHE walked in.

Julia Grant saw him from the open door and paused on the threshold for a second, unsure of whether to continue with her decision to have a quiet drink before having her hair done for the dance that evening.

To her consternation, as she stood there, despite all her good intentions to the contrary, Julia felt her heart begin to race at the sight of him. He was wearing that same beige linen jacket he had worn on their first real date. It was at a garden party held in aid of Tory funds in a neighbouring constituency. His wife could not attend, and he had introduced her as his personal assistant. "Just exactly how personal would you like me to get?" she had smiled, as they had moved on to greet others of the Party faithful. Their eyes had met and she could have sworn she saw the faintest hint of a blush as he had squeezed her elbow and replied quietly, "That's entirely up to you."

Simon's eyes fixed on hers for the whole of the long walk from the door to the bar, where he sat, nursing his drink.

She walked straight up to him and smiled. "Mine's a G and T," she informed the barman. "Make it a large one."

Simon went to get his cruise card to pay, reaching for his inside pocket where he normally kept his wallet, then withdrew his hand as if stung when he remembered the knife. "I'll pay for this," he told the barman. "Charge it to my cabin." There were some advantages to having a famous face.

"Cheers!"

He lifted his own half-empty glass in response, then downed the contents in one and motioned for the bar steward to refill it. "I see you don't have your Inspector Glum in tow," he mused, glancing around the almost empty room. "Is he too busy sleuthing to find the energy for romance?"

Julia took a sip of her gin and tonic before setting it down gently on the bar-top. "You really can be a bastard at times, Simon," she said softly. "A real bastard."

"But only at times." His blue eyes were smiling into hers and his voice was disconcertingly low, with that intimate tone he reserved only for her. He could not believe he was actually next to her. By rights she should be dead. A sick feeling came to the pit of his stomach at the thought. His own wife had tried to kill her. It was like some crazy nightmare from which he would soon wake up.

Julia was standing disconcertingly close, her left thigh almost touching his right knee as he rested his left elbow on the bar and scrutinized her face. She was just as beautiful. Too damned beautiful for her own good. That much had already been proved by Brenda's crazy actions. "Why exactly are you here, Jools?" He only ever called her that when they were particularly intimate.

Julia gave a light laugh and tossed her hair back. "I fancied a drink, that's all. Adrian has been tied up with that stupid enquiry and I was at a loose end."

"Forget bloody Adrian. Why are you here – on this cruise?"

His voice had an intensity about it that she knew she could not brush off with another flippant riposte. She watched him down half of his fresh drink in one gulp then answered truthfully, "I signed up because you were on it."

The frankness of the reply took him aback. He had been prepared for a game of cat and mouse such as they had so often played with one another. Honesty had never figured large in their relationship. On both sides it had started as a simple case of enjoy the sex and ask no questions. But life was never quite as simple as that. He could feel the short hairs at the back of his neck begin to stand on end and a physical tremor ran through him as she laid a hand on his thigh. "I admire your honesty," he said softly.

Her left hand remained in place as she raised her glass with the other. She ran her tongue along her lower lip. Her mouth was parted slightly and the action made her lipstick glisten in the soft lights of the bar. There was an electricity between them that was almost tangible.

"Well, well, who do we have here?"

They both started abruptly at the soft Geordie accent. Adrian Clarke was standing just behind them, looking curiously from one to the other.

Julia removed her hand from Simon's thigh like a shot and for a fleeting second disappointment registered in her eyes before her lips broke into a smile. "Adrian, darling – at last!"

She turned to Simon. "You don't mind if my friend joins us, do you?"

"Do I have a choice?" Simon's voice was almost child-like in its petulance. The last person on earth he wanted to see right now was Super Sleuth.

"I'm afraid Simon's not very sociable at the moment," Julia smiled. Her eyes rested on the plaster on his forehead. "Probably due to his recent accident. What on earth happened to your brow? Did you walk into a door or something? Or was it a mite more exciting, such as getting into a fight defending my honour with Adrian here?"

It was meant as a joke, to lighten the atmosphere, but neither man was amused.

Simon shifted uneasily on the bar-stool. "Look here, I'd better be going. There's someone I have to see." The knife in his pocket was like a ton weight on his mind. He had decided to go in search of a litter bin.

"See you at the dance tonight, perhaps?" Julia's voice rang in his ears as he took his leave but he made no reply.

The three whiskies he had downed in quick succession were having their effect. He felt emotionally punch drunk, reeling from one shock to another. He shook his head, trying to clear his brain. He must stay in control, he must hold onto his composure or he would be finished. Brenda would drag him down into the gutter with her.

Julia could see that he wasn't himself as he walked out and felt worried. "Just check he's all right," she asked Adrian, "and give him these." She passed a slim packet of panatellas, which Simon had left on the table, to the detective. Adrian did his best to hide his annoyance and went after the swaying figure of his rival. He did not wish to appear sulky or childish in front of Julia. He also wanted the opportunity to warn Daviot off setting his cap at Julia again. The poor girl had been through quite enough at his hands as it was.

Simon couldn't see a litter bin anywhere and he was to panic. Now that he thought about it, he didn't remember seeing one anywhere on the ship. In his anxiety the plastic bag seemed to be growing in his pocket; he began to imagine that he couldn't walk naturally with it sticking into him and that everyone was staring. There were too many people around him to think about throwing it into the sea, he didn't want to end up being interrogated by Adrian about a mystery object going overboard. Suddenly he spotted a sports bag that someone had left on a seat, perhaps while they went into the bar for a drink. It was not fully zipped up and there was a tennis racket sticking out of one end.

As he sidled towards the seat he was totally unaware of Adrian watching him from the door to the bar . . .

Taking the packet of panatellas from his pocket Adrian was about to shout the MP's name when he stopped in his tracks. Daviot was taking something green from his inside jacket pocket and furtively pushing it down as far as it would go into a sports bag which appeared not to be his.

Adrian Clarke's professional mind went into overdrive. He was across the twenty yards that divided them in a few strides as, totally oblivious to the fact that he had been seen, Simon Daviot walked off in the direction of the stairs.

The retired detective plunged his hand into the sports bag and pulled out the green plastic bag. He was in the process of opening it when Julia appeared at the door.

"What kept you?" she called, hurrying across the deck to join him. She had suddenly had a vision of the two men getting into an argument once out of her hearing. "What's wrong, Adrian? What's that you've got there?"

Adrian Clarke's tanned face was drained of colour as he gazed into the plastic bag in his hands. His stomach lurched at the sight of the knife and he now closed the bag quickly as Julia approached. "It – it's nothing . . . nothing that need worry you."

"Of course it's not nothing!" Julia insisted. "I can see for myself it's something . . . Here, let me see!" She reached across and attempted to grab the bag from Adrian's hand. "Ouch!" In doing so she pushed the knife through the plastic and felt the tip of its blade.

She stared aghast at the bag still clutched in her friend's hand and then at the spot of blood just beginning to appear from the nick in the skin of her palm. "Good God, Adrian, what's in there?"

There was no point in trying to deceive her any longer. Slowly the retired detective leaned towards her and held out the open bag. Julia gazed inside it and let out a horrified gasp. She took a step back and stared at him, then back at the bag, as her hand went to her mouth. For a moment she was totally speechless, then she managed to stammer. "It – it's the murder weapon, isn't it? It's the knife that killed that poor young woman." Adrian nodded gravely, not trusting himself to speak. "Where did you get it?"

He jerked his head in the direction of the bag. "In there."

Julia stared in horror at it. "My God! But if we can find out who owns the bag, we've got the murderer, haven't we?"

"No, I don't think the owner of the bag knows anything about it. Someone has just put this in there."

"How do you know that?" She was impressed with his certainty. He must be a hell of a detective.

"I just saw them do it."

Julia gasped. "You're kidding! You really saw who put it in there?"

"I really did."

"Then who was it? For God's sake, who was it?"

He looked straight into her eyes. He was going to hurt her, he knew that. For no matter how much she might like him, and no matter how well they might get on together, he had not the shadow of a doubt she still loved the guy. Despite all her protestations to the contrary, she was still in love with . . . "Simon Daviot. It was Simon Daviot."

"NO!" Her hand flew to her mouth again as she stared at him. "NO! That's just not true! Simon may be a bastard in many ways but he's not a murderer!"

"I'm not saying he is," her friend replied quietly. "That's for the court to decide. All I'm saying is that I saw him putting this bag with the blood-stained knife into this sports bag. How he came by it is not for me to say."

Julia felt physically sick and she could feel the hot sting of tears in her eyes. Her thoughts were racing. Never in her wildest dreams could she accept that Simon was a murderer. She had to get to him. She had to warn him.

Blindly she began to run in the direction of the stairs, leaving Adrian Clarke standing clutching the green bag.

For almost twenty minutes she searched the main social areas on the other decks in vain. She even managed to find out which cabin number was allotted to Simon and his wife, but several minutes pounding on the door had no effect. He wasn't in there.

She was almost on the point of giving up, and was retracing her steps from the Daviots' cabin suite when she saw Brenda coming towards her.

"Mrs Daviot!" Julia found herself almost shouting Brenda's name. "Oh Mrs Daviot, it's terrible! We've got to do something!"

Brenda looked puzzled as the young woman took her arm and propelled her back in the direction of the Daviots' cabin door.

"What on earth is all this about?"

Brenda had just spent an enjoyable couple of hours in the company of Sandra Van Horn and that lovely Indian doctor, Horatio Patel. Ray, as she now called him, had promised to look out for her at the dance that evening and her heart had skipped a beat when he had held her hand just that bit longer than necessary on parting. She was sure he quite fancied her. The caring way he looked at her and the questions he asked; it was as if her problems really mattered to him. And dear God she had problems in plenty these days. Terrible problems that she doubted she could confide to anyone, even him . . .

Ignoring the older woman's protestations, on reaching the cabin, Julia insisted Brenda listen to her and pour them both a stiff drink from the personal fridge before she divulged her shattering news.

Brenda Daviot sat quite still, nursing her drink in her lap, as she listened in silence. She looked at the young woman more in confusion than horror when Julia had finished and shook her head vehemently. "You must be joking! I simply don't believe it. My husband hasn't the physical courage to kill anyone."

The matter-of-fact reaction took Julia by surprise. "But it's true," she insisted. "Adrian . . . ex-Detective Chief Superintendent Clarke saw him do it."

"The murder?" Brenda's pale brows rose sceptically.

"Of course not. Dispose of the weapon, I mean."

"Hmmm . . ."

Brenda was obviously not convinced and her scepticism had a momentary calming effect on Julia who finished her drink and stood up. "Look, I appreciate your not believing Simon could do such a terrible thing but, whatever you say, Adrian Clarke saw him getting rid of the weapon and there'll be a hunt for him all over the ship at this moment. Adrian will have had no choice but to go straight to the authorities. You have to try to find Simon and warn him. Perhaps you'll have a better idea where to find him than I do."

With that, Julia rushed from the cabin and out on to the deck. The sun was streaming out of a clear blue sky and seagulls swooped and soared far above her head, their raucous cries eddying on the slight wind that caused white horses to cavort on top of the surface of the water. It didn't seem right somehow that such a dreadful thing should have happened on such a perfect day. There had to be some totally rational explanation. But somehow, as she stood there, leaning on the ship's rail, she could not think of one.

It had been a crazy idea coming on this cruise. Somehow she felt it was her fault that Simon was in trouble. Perhaps if she hadn't been so intent on following him and making life awkward for him he would never have found himself in this mess. She felt almost sorry for Brenda in her Easter-chick yellow frock. She already had the defeated look of a woman who had given up on life. What was this holiday supposed to do for their marriage anyway? No matter how glamorous the surroundings, they were still the same people at the end of the day. Simon had fallen out of love with his wife a long time ago and no amount of blue skies and fresh sea air could ever change that fact.

She had been stupid, Julia decided. If she had played her cards right and waited patiently until they had returned home, she could have had him eating out of her hand, begging her to take him back. Yes, cooped up with pathetic old Brenda for two weeks, no matter how wonderful the surroundings, would have had Simon climbing the cabin walls and been just the boost their affair needed. But the milk was spilled now. They were stuck in the here and now. Nothing she could do or say now could help Simon and she only prayed that if there really were such things as guardian angels, Simon's was looking after him at this moment when he really needed it.

As Julia continued her search, someone was opening the door of the Daviots' cabin suite. Charlotte Daviot looked about her as she edged the door ajar and slipped inside, closing it quietly behind her. Her face was flushed and she breathed a sigh of relief as she pushed a long strand of blonde hair back from her eyes. Neither her mother nor her father appeared to be in.

"Mum? Dad?" She had to make sure. She leant back against the door and listened, the woodwork cool against the bare skin of her sunburnt shoulders. No replies came. "Thank God for that!"

Lightly she ran across the carpet and opened the bedroom door, making for the dressing table. She frowned slightly at the sight of the bottom drawer hanging half open. Had anyone been in there? Her heart lurched at the thought.

Her mother's new underwear lay in a tangled mess within. She could feel her heart begin to race as she knelt down and felt frantically inside the disarray of silk undergarments, the cut-glass stone in the ring on her little finger snagging on the flimsy material.

"Blast!" She tugged at a long wispy silken thread attached to the ring and snapped it impatiently, casting aside the camisole it belonged to.

She had deliberately chosen this drawer knowing it was used only for her mother's infamous 'spares' and that it would never be looked into again until they were ready to pack up and leave the ship. That would give her the breathing space she needed to dispose of the thing. It would have been disastrous leaving anything in the cabin she shared with Sophie. Soph had a nose like a ferret when it came to sniffing out things that didn't concern her.

Charlotte's brow furrowed even more and she could feel herself begin to sweat as her hands searched more frantically, pulling knickers and bras out of the drawer and scattering them on the floor beside her.

"It has to be in here somewhere!"

Out came the toilet bag with her mother's duplicates, then the travelling iron. Jeez . . . it had been right next to that! Where the hell was it?

She could feel the panic rising in her as the awful truth began to dawn. At last she was looking into a completely empty drawer.

It had gone. There was no sign of the knife.

"Oh my God, NO!"

Aghast, she crumpled against the empty drawer and gazed at the mess of discarded underwear around her. IT HAD GONE. THE KNIFE HAD GONE.

She – Charlotte the capable one who was never at a loss for anything – stared blankly in front of her. She had had it all so cleverly thought out. No one would ever know. She would have outwitted them all – that stupid Clarke guy who had been so mean to her father – the whole damned lot of them. The knowledge had given her a feeling of power she had never known before. Not even Sophie would have guessed her secret. Now all her plans were for nothing. Someone had found it. THE KNIFE HAD GONE. The thought made her want to throw up. She was totally at a loss as to what to do.

For the first time in years Charlotte Daviot began to cry.

chapter TEN

Julia emerged from the Iberia Room. Her heart was thumping and she was close to tears. She crossed to the rail and scanned the Riviera Pool and its open-air bar on the deck below. She had never stopped to consider before just how vast *Oriana* was. By this time she was carrying her once-comfortable Ralph Lauren canvas mules in her hand, her heels feeling raw and blistered.

Simon Daviot was nowhere to be seen. She had scoured Anderson's, the Curzon Lounge, the Royal Court and Knightsbridge shopping mall, the Crow's Nest with its panoramic vista as the ship scythed its imperturbable way through the sparkling blue waves towards Alexandria.

Below her, all she could see were her fellow passengers lounging on comfortable steamer chairs, basking in the sun's considerable heat, reading, talking, laughing, sipping long cool drinks, or just dozing, faces plastered in sun-cream.

Julia was not normally misanthropic but she experienced a sudden surge of pure . . . hatred . . . for all those so bloody normal, happy folk, oblivious and no doubt uncaring when her entire world was collapsing around her.

She hurried along the Sun Deck, heading to the back of the boat – all right, all right she thought to herself, remembering Adrian's gentle chiding, the stern of the bloody boat, ship! – past a laughing group playing deck tennis and others preparing to shoot at clay pigeons, fired out to sea.

He had to be right at the back, of course. Okay, the stern. Sod's law. And there he was, propping up the Terrace Bar and downing a very large tumbler of Jack Daniels sour mash whiskey, clunking with chunks of ice.

"Yes," said Julia to the barman, "I'll have one of those . . ."

"What the hell do you want?" asked Daviot, ungraciously. "Your antique toy boy ditched you or was it all over too quick and you want seconds?"

Julia slapped his face hard, before she knew it had happened.

"Bloody hell, Julia!" exploded the Member for West Somerfield, and clapped a hand to his stinging cheek. Then, sensing the bar steward and a couple of other passengers, the American heiress Sandra Van Horn, that daft old bat Annie Young and her not unattractive niece Chrissie, were all watching with undisguised interest and amusement, he grinned his widest, most likeable-decent-chap grin (he regularly practised a whole repertoire of photo-opportunity smiles in the mirror) and threw his arms up (in body language this meant he had nothing at all to hide), chuckling ruefully.

"Good Lord, my dear young lady," he exclaimed in a loud, good-natured voice. "When I said I approved of foxhunting, I had no idea you felt so strongly! I compliment you on your depth of commitment to the anti-blood sports lobby. Of course I don't actually hunt, myself, you know."

Julia smiled, although she felt terribly shaky. "I'm so sorry Mr Daviot, I don't know what came over me."

"Consider it forgotten, we suffer much worse during the BBC's 'Question Time'," replied Daviot, lowering his voice and relieved to see the others lose interest and return to their own affairs.

Julia said, very softly, "Adrian saw what you pushed into the sports bag. He's recovered it, Simon, and he's looking for you."

For an instant it looked as if Simon Daviot was going to pass out. He clutched at the bar counter and swayed.

"Here," said Julia, "drink this," and pushed her untouched tumbler of Jack Daniels at him.

Daviot swallowed a couple of gulps of the stuff. His brow had broken out in a sweat.

"Go on, go on," he murmured, glancing around to ensure they were not being overheard. He touched his bright red cheek and let his eyes focus on his former mistress.

"There's worse," went on Julia.

"What could be worse?"

"I've told Brenda."

"Oh my God, you've told Brenda about us?"

"I told her about the knife you bloody fool, but everybody's going to know about us when this hits the press anyway."

Daviot buckled at the knees. "The press?"

"Murder does tend to get into the papers, Simon, you really should have thought of that."

"Oh no, oh no," intoned the MP in a chant-like voice, as if praying. For a second his eyes roved wildly around the deck and he seemed to be judging whether he could make a dash for the sea rails and blessed oblivion.

"You'll never make it, Daviot," said the voice of former Detective Chief Superintendent Adrian Clarke.

Daviot turned to face his rival with a look of resignation. Julia was surprised by the expression on Adrian Clarke's face; just for the merest moment it was one of quite alarming anger. She was mildly gratified to have aroused such jealousy in a man so patently mild and not given to demonstrations of emotion.

Clarke took a deep breath and controlled his feelings. "Simon Daviot," he said, "as the police officer investigating the murder of one Olivia Catherine Harman, I must ask you to accompany me to my office, where I require you to assist with my enquiries."

Daviot flushed and felt his heart leap around his chest. He was aware of the other passengers staring, the buzz of conversation stilled.

"Well, I am always ready to help and advise on matters judicial," he heard himself saying. Then the survivor that was Simon Daviot MP added, "But I do insist on a third party being present, in order to corroborate our conversation."

Adrian Clarke stared at Julia's former lover (former? It hadn't looked all that former in the Tiffany Bar, about forty minutes earlier). A witness to his interrogation was, of course, Daviot's right, no question of it, and Clarke was first and foremost a professional and conscientious police officer, with ingrained instincts which eighteen months of retirement had not blunted.

"And who would that be, sir?" he enquired, in a tone suggesting any answer would be an admission of guilt.

The MP thought fast. Julia was right there and could probably still be relied upon to back him up, should there be any variance over who said what, back in Clarke's 'office'. But it was now unavoidable that this whole mess was going to be in the media and he needed Julia to be further involved like a hole in the head. Also, hadn't it been said that the dead woman was almost the double of Julia? There was just a chance, and he saw that she was looking at him rather oddly, that his ex-mistress imagined he had mistaken the murder victim for herself.

But who else was there? Brenda? No way. If Daviot was going to get off the hook, he would have to be completely frank with this PC Plod. And if he was going to be frank, he could hardly afford to have his dearly beloved wife present. No, it would have to be a man. But who? Certainly not that foppish professor with the black eye.

"The ship's captain," he finally said, with such quiet confidence that it must have been clear to anyone present that he had absolutely nothing to hide.

Adrian Clarke raised an eyebrow at this pompous nonsense. Just what he'd expect from a politician.

"I'll see if he's free. Let's go below, shall we?"

Simon Daviot accompanied the retired detective to his office, both of them unaware of the drama unfolding back in the Daviots' stateroom.

While Julia Grant had been searching the vast cruise liner for her old lover, desperate to warn him about Clarke's witnessing him in the damning act of disposing of the murder weapon, Brenda Daviot had decided she was too upset to indulge herself at the bar and had returned to her cabin. The calm exterior she had shown to Julia had now crumbled. Contrary to what she had told Julia, she could quite imagine that Simon could murder someone if he thought that his career required it and that he would get away with it. There were now two questions on her mind; why would he have murdered this particular girl, and who was the woman who had come to tell her about it? Brenda assumed that it all had something to do with sex, but she couldn't imagine that Simon would be sufficiently worried about a sexual revelation to actually kill someone. He had never been that bothered about protecting his family from scandal in the past. It was all very unsettling.

She had stepped into the sitting room and closed the door, leaning against it and letting out a deep, shuddering sigh. Simon a murderer. She shook her head. Life was becoming a never-ending nightmare. Brenda had suspected he was up to something on the ship the night they came back from Knossos. She had come to recognize the signs, the way he would pick a fight with her and the extra care he would take over his appearance. Was this the girl? Had she threatened to expose him over something? Would he care enough to kill her? More likely she had threatened to go to the media, for that, certainly, was Simon's Achilles heel.

Then Brenda became aware of the sound of sobbing. She frowned, it was coming from the bathroom. Had one of the cabin maids some personal problem that had become all too much? Brenda Daviot could certainly empathize with that and in the blink of an eye she changed gear, back into her MP's wife mode, the constituency rock, a shoulder to lean on, and opened the bathroom door.

To her astonishment, she saw not a blubbering chambermaid but her normally cool and self-possessed daughter, Charlotte. The girl was sitting on the floor by the lavatory, and she was weeping as if she might never stop.

For the first time in years, a wave of tenderness for the child swept over Brenda and she hurried to her side, sitting down on the floor beside her and cradling Charlotte in her arms, rocking her gently.

"There there," Brenda intoned. "There, there, there . . ."

"Oh God, Mummy." (Mummy? Things had to be very bad.) ". . . I've done something terrible."

Brenda's heart froze. "Charley . . . don't tell me, I can't bear it. It was you . . ."

"I was trying to help Dad," sobbed the distraught girl, "and now it's gone . . . somebody's found out . . . oh Mummy I don't want to go to prison . . ." and as her shoulders shook, Brenda started to weep with her.

In Adrian Clarke's office, Captain Moore sat and impassively listened, as the formal interview of the prime suspect in the murder investigation went on.

"So you do not deny," enquired Chief Superintendent Clarke, in that understanding, slightly ominous monotone detectives seemed to reserve for such occasions, "that you dropped this item," he indicated the green plastic-wrapped knife, "into a sports bag." Bloodstains were visible on the inside of the plastic, on his desk. The whole thing was sealed inside a clear plastic bag and neatly labelled.

"I do not deny it," replied Daviot, who had regained some of his composure.

"And this is the knife you used." Silence.

Captain Moore watched Daviot with interest. The MP remained expressionless.

"You are," said the policeman, "entitled to remain silent. But you should be aware that juries are sometimes inclined to interpret that in a way that might not help you."

"I did not use that knife or any other, Mr Clarke. I am not your murderer."

Clarke did not seem to have heard. "Your attempts to dispose of your bloodstained clothing were not a success. You know that?" he glanced up at Daviot, letting his eyes bore right to the back of the man's skull.

"My clothes were not bloodstained. I was nowhere near the incident and I did not murder the girl."

Adrian Clarke wrote this painstakingly on his lined note-paper. "I did . . . not . . . murder . . . the girl," he mouthed, as he wrote. He studied the words, as if they held some clue.

"So it was not murder, then. I can see that." He looked up once more. "She provoked you. Manslaughter. You acted without thinking. She attacked you? Enraged you?"

Moore was impressed by the calmness of Daviot's response.

"I found the knife. I was very stupid. I panicked. I knew that the dead woman bore a remarkable resemblance to someone I recently had a . . . relationship with." Captain Moore noticed a glint of some unpleasant emotion in the policeman's eye. He also noticed that Simon Daviot was staring directly at the policeman, almost as if he was challenging him. Very rum, thought the captain. But interesting.

"Go on, sir," said Adrian Clarke, writing all this down in his neat hand.

"Well, we politicians have been under a three line whip not to embarrass the government. You know, what with all the scandals, all the allegations about ministers and MPs."

"What sort of allegations," enquired Clarke, "exactly?"

Daviot shrugged, it was hardly very important. "Oh you know . . . sex, sleaze, money for questions."

"Sex," muttered Clarke as he wrote. "Sleaze. Money for questions." He frowned. "Murder. Yes I can imagine that would be something of a sickener." He tapped his pen against the desk, then said, "And you didn't think disposing of vital evidence in a brutal killing might embarrass your masters, threaten your, um . . . good standing?"

"Well I rather hoped not to get caught, didn't I?" answered Daviot with angry candour.

And Clarke wrote that down, too. "Where did you find the knife?" he asked.

"I'd rather not say," replied Daviot, and from his expression it was obvious the man did not expect to be believed. For a moment, Captain Moore felt sorry for him.

"Mr Clarke, I'm not an expert," said Captain Moore, with some diffidence, "but would it not be helpful to see if Mr Daviot's fingerprints are on the knife?"

Adrian Clarke pushed his chair back and put his fingers together, deep in thought.

Then he said, "If they are on it, on the hilt, and suggest a grip commensurate with stabbing or slashing, then I would ask you to lock Mr Daviot up, pending our arrival at Alexandria, where he should be handed over to the local police, until the arrival of an escort from Scotland Yard." Clarke gazed at the plastic bag and the bloodstained knife. "I have a report here from the ship's doctor," he slid a piece of paper from the medical officer across the desk, "confirming that the blood group on the knife and its plastic wrapper corresponds to that of the dead woman."

Simon Daviot seemed much relieved, "Thank you Captain. So let's get on with it."

"But if I don't find your prints, sir, it does not, I'm afraid, let you off the hook."

"What do you mean?"

"You could have worn gloves," Clarke smiled coldly. And at this point there was an urgent knocking on the cabin door.

Captain Moore exchanged glances with Clarke then crossed to the door and opened it slightly. A junior officer was outside and a muttered conversation took place. Then Moore turned to the detective and said, "It seems there might be a new development, Chief Superintendent."

"Wait here please," Adrian Clarke said to Daviot and he stepped out into the companionway.

Brenda Daviot stood there, with her daughter Charlotte. Both looked as if they had been crying and they were extremely agitated.

"Simon did not put that knife in my drawer, Chief Superintendent."

"Is that a fact?" said Clarke, who seemed unsurprised. "Might I enquire who did? Was it you, Mrs Daviot?"

"I put it there," said Charlotte, looking pale and apprehensive. Adrian Clarke regarded her thoughtfully.

"In that case you had better go and wait in that room over there," he said, indicating an empty administrative cabin across the corridor. "I'll take your statement in a minute. Perhaps you would be good enough to stay with her, Mrs Daviot."

Clarke went back into his office and gazed thoughtfully at his prime suspect and rival in love.

"I'm not at all convinced we should not lock you up, sir," he said solemnly. "But for the time being, that's all. Your wife and daughter seem to have something to say about the case."

"I really do insist you take my fingerprints, Inspector."

It's Chief Superintendent, Mr Daviot. And when I want your dabs I'll let you know." He stepped aside and indicated the open door.

"If you are going to interrogate my wife, I demand to be present," said the MP.

"Really, sir?" replied Clarke, "but you didn't insist on her being present when we had a chat."

Moore almost smiled. The wily copper had got the too-smooth-for-his-own-good politician pinned to the wall.

"I'll be happy to stay here," said Moore.

With considerable misgivings and anxiety, not least at what his wife and daughter might say about him, Simon Daviot left Clarke's office and headed for his stateroom. He needed to take a shower and lie down. He needed to get back in control again. He decided that when he had freshened up he might visit the ship's gym. A few minutes on the exercise bike and the rowing machine would do his image no harm. Plus he had noticed the interesting-looking Chrissie Young coming out of there from time to time. She seemed to be just the type to be able to distract him from his current dilemma. If he was going to have his name dragged through the mud he might as well enjoy it and go down with style. Simon Daviot smiled at his own insouciance under pressure. When all this was over, he might pen an amusing piece for the Spectator or the Sunday Telegraph. Daviot had assumed that Adrian Clarke did not believe he had murdered Olivia Harman, and from that point of view he felt the worst was over. But poor Brenda would not stand up well to Clarke's gently persuasive interrogation technique.

Had his wife murdered the Harman girl? What was the tearful, whispered conversation outside Clarke's office door all about?

Poor old Brenda. Well, he would hire the best lawyers money could buy. The scandal of Julia and his wife's manslaughter – yes, manslaughter, that was it – of a stranger she mistook for his mistress might not be all gloom and despair. After all, just think what a publisher would pay for his book on the trial and events leading up to it. Provided Julia did not get in there first. She was no slouch at spotting an opportunity.

Daviot contemplated phoning an agent there and then. He had been approached by a chap not long ago wanting to handle his memoirs, he would look up the number.

But better to wait and see what they charged Brenda with. Murder might be more lucrative than manslaughter and God knows he was going to need something to fall back on if his political career went down the tubes.

Lisa woke up in a mess. Her hairpiece had come half off and her knickers were round one ankle. One of the incredible hunks was asleep on the floor, snoring softly, bollock starkers. Jazzy, too, was fast asleep, arms and legs entwined with two of the blighters, none of them wearing much. There were six empty bottles of Frascati and the stale smell of sex and too many cigarettes.

It had been like this ever since the two girls had managed to hunt down the men they had assumed were detectives on account of the way they had looked neither to the left nor to the right and because of the straight suits they wore, which had failed to hide their fabulous physiques.

After disporting themselves around the exercise area of the Oasis and the sauna rooms (Jazzy had been shameless), and a few drinks at Harlequin's Disco bar, the lads had been like lambs to the slaughter.

They had hardly left the girls' cabin ever since and the permutations of coupling between two randy female ravers and five athletic, if slightly dumb, blokes had been fully explored.

Lisa shook her head at such memories. Never in her wildest, most lustful imaginings had she thought this cruise would have turned into such a marathon. She smiled at the recollection that she and Jazzy had thought the blokes were coppers. Even that first night when all the fun had really started. Coppers – no way. This was the bow-tie and G-string troupe, the Davenports, a gorgeous quintet of perfect torsos and rippling muscles who formed part of the cabaret booked for the last three nights of the ship's cruise, second billing on the Theatre Royal's variety show.

As one of the sleeping hunks, bronzed and delicious, stirred and began to wake up, Lisa rolled, ungainly but willing, off her bunk and onto the floor beside him. The poor man's eyes widened as he took in the full horror of his situation. "Oh please," he moaned. "Not again . . ."

Adrian Clarke scribbled intently in his lined notepad. Then he raised his head and looked at Charlotte Daviot and her mother. Captain Richard Moore sat on one side, the impassive observer. Charlotte and Brenda looked extremely worried. "Let me get this right," Clarke addressed the daughter. "You were on the Sun Deck, around midnight, when you saw the knife, wrapped in green plastic."

Charlotte nodded, speaking in a small tearful voice. "Well, I sort of, half knelt down and picked up the plastic. And inside was something heavy."

"And did you look into the package there? Or did you go back to your cabin?"

"I started to open it. Then I realized it was a knife. I put it under my cardigan and went to one of the ladies loos. It was horrible. There was obviously congealed blood inside and this ghastly, very sharp sort of . . . dagger."

In the silence that followed, Adrian Clarke wrote neatly and swiftly. Then he asked, "Why did you hide it?"

"Well, I wanted time to think. I mean, Dad was terribly upset. I think he felt you suspected him."

Well he is still my first choice in the frame, thought the detective. "And you wanted to protect him," he said.

Charlotte seemed confused. She started to reply, then stopped. She spread her hands, "It's so difficult to explain. I was feeling guilty about being there." She cast an embarrassed look at her mother. Brenda was sitting with her head bowed, staring at her hands.

"Why did you feel guilty, Charlotte?" Adrian asked gently.

"I had gone to meet someone," she muttered.

"Meet who?"

"A man."

"What man?"

"I don't know who he was," she blurted out, close to tears again. "He didn't tell me his name, just a man I'd met in the pool during the day. He stood me up anyway." Now both the mother and the daughter were staring at their hands.

God preserve me from near-hysterical adolescent girls, thought Adrian Clarke. The moonlight, an assignation with an elusive stranger, a plastic bag with a blood-stained dagger. He had heard that cruises could lift people away from reality, but Charlotte Daviot seemed to be in orbit. It was clear this was a lass whose hormones were racing around like a million cupid's dart targets, just gasping to get the old golden arrow.

"You know, um . . ." he consulted his notes, "Charlotte. I think I actually do believe you." Brenda and Charlotte sagged with relief. "But withholding evidence is against the law you know. So you are going to have to be very, very honest with me and answer everything I ask you absolutely straight. Do you understand?"

Charlotte nodded meekly. "Yes, sir," she replied.

Two hours later, Julia Grant saw Simon and his wife strolling pensively past the Crystal Pool, filled with happy youngsters and laughing adults. The couple were deep in conversation. Julia was desperate to know what had happened after Adrian had more or less arrested Simon. Why was Simon now walking around free? And what had brought him and Brenda so seemingly close in such a short space of time?

She seemed to have spent that entire day in a fruitless search for each of the two current men in her life. First Simon – God how her chaffed heels stung – now Adrian.

Julia wanted to soothe Adrian, who clearly had seen her with her hand on Simon's thigh in the Tiffany Bar, and let him know how strong her affection was for him. But the former policeman was nowhere to be seen. His office was locked and in darkness. She felt abandoned and surplus to requirements.

Adrian Clarke was in fact in his own cabin. His jealousy had long since abated, however, and he read for the second time the cable the ship's communications officer had brought to his office, just after he had released the Daviot girl.

That knife had certainly done the rounds, since it had so viciously ended the life of Olivia Harman in Rosamund Westcott's cabin. Reluctantly, he had to admit he could understand the pompous, adulterous, but basically straight Daviot trying to dump it, wrongly believing it to be evidence that one of his family had done the deed.

The cable, marked STRICTLY PRIVATE AND CONFIDENTIAL, was from the Assistant Commissioner (Crime) at New Scotland Yard. It thanked Clarke for taking charge of the initial investigation and complimented him on the thoroughness of his notes. It agreed with all the steps he had taken. It asked him to continue with the investigation until further notice.

Captain Moore had also received a secret cable from the Assistant Commissioner (Crime) at New Scotland Yard.

"Dear Captain Moore," the cable had read. "This is very strictly for your information only."

"We have run a comprehensive check on the murder victim, Olivia Catherine Harman. Before emigrating to Australia she was employed by Huddersfield Police Headquarters as a civilian employee. This is where former Chief Superintendent Adrian Clarke was Head of the CID. We are perplexed as to why he has not disclosed the fact that she worked in his building, which is not large.

"Despite our concerns about his not disclosing this information, I have asked him to continue with his investigation into the murder.

"I would be grateful for your complete discretion. Please take steps, however, to ensure the murder weapon does not disappear once again."

Well . . . thought Richard Moore. Yet another one for my memoirs. He shook his head and reached for his cap.

During his long years of service the captain had discovered that it was best to remain uninvolved with passengers' squabbles, but when it came to murder he could hardly hope to remain completely aloof from the proceedings. He had also learned to be extremely cautious where judgements were concerned, especially where people on his ship were working in some official capacity, as Clarke was. He didn't intend to go leaping to any premature conclusions. He would wait to see what happened next.

Lost in thought, he stared out at his mistress. She was vast, bigger than even he could have imagined possible when he was young and first fell in love with her. Still beautiful though, and restless of course, but then great beauties were often restless, as if they sought by their constant changes of mood to keep every eye on themselves. Despite everything he was still in love with this first great passion of his life, still unable to keep from being mesmerized by her, still as much in her thrall. The sea had always been his first love. It always seemed too big and too grand to be bothered with the petty spites and jealousies of the human race.

With a deep sigh, he tore himself away from the view and went back to work.

chapter ELEVEN

Hilary Brown was feeling simultaneously trapped and intrigued. She felt trapped because Warren had managed to catch her reclining on the Sun Deck in full sun-cream, and intrigued because he seemed intent on pouring his heart out about Sandra Van Horn, a woman whom Hilary realized from his description she had noticed around the ship a great deal. Warren had simply come up to her, asked if she was the 'famous psychologist' and then begun his monologue of complaints.

"She's changed so much in recent months," he started. "I would really value your professional advice. Normally she is so calm and well organized . . . completely in control of her life. Recently she has become disorganized, nervous and tense, like a coiled spring, threatening to fly out of control at any moment. This cruise seems to be making her worse. I just cannot get her to socialize and on one of the shore trips she took she seemed to have a panic attack and came scuttling back to her stateroom."

At Antalya, on the southern coast of Turkey, Sandra had told Warren she was meeting her agent who had travelled from Istanbul with the icons she wished to purchase, but had become funny when he offered to come with her. Later, when he met up with her for dinner, she seemed very on edge and was drinking too much.

"She told me," Warren confided in Hilary, "that things had not gone strictly to plan. To her expert eye, the authenticity of two of the icons was dubious. Normally she would have dealt with this erring agent with cold disdain and dismissed him scathingly, but with dignity. This time apparently she could not control her anger. It boiled over so that she found herself screaming abuse and coming close to hitting him as she berated him for being a fool and for not realizing that she was not some rich stupid collector but an expert in her own right. I had to drag all this out of her, she was so upset.

"Worse was to come when, upon studying the documents for the third and genuine icon – necessary for the export of any ancient treasure from Turkey – she had noticed what looked remarkably like an erasure, close to the signature of the minister responsible for the release of artefacts.

"This whole transaction was beginning to stink, she thought. If anyone was going to rot in a Turkish jail for smuggling antiquities it was not going to be her. Despite the agent protesting that all was in order, that it was the minister himself who had made the erasure and that the providing of new papers could take days or even weeks, she persisted in her demands. Nor would she delay her departure and catch a plane to rendezvous with the ship later, not with her fear of flying. 'Meet me in Haifa or Port Said,' she told him and then she swept out.

"This whole incident seems to have shaken her to the core. She is not used to losing control in such an unseemly way, even with someone she was convinced was an out and out crook."

"So what happened in Haifa?" Hilary asked, fascinated by this glimpse behind the cool, expensive façade of the American collector.

"She was wrong," Warren shrugged. "The man was awaiting *Oriana* at Haifa with the one genuine icon, with its paperwork in order and with a charming note from the minister himself to reassure her that all was well and wishing her happiness with her new acquisition."

"You went with her this time?"

"No," Warren raised his hands, as if this proved that his friend was losing her grip, "she just told me this afterward. I think she was embarrassed to have divulged so much to me before and wanted to pour cold water on the whole story.

"The other odd thing is that she didn't seem to take any pleasure from the acquisition. Normally she would have rushed to her stateroom, ordered the icon unpacked and spent hours gloating over it. Instead, this time, it remains in the Purser's strongroom and she appears to feel no burning desire to see it again."

Warren continued to whine about how neglected he felt, and how unfair it was since Sandra had invited him on the cruise in the first place, until Hilary couldn't stand it any more and made her excuses to return to her cabin. But Warren had tickled her interest and she would now watch Sandra's elegant progress around the ship even more closely.

The great ship steamed south before turning west along the coast of Egypt. At night the sky was the deep purple of a pansy, stabbed with stars that shone with a much brighter light than farther north. The land on the port side seemed to pulsate with the stored heat of the day and with the mystery of the great continent that lay sleeping beyond it.

Sandra barely seemed to emerge from her stateroom for the next few days. Warren tried in vain to coax her out.

"It's not like you to do a Garbo, Sandi my sweet. You're not going down with anything are you?" He shuddered, for he loathed ill health of any type. It made people look so ugly – even the common cold – and if there was one thing Warren could not tolerate, it was ugliness.

"Of course not. It's just that I don't feel like being with people at the moment."

"You're not becoming menopausal?" Warren shuddered even more as he whispered the word in a voice brimming with horror. "I just couldn't bear that," he sighed exaggeratedly.

"Really Warren, you can be so very impertinent. If I were, it would be me who would have to bear it, not you." She laughed at his horrified expression.

"Tut, forgive me, do. But you did not know my mother, how she suffered, the poor dear . . . I wouldn't want that to happen to my worst enemy, let alone a darling like you."

"And it won't, don't fret." She smiled, remembering the impossibly hypochondriacal mother Warren had been cursed with. "You go out, I'm fine here." And Warren had rushed to the door with somewhat obscene haste, she had thought. "Recruiting again, Warren?" she teased him, and he confessed that he was counselling a repressed homosexual, helping him to 'come out'.

"Maybe he doesn't want to 'come out'. Perhaps he's happy as he is."

"Sandi, you do talk such rot at times. Of course he isn't happy, how can he be? He needs to be liberated."

"Has he a wife?"

"The dreariest soul," he sighed.

"Then maybe you should think of her and the pain it might cause her. Have you thought that perhaps that is the reason your friend is not so keen on 'outing'. Has it crossed your mind he might love her?"

At these words Warren's shudder was volcanic. "Don't be obscene," he'd said and made a dramatic exit from her stateroom.

She missed him when he wasn't there. Despite her books, her music, the hours she devoted to her beauty routine, she found that the days stretched endlessly ahead of her. Maybe Warren was right and she was menopausal, which was a thought she did not welcome.

She must make more of an effort, she decided, or she was liable to become seriously depressed.

That evening, as she sat in a deep leather chair in the infinitely clubbable atmosphere of Anderson's, she looked about her while she took the occasional sip of her champagne cocktail. She had chosen this bar since it was quieter and had a more sedate atmosphere than the others. She felt that she was not yet ready for too much noise and too many people.

Warren, she was sure, had seen her from the other side of the room as she had entered, but for reasons of his own was choosing to ignore her as he continued his deep conversation with the man she recognized as Patrick Westcott, whose books she had read and admired. So he was the poor man still lurking in the closet. Now she did not feel so much sympathy for the 'poor' wife. She had briefly met Rosamund

Westcott and had found her insufferably smug and pleased with herself, for no particular reason as far as Sandra could make out.

A few tables away Sandra took stock of the attractive, mid-thirties woman, dressed, if she was not mistaken, in Lacroix, and nervous. Sandra wondered why. She knew women like that, taut as wire, self-contained, afraid of emotions, of letting go – she should know, she was one herself. She smiled at this new found self-awareness. She also smiled when she saw the face of the other woman light up as a tall, broad-shouldered man approached her table. Sandra recognized him as the man who had been asking questions about the murder – a former detective someone had said. He was attractive, she could not help but wish she had seen him first, she liked dark-haired men. His grey eyes looked even greyer in his evenly tanned face.

"So you found the time, Julia. I am surprised," he said and Julia blushed at the sarcasm in his tone.

"Adrian, please!"

"Where is he then? Stood you up? Where's Simon?" His voice was bitter, his handsome features suffused with anger.

"You don't understand."

"No, I bloody well don't . . ." Then Sandra could hear no more as a chattering group of passengers moved into Anderson's and began noisily to decide what to drink. She did notice that a grey-haired woman swapped her seat for one nearer to the arguing couple. She opened a blue note-pad and began quickly to scribble in it. What extraordinary behaviour, thought Sandra. Surely she was not taking notes of their discussion, though it certainly looked as if she was. Sandra had also noticed this woman on the trip to the gorge and had avoided her then. She did not like her type. It was not just because of her nosiness but her way of dressing, too: she looked like a refugee from Woodstock. Like most of those superannuated hippies it had been Sandra's misfortune to meet, this one had the same expression; she smiled to herself as if solely aware of the secret of the universe when no one else was. If she conformed to the usual pattern then she would have taken tolerance and reasonableness to such an art form that Sandra knew she would long to strangle her.

Into the room, waving cheerfully to left and right, stalked a young man confident in his looks and charm. Sandra watched him as he paused to speak to the arguing couple. Julia, however, barely acknowledged him but got to her feet and virtually ran from the room. Blithely the young man continued until he had joined the grey-haired woman.

"So, Annie, what's your poison, the usual?" he asked.

Her fresh drink arrived, she watched them surreptitiously over the rim of her glass. Was she getting paranoid as well, for she was certain they were talking about her. Annie even blatantly turned and stared at her. Sandra averted her gaze and studied the bowls of nuts and olives the waiter had left her instead. When she looked up again it was to find Annie, a kaleidoscope of trailing scarves, standing at the table.

"It is Sandra Van Horn, isn't it? Several nights back I saw you in the Crow's Nest I think it was. We wondered where you'd got to, didn't we Rupert," she called across to her young companion. "Mind if we join you?" Annie did not wait for a reply before taking a seat. "Bring the vodkas over, Rupe, there's a pet."

Sandra needed people, she had acknowledged that, but she was not sure if she was ready for the easy familiarity and chatter of the Annies of this world. "Of course," she heard herself say and despised herself for doing so.

"Excuse me," a young man said politely. "Annie, have you seen Chrissie? Only we arranged to go ashore to look round Alexandria together and she never showed up."

"No, Mike, sorry. She's none too happy with me, can barely speak to me. Have you seen her, Rupert?"

"I'm not flavour of the month either. I saw her at the swimming pool at lunchtime. She said she was tired and needed to have a nap – I thought she was avoiding me."

"Right, well if you do see her tell her I'm in the Crow's Nest, would you?" And he waved and was gone.

"What about the murder then?" Annie said to Sandra with a somewhat tasteless enthusiasm. "I tell you, this cruise has everything, wonderful food, drink, entertainment, weather and then a mystery worthy of Agatha Christie." Annie laughed. "Have you met our own Poirot? Adrian, come and join us." She gestured expansively not waiting for a reply. Sandra was aware that her heart was racing in a very unusual way as Adrian stood, collected his scotch before the steward could do it for him, and joined them. Everyone shuffled their chairs around to make room for him.

"Adrian Clarke." He bowed over her hand.

"Sandra Van Horn," she replied, and felt flustered just saying her name.

"How's the investigation going, Adrian? Any suspects?" Annie asked.

"Now, would I be telling you if there were, Annie?" He smiled good naturedly at her.

"That's a lovely dress, Mrs Van Horn, if you don't mind me saying so." Rupert was smiling at her.

"Thank you."

"And such a pretty necklace, the colour of your eyes," he continued. He was flirting with her!

She looked at him with panic in her eyes and pressed herself back into her seat.

"Are you all right, Mrs Van Horn?" she could hear Adrian asking her as if from a long way away.

"Yes, I'm fine," she lied. She wasn't, she felt sick – this man looked just as she imagined her son would look now, if he had lived. She judged him to be the same age, too, and he was flirting with her! It was an abominable thought.

"I can tell you one thing that might help you, Adrian, if you haven't found out already."

"What's that, Annie?"

"The identity of the corpse, I mean how do you know she was who you are all saying she was?"

"A process of elimination. When we discovered who was missing from their cabin it was easy to deduce from the papers we found there," he said calmly, looking none of them in the eye.

"Well, how is it then that her name wasn't on the passenger manifest? I checked it. Was she sailing incognito and if so why, for there's no Olivia Harman listed?"

At that moment Rupert winked at Sandra and she fainted dead away. Annie immediately snatched up her notebook and stashed it in her bag.

Sandra came to on the bed in her own stateroom. "How did I get here?" she asked, aware that her head was throbbing.

"Mr Clarke and I carried you." Dr Patel was speaking. "You weren't totally unconscious or I would have taken you to the sick bay. Have you eaten today?"

"No," she lied. "I knew it was a mistake to have those champagne cocktails on an empty stomach." She managed a good attempt at a laugh. "I'm fine now, Doctor, really I am."

"Just call me if you think you need me," Dr Patel pointed to the telephone as he stood up. "Well, if you're sure, I've one or two patients with gyppy tums, I told them to be careful what they ate on shore, but do they listen?" He fussed his way to the door and Adrian began to follow him.

"Mr Clarke, may I speak with you a moment?" Sandra asked.

"Of course, but please call me Adrian." She was not sure why such a simple sentence could make her heart turn turtle, but it did.

"Adrian," she said almost shyly. "I've always liked that name. I'd prefer it if you called me Sandra." And this time to her surprise she noticed that she sounded almost demure. She caught herself wondering what the woman called Julia meant to him and suddenly realized it mattered to her very much. And then she put her hand to her lips, shocked in the circumstances that she would be even thinking this way. "Oh dear, I hardly know where to begin."

"Was it really the champagne cocktails that made you faint?" he asked kindly.

"No, I lied to the doctor, but it's so complicated." She brushed her hair back with her hand and he waited patiently for her to begin.

The telephone on her bedside table rang. She looked at it with alarm, not sure why. "Would you like me to answer it?" He picked it up. "Yes," he said abruptly. "Speaking." He sat silent as he listened to the voice at the other end. Suddenly he stood up. "I'll be along immediately."

"What is it? What's happened?" she asked, immediately picking up his seriousness.

"Can I ask someone to come and sit with you? Do you know any of the other passengers?"

"Why, what is it, what's happened?" She was kneeling up on the bed now, her face twisted with anxiety.

"There's been another murder."

chapter TWELVE

The announcement was made at eight the next morning, and permeated through to all corners of the ship. Discreetly placed loudspeakers relayed the words to every bar, to every breakfast table, into the privacy of every passenger cabin. Even early risers lounging by the top deck pool 'catching the southern sun before it became too hot' were treated to the calm voice of instruction:

"The captain requests that all passengers return to their cabins by eleven o'clock this morning, and remain there until further notice, for the purposes of a routine passenger check. We regret any inconvenience this may cause and would like to . . ."

Responses across the ship varied. Jasmin and Lisa groaned almost in unison. Ever since the five Davenports had been located and removed by the theatre manager – who had seemed shocked at their pallor, and had given the two girls a look of disgust – things had been depressingly quiet. The night before they had tried their luck at the disco, but had ended up with nothing more than slurred speech and the complex pattern of bruises caused by falling down some steps.

"Eight o'clock in the morning! Who do they think we are?" grunted Lisa from a fog of sheets, bad breath and hangover. "If they'd left us to sleep we'd have been here anyway."

Rosamund Westcott was not altogether sure she had heard the announcement correctly. She was lost in the folds of a dress she was pulling over her head at the time, looking a little like somebody fighting with a tent. As her head popped free into light and air the words of authority were repeated and she caught them clearly enough.

Surely that could not mean . . . ? Her thoughts flew back to the shock of that memory: the still, bloodied girl, lying on the bed in her cabin. Her heartbeat quickened. Though even now she could not find it in herself to exactly feel sorrow for the victim. Her pity was snagged on the remembrance of that thin waist, the young skin, still clear. A hussy probably. The sort who brought things upon themselves.

From behind her she heard the faint sound of her husband blowing his nose. "What was that about, Rosamund?" he asked. "I didn't quite catch it."

She didn't turn round. The fact was, in the last few days everything he did seemed to irritate her. Perhaps it was the chance she had found of meeting other men. Like the charming Dr Patel. She simply could not see her husband as she had done before.

"We're to come back to the cabin at eleven so they can make a check."

There was a pause of evident bewilderment. "Just us?"

How had she managed to put up with somebody so vague, so uninterested in the world, for all these years? In the past she had at least thought him clever in his work. But now she found it hard to believe even in that. "No, not just us. All the passengers."

Another pause. Then annoyance. "But that means they won't be able to get to my lecture on the Roman province of Africa. And, for that matter, I won't be able to give it."

Rosamund held herself in. "I'm sure you'll all survive."

Julia Grant and Rupert Revell had been having an early morning sibling row. "You've creased my best dress," Julia complained, brandishing something that seemed to be made up mostly of gaps and strings. "I told you to take care putting your stuff away."

"You shouldn't have brought so much," Rupert retorted petulantly. "Just because you've filled your whole wardrobe and need space in mine . . ."

Julia was just about to bring in the heavy guns – that she was paying for the trip – when the slow voice of the announcement began. Both listened without a word.

"Can't be another one, surely," said Julia, at last. Her voice had changed, uneasy now.

Rupert said nothing.

Simon Daviot had been engaged in the delicate process of shaving and at the same time admiring his chin, when the radio fell into silence and the announcement began. He listened, then called out to his wife in a tone of stock scorn, "The captain requests, eh? It's a bit much. Treating us all like children, considering what we've all paid."

Brenda did not answer. She had been very quiet during the previous few days.

Simon smoothly removed a last outpost of hairs on the end of his chin. Such a good chin, he considered. Who was it who had said it was the chin of a statesman?

He pondered a moment on one of his pet theories: that a man's worth was always reflected in his appearance. Take that ghastly would-be policeman, for instance. Clarke. A man with a face that was ludicrously square. A face with no meaning to it, no distinction. Clarke was a rough summary of everything Simon Daviot detested. Conceited. The sort of person, he considered, who thought he was special just because people just as bad as himself endured him and remembered his name at the local pub. And he wasn't even a real copper any more. Retired until this voyage.

If only he could get the man off his back. Better still, get even in the process. Smoothing his chin with his hand, he imagined himself striding into the man's office. Giving him a good scare. Telling him how an MP was used to being treated with some respect, rather than having his family needlessly accused and upset. "And I should tell you," he could see himself saying, "that I am not without connections in the police. Chief Constable Davies was a guest at our house only last month. So you needn't worry yourself that my complaints won't be properly heard. They'll be heard as clear as can be."

Adrian Clarke was happily unaware of his imagined dressing-down. He was standing on the bridge of the ship, among all manner of impressive electronic gadgetry – devices displaying their position, others relaying the workings of the ship; radar images showing other vessels in the vicinity; communications coming in. And of course, a weather chart that showed the ship leaving a largely blank area, and approaching a complex pattern of thick lines and circles within circles.

"The passenger check should be complete by noon," he told the captain, "so there should be no interference with lunchtime arrangements." This time there had been no problem identifying the murder victim. But there had still been need of a check, in case the murderer had slipped away. Although the body of Chrissie Young, her tender throat slit wide open, had been discovered two hours after the ship left Alexandria, Dr Patel had considered the likely time of death as between three and four hours earlier.

Captain Moore, like most ships' captains when standing on their own bridges, had an air of solid immovability, the aura of unchallenged importance in a small place. "I'm glad to hear it," he answered, a touch wearily. "The last thing I want is a lot of angry passengers. And they don't like being stuck in their cabins."

"We have to think of their safety," Adrian Clarke insisted. He liked Captain Moore. Could see he was a reasonable man struggling with a difficult job. But this crisis had set them at odds. Different priorities. "If anything else happens we may have to insist they stay in their cabins permanently."

The captain peered out across the horizon. "That's the last thing I want. I have to think what these people expect. This is their holiday, after all. They expect to enjoy themselves, and can get very difficult if things aren't as they want." He crossed the bridge and opened a small metal locker. "It's your job to sort this out, and quickly." From the locker he took a small walkie-talkie radio. "This is something I thought might be useful. It's standard for the crew when we're docking. This one's tuned into the bridge here, and also the communications room."

It was a sensible thought. Adrian Clarke took it gladly. "Thanks Captain." He would have liked to have said something confident. To have predicted an imminent solution. But he had so little to go on. "I'll let you know at once if there are any developments."

The captain nodded. "You know that tonight's the opening night of *Salad Days* in the ship's theatre. It looks as if it'll be a full house. Perhaps your murderer will be there."

"I'll keep a good look out."

As he walked down the corridor towards the main area of the ship, Adrian Clarke could feel the pull of exhaustion. He had been up till after four – not so long ago – talking to Chrissie Young's two relatives. The brother, Mike, had been too upset to be of much use. Just kept blaming himself for not having been there at the time to save his sister. The aunt, Annie Young, had been much more collected. In fact she had been so cool she had slightly given him the creeps. She seemed to be almost enjoying the whole thing, flipping through her notebook, playing detective, with one of her own family dead. And she had lost no time throwing suspicion about. She had pointed the finger at just about everybody who had had the misfortune to speak to her. Though most of her ponderings had not added up to much.

The fact was that this latest murder seemed to make matters even more fog-bound than before. Chrissie Young had no connection that he could see with the first death, except that both victims were young and attractive. And there had been no evidence of any sexual assault. Jealousy, then? Or just some deeply disturbed mind? Yet Clarke had checked all of the names on the passenger list against English medical records, and nothing had come up except a number of instances of depression, which included Dr Patel, the ship's doctor. As for actual crime, there had been nothing more violent than a few ancient fraud cases, plus the inevitable flood of traffic offences.

Hardly the stuff of serial murder.

Clarke had reached the entrance to the restaurant, and was being reminded of how hungry he was by a delicious coffee smell, when the walkie-talkie began to bleep.

"Inspector Clarke? There's a call coming in for you at the communications room. From a Chief Superintendent Ferris at Scotland Yard."

That was all he needed. "I'll be right along."

He guessed Ferris would be in a foul mood. After all, there was the time difference. Quarter to nine here meant quarter to seven in London. The Chief Superintendent – a man not known for his sweet temper – must have been roused in the middle of the night.

Nor was Adrian Clarke wrong.

"I thought you said you had a suspect," a voice loaded with sarcasm demanded through the atmospheric hiss and crackle. "Where was he when this happened?"

Adrian Clarke determined not to sound apologetic. He felt he had nothing to apologize for. "That's one of the things I intend to determine, sir."

It seemed this was not the desired answer. "You mean he was wandering about, free as a bird? You weren't even keeping an eye on him?"

"It turned out we didn't really have much on him, sir. Not enough to hold him."

Ferris was not impressed. "You realize the press have got hold of this. They've been ringing all through the night."

"Here too, sir." Several times his conversations with Mike and Annie Young had been interrupted by calls from hard, hungry voices trying to lure him into saying something foolish.

Ferris's voice softened a little. "You have to understand, Clarke. This is just getting too hot."

Adrian Clarke saw that Ferris had been leading up to bad news. "You're taking me off the case?" he guessed.

"I'm sending out a team of three. Chief Inspector Williams, Sergeant Clive and a lab man called Peterson. You will work under Williams."

Clarke knew Williams from the past. A pompous, crude man. And to be taken out of charge of the case just as he was getting interested . . . "Are you sure that's really necessary, sir? If only I could have a little more time, I'm sure . . ."

Ferris was not to be swayed. "It is necessary, Clarke. And you will work under Williams. You'll clean his boots if that's what he tells you. They're flying out later this morning. We've arranged for them to land at the squaddies base at Cyprus. Then an RAF helicopter will take them direct to your ship. They should arrive about seven this evening your time. Make sure you're there to welcome them. And that you're friendly and co-operative."

Walking back to the main part of the ship, Adrian Clarke found himself regretting that he had ever been flattered into accepting his re-appointment. If he had declined, he would now be enjoying a holiday, rather than being hassled by superiors and pressmen. Blamed for what he had not done.

Nor would he now have the prospect of working under Chief Inspector Williams.

But a hearty breakfast and two cups of black coffee made matters seem a little better. After all, he pondered, he wasn't finished yet. He glanced at his watch. Five past nine. The new team wouldn't arrive till seven. He glanced about him at the other diners. If the murderer hadn't got off at Alexandria, he or she was quite likely to be eating breakfast at this very moment. It should be possible, surely, to crack this one. And how satisfying it would be, if he could achieve a breakthrough before the others arrived.

The cabin check began at eleven sharp. It didn't take long for the staff responsible for each deck level to knock on doors and check names against the passenger list. But matters were slowed by the fact that a number of passengers had not listened to the announcement, or had forgotten. All the ship's bars and restaurants had to be searched several times. It was half past noon before the chief passenger officer brought Adrian Clarke a final list.

"Looks like they're all still on board," he reported. "There's only one passenger who disembarked at Alexandria, and we know about him. Chap called Hermann Klaus from Stuttgart. Had to fly home because his brother was ill."

Clarke felt relief. So one of the deck stewards had probably been happily chatting to the killer within the last hour or so. An eerie thought. "And none of your staff noticed anything unusual during the check?"

"Nothing that they mentioned."

But he or she was still aboard. And that, in a way, was good news.

Jasmin and Lisa did not make it onto the deck to sun themselves until well after lunch. They were delayed not only by eating, but also by the need to pause and comfort one another as they pulled on their bikinis.

"Honest Jazzy, you've nothing to worry about. Like a bean pole, you are, pretty much. It's me that's put it on."

"That's not true at all, Lisa. You don't look bad. Really you don't. Especially round the hips. It's me needs to watch myself."

They had soon depressed each other so much that they had to stop off at the Crow's Nest for a quick one. Or two. They were well warmed by the time they reached the swimming pool.

"Funny weather," observed Jasmin, as they lay down, glistening with sun-cream. "I mean the sun's out and that, but the sky's not usually that colour."

She was right. It had a discernible purple hue to it. A kind of purposeful haze, that seemed to have robbed the sun of some of its bite. Though it was hot enough. Humid. Even the movement of the ship could not dispel the heaviness of the air. Both girls found themselves perspiring heavily through their sun-cream.

"Quite turns me on," murmured Jasmin. "Makes me feel just ready for a nice bit of . . ." her words trailed away into the heat.

"Could be your lucky day, Jazzy," Lisa was sitting up. "Over there, by the diving board. It's Ned."

On the other side of the swimming pool an over-muscled figure in tiny swimming trunks picked his way furtively past the sunbathers. The unmistakable shape of a Davenport. So great was the weight of flesh about his chest and shoulders, and so thin was his waist, that his whole walk had a strange quality to it, almost as if he were wearing high heels.

Jasmin sat up, too. "Cooeee Ned!"

"Ned . . . where've you been?"

He looked their way only for a second, seeming not quite to see them, then turned about and slunk off in the direction of the bar.

"The rotten bugger!" exclaimed Jasmin. "He's hiding."

Lisa glanced at her own glistening stomach, then looked crossly away. "As if we're interested in him."

Jasmin thought for a moment. "Quite. Only wanted to say hello, didn't we? As if we'd want to have anything to do with a bloke like that. With his stupid poncy walk. Once was enough."

"More than enough. Once too many, I'd say."

They both laughed noisily. Then lay back on their sun-chairs and lapsed into gloomy silence.

Adrian Clarke turned up the air-conditioning in his office. Touching the window, he could feel the heat outside.

After all his earlier hopes, it had proved a frustrating afternoon. He had conducted several interviews, but not one of them had yielded anything substantial: anything he could work on, and time was ticking by. The Scotland Yard team would arrive in two hours.

Rupert Grant, or Revell as he preferred to be known, had been the first passenger he had questioned. Clarke had been interested in him because he was the only one who had a connection – if a very tenuous one – with both the murdered girls. He had been seeing a lot of the second victim, Chrissie. At the same time his sister, Julia, was a dead ringer for the first.

Of course Clarke had come across him before now. Hadn't taken to him much, either. Too damn casual. Too pleased with his soap opera good looks. Nor did it help that he had been playing a game of being Julia's husband. He had admitted that openly. Clarke felt a twinge of anger and then regret that he had let himself get so close to the girl. And all the time she had only come on the cruise so she could win back that awful pumped-up MP . . . with brother Rupert's help.

Not that Clarke would have allowed this personal annoyance to affect his judgement. He was too good a policeman for that. And he knew that he had nothing on Rupert. Nothing that would be worth telling his superiors about.

Though he did have a slight feeling of disquiet. During his questioning he had never actually caught Rupert in a lie, but there had been something about him. His manner seemed slightly overdone. Like someone over-playing his part. Overdoing his performance as the reasonable man eager to help. Clarke was all but sure he was concealing something.

Nor did he have much of an alibi. He had looked round Alexandria with Julia, but they had come back early, as it had been too hot. About the time of the murder Rupert claimed to have been taking a nap in their cabin, while Julia had been off taking a dip in one of the swimming pools.

Another interviewee who had surely been hiding something had been the lecturer, Patrick Westcott. A funny-looking chap. And very nervous. He had become very uneasy when questioned – this was the second time – about why he had missed the boat at Crete. Started to bluster, complaining that he had been through all of that already, and that he had nothing to add. A sure sign that he did. Nor had he provided much of an alibi for the time of Chrissie Young's murder. He hadn't bothered himself with the Alexandria city tour, and claimed to have spent the whole afternoon alone in his cabin, preparing his next lecture.

But that didn't make him a murderer. And – as with all the others Clarke had interviewed – he did not seem to possess any real motive.

Here lay the real problem. There was nobody on board who seemed to have an obvious reason to murder either the Harman girl or Chrissie Young. Let alone both.

Just then the phone rang. It was a female voice, sounding troubled. "Chief Superintendent Clarke?"

"Speaking."

"My name's Roman Brindle. I shouldn't be bothering you. It's probably nothing important – probably just a stupid joke – but I thought you might just be interested. You see I've found this note pushed under my door . . ."

It sounded as promising as any of the other leads he had been following. He decided to go over to her cabin.

"It's rather a mess in here," she apologized as she opened the door. "I hope you don't mind." Domestic politeness. It didn't hide the fact that she was scared.

She had evidently been practising her singing, and the room was strewn with music scores. "It's a pretty likeable sort of mess," he answered, and wondered at his own words. Flirting. It was hard not to on this ship. It was in the air. Everyone seemed to be flirting all of the time. Besides, she was a nice-looking girl, very shapely. It occurred to him that this could in itself put her in danger. Judging by the previous two victims. "Now where's this note?"

"Here, I found it on the floor. As I said, it must have been pushed under the door."

He examined it. The paper itself was the corner of a copy of the dinner menu. Nothing special in that. They were printed out differently for every meal. Throwaway things. Nor was the writing helpful. Block capitals, neatly drawn. Signatures on the passenger list would be difficult to compare. Though he would fax a copy back to London for examination by handwriting experts, just in case.

DEAR ROMAN,
I NEED TO SPEAK TO SOMEONE. SOMEONE TO TRUST. I KNOW SOMETHING ABOUT WHAT HAS BEEN GOING ON. PLEASE LET ME TALK TO YOU. I WILL COME TO YOUR ROOM TONIGHT AT HALF-PAST EIGHT. DO NOT TELL ANYONE ABOUT THIS. FOR YOUR OWN GOOD.

PLEASE DO NOT HIDE FROM ME. BE THERE. I NEED YOUR HELP.

It was unsigned. Not even a cross, or YOUR FRIEND. Adrian Clarke frowned. "There's nobody you know who might have done this?"

She shrugged. "Nobody I can think of."

"Quite a mystery. I'm glad you let me know."

She was looking nervous. "D'you think it may be . . ." she ran out of words for a moment. "Him?"

He smiled, trying to calm her. "Probably not. Probably just some nasty individual playing a joke. You've no idea how sick people can get."

It probably wasn't the most reassuring thing to have said. She looked far from comforted. "What are you going to do?"

"We'll certainly treat it as serious. A police team should be flying in later today, and it'll be up to them to decide how we handle it. But don't worry. We'll sort it out. In the meantime I wouldn't let anyone into your room."

Privately he was more than a little puzzled. If it was the murderer, surely he, or she, would realize that he, Clarke, would hear about the note – that somebody would be watching. Unless the murderer was out of control, not thinking in a logical way. And that sort of behaviour would be noticed by other passengers. He'd have heard, surely.

He glanced again at the piece of paper. Something – an itch – made him feel that this was important. More than just a nasty prank.

Eight-thirty. If only the note-writer had chosen an earlier time.

Across the ship, passengers were preparing themselves for a night at the theatre. There is something about a cruise that brings out the desire in people to dress up – even the English. And though London theatre has long been stubbornly informal, the *Oriana's* cabins were filled with people fiddling with zips, buttons and tie knots, even the occasional collar stud. These tasks were made a touch more interesting by the rocking of the ship which was not uncomfortable, but strong enough to be inconvenient. When a large wave struck, across the vessel hands abandoned their tie knots, hooks, collar studs and bra straps, and hurriedly reached out for something to clutch, letting pieces of garment fall or sag or fly away to freedom. The fainter hearted were already well dosed with sea-sickness tablets.

Sandra Van Horn eased herself into a seven thousand dollar dress, wondering why on earth she was bothering. *Salad Days*, of all plays. A moronic English romp of the kind usually performed by amateur theatre groups, or unimaginative students, destined for careers in insurance or small town legislation. Not the sort of thing she would ever usually bother with. Normally she would only trouble herself with a text and production of acknowledged depth. The sort of theatre that all the right people would attend.

But Sandra knew well enough why she was going. Distraction. She inspected her face in the mirror glumly. She looked so tired. Quite unlike herself. But then she had

had so little sleep. It was ridiculous. Worse than ridiculous. She had become scared of being asleep. Of her own dreams.

She looked away from the mirror. Absurd. Only dreams. But she could not seem to get them out of her head. She looked again at herself in the mirror.

Hands twitching as they worked, eyes intense and troubled, she prepared herself for the theatre.

Rosamund Westcott was growing impatient with her husband. "For goodness' sake, Patrick, it'd do you good to come. You should spend less time with your nose in books."

It wasn't that she actually wanted him to go with her. More that she wanted to goad him into something. Find fault with him.

"I really can't, dear," he answered peevishly. "I haven't time for silly plays. You know I have to prepare for tomorrow's lecture on Carthage and Rome."

"Well I'm not going to sit here all evening," she declared firmly. "If you won't take me out, I'll go by myself." In fact this was pretty much what she had intended to do all along. Perhaps it was a touch of guilt that had made her try and bully Patrick into joining her.

Her thoughts turned to that nice doctor she had spoken to a few days earlier. Wondering if he was the sort who would go to the theatre.

Simon Daviot was practising his skills of people control, the people in this case being his family. "You can't just lounge around doing nothing. In this world you have to be active, be seen."

It was his daughter Charlotte who was resisting. "But I don't want to go to this stupid play. If you'd asked me, instead of just planning for everyone, I'd have told you so."

The fact was, Simon Daviot was not himself greatly interested in the production. He had decided to take the seats from a sense of self-protection. After the goings-on of the last few days, and the suspicion that had fallen on them, it was essential to play the part of the untroubled family. Be visibly happy.

"Theatre's good for you," he insisted flatly. "Better than wasting your time lounging about watching rubbish on television."

Not that Charlotte had intended doing any such thing. But here was her weakness in the argument. She could not tell her father what she did want to do. The fact was, this afternoon by the pool, she had found herself being chatted up by a smooth type with a pony tail and a Birmingham accent who had lost no time in telling her how he ran his own recording studio. He was everything her father would hate. He was even called Dave. Perhaps that was why she had rather liked him. And he had given her his room number, and an invitation to "Drop in and have a scotch or three." Charlotte felt a delicious thrill run through her: the thrill of a wicked adventure anticipated.

Julia and Rupert were enjoying their second sibling row of the day. Though this one had rather more substance to it than the first.

"It's crazy," Rupert claimed. "We both want to go. We both can go. Neither of us has anybody else to go with. Why on earth shouldn't we go together?" The fact was, he was feeling the need for some sisterly company. The comfort of the familiar. He had been rattled by the interview with Adrian Clarke that afternoon. Not that he had pinned him down, but he had been so suspicious. It was scary. Having someone you know murdered was proving more unsettling than he would ever have imagined. He felt his whole world had wobbled and he wanted his sister to be a rock for him to steady himself on. He wanted her to appreciate the masterly performance of grief he was giving. She was being most unobliging.

"It's up to me who I go with," said Julia threateningly. She was in a bad mood, and Julia's bad moods left most other people's far behind. "You're a big boy now. Surely you can find your seat by yourself, without big sister holding your hand."

Sarcasm directed at his manhood. It was enough to rile Rupert into attack. "It's that bloody copper, isn't it? Clarke. You want to go alone so you can chat him up."

It was. "What if I do? Just because you don't like him."

"I certainly don't," Rupert agreed. "You should've heard the way he was talking to me this afternoon. Really sneaky and nasty."

Julia gave him a strong look. "And what did you tell him, Rupert?" And all at once they had reached what they were really arguing about. "It must have been pretty bad. In the restaurant just now he walked past me as if I wasn't there."

Rupert was affronted. "I just answered his questions, and tried not to let him find some excuse to charge me with a couple of murders."

"What did you say about me?"

Rupert found himself on the defensive. "I had to tell him the truth."

Her look hardened. "Did you tell him that I'd asked you to play the part of my husband?"

He said nothing.

"Did you tell him I'd come here with the idea of making Daviot jealous?"

Again he didn't answer. Which of course was an answer.

"You little shit, Rupert." She practically spat the words. "I should never have brought you along."

Rupert decided he was being unfairly criticized. "So it's more important to you to impress this squarehead Clarke than if your own brother ends up wrongly imprisoned for the rest of his life? Well thanks very much."

They went to the theatre separately.

Adrian Clarke stood, a touch stiffly – this was not a moment he had been looking forward to – with the staff captain beside a pile of tennis nets on the games area of the main upper deck. These had been taken down to make room for the Scotland Yard team of three to be winched down from their helicopter.

"That must be them." Staff Captain Harcourt had sharp eyes, and it was a moment or two before Clarke made out the tiny illuminated dot just above the horizon. It was almost sunset – though the sun had vanished behind darkening clouds – and the aircraft's lights were almost exactly balanced with the light of the sky. He watched, trying to quash his disappointment, as the machine sped towards them. It was soon overhead, casting down its own vertical gale.

"They've picked a day for it, all right," said Harcourt.

Clarke could see what he meant. The hovering helicopter above seemed to be swaying back and forth: an illusion, since it was in fact the ship that was doing the moving, rolling with the heavy swell. There was quite a wind up, too.

Looking up at the helicopter, he could make out the three policemen, peering out of the side. After a moment's staring he recognized Williams. Heavier than the others, with worrying hair that seemed to grow where his forehead should have been. He looked almost ludicrously well prepared for warm weather – in a way only the English know how – wearing a billowing khaki safari suit, a sun-hat, and sunglasses, though it was now dusk. Probably he could hardly see a thing.

"You think you can? It's getting up." Harcourt was speaking through his radio to the helicopter pilot. "Very well, if you're sure."

It was clearly a drama worth watching, and the few evening time pool-side survivors stood to watch. Jasmin and Lisa – both now coloured a deep pink, despite the sun-cream – were at the front of the little crowd. "They must be important," observed Jasmin. "Wonder who they are?"

"This one doesn't look like a copper," added Lisa, as a figure in a safari suit swung violently above them, lodged in a kind of ring at the end of a wire. "More like a soldier."

"Or someone who's been hunting elephants."

A sudden gust neatly caught him, and sent him veering off towards the funnel. The wire was hauled quickly upwards, then began another slow descent.

"But then why'd they want someone like that?" pondered Lisa. "I mean there's no need."

Jasmin thought. "Perhaps there's a problem. You know, vermin."

Lisa studied him as he grew nearer. "Whatever he is, he looks quite dishy. Nice shoulders."

But at that moment a second gust hauled him off towards the radio tower, at the same time neatly plucking off his white sun-hat, which flew off at speed somewhere in the direction of Libya. He was hauled upwards again, and this time was taken all the way back up to the helicopter. After a moment's uncertain hovering, the aircraft turned about and vanished into the dusk.

Jasmin shrugged. "So much for that. Let's get ourselves a nice drink."

Staff Captain Harcourt frowned apologetically. "I'm sorry, sir. It's just too strong tonight. If they're willing to try again, we might be luckier tomorrow." He pocketed his radio. "You must be disappointed."

Adrian Clarke shrugged, trying to hide his relief. "These things happen."

The audience were taking their places in the Theatre Royal. Not as easy as it might have been, as the theatre – being placed close towards the bows – felt the movement of the ship especially keenly. Passengers in the aisles found themselves staggering as they sought their seats, falling into one another. Some looked more than a little pale. A few took their places, then had second thoughts and fought their way back against the flow of arrivals. Above the hubbub could be heard the deep grumble of thunder.

"Dad, I really don't feel well," protested Charlotte Daviot. Though she looked well enough.

The truth was that – like her father – she was a good sailor, and felt fine. If the heaving of the ship was having any effect upon her, it was of quite a different kind – reminding her of the strangely sensual pleasure she had discovered during her early teen adventures on centrifugal machines at funfair parks. No, rather than causing queasiness, the movement of the ship seemed to have had an unloosening effect upon her imagination, along with the drama of the rising storm. She found herself dwelling on what it would be like to do it this very night. The thought of it. To let herself go in a near-stranger's cabin, on a cruise ship surging and heaving in a Mediterranean storm.

"Don't be so wet," her father said sharply. He had a tendency to bully the girls, almost like a sergeant-major ticking off new recruits. Probably it stemmed from lingering annoyance – and uneasiness – at his failure to sire any sons. "Stop moaning and you'll be fine."

There must be some way, Charlotte pondered, that she could escape.

Adrian Clarke was doing his best to reassure Roman Brindle. "Don't worry. Nothing can go wrong. Just make sure you keep the door closed. He'll be able to hear you right enough. And we'll be able to hear him."

She didn't look reassured. "It's just the thought of it all. I mean if he really is the . . ." Her words tailed off.

"Like I said, it's probably just a practical joker," Adrian Clarke suggested encouragingly. And a touch guiltily, as he didn't believe his own words.

They were in the cabin just across the corridor from hers. The most sensible spot for a stake-out. The steward, whose cabin it was, had been moved to another part of the ship. A workman crouched in the entrance way of the cabin, drilling a spy hole in the door, so Clarke would be able to see out into the corridor. He had thought it wise to call in help, and further into the room was sitting the ship's security officer. Also one of the crew, chosen for his size. Just in case.

Adrian Clarke hoped the note-writer didn't have it in mind to pay an early visit to the corridor. It was hard to imagine a more obviously suspicious scene.

"Now just don't let yourself get worried," he advised again, ushering Roman past the workman and back towards her own cabin. “I’d switch on the television or something. Keep yourself busy.”

She still looked troubled. “But what should I say to him?”

A bright flash erupted outside her cabin window, momentarily illuminating the sea a lurid green. Seconds later the thunder rumbled across the waves to them. “It really doesn’t matter. Just encourage him to talk. Find out what he wants. The important thing is for us to be sure this is the one who wrote the note.” He took her by the arms for a moment. “And remember, you’re not alone. We’ll be right here, ready to jump out and grab him.”

There was no doubt about it: the theatre audience was steadily shrinking. From having been almost full when the curtain went up, the auditorium now showed an unhealthy patchiness. Nor were things too good on the stage. The cast, in their blazers, boaters and summer frocks, were fast beginning to wish there had been a bit more scenery. If only this had been an old-style production, with chunky tables and chairs and drinks cabinets to grab hold of, rather than a fashionably minimalist bare stage, where all you could do was sway. Some were also beginning to feel worryingly queasy, despite all the pills they had swallowed.

“Buck up, Charley,” Simon Daviot commanded. “We’re here now, and we’ll damn well enjoy it.”

“But I’d rather go back and read my book. This just isn’t my sort of thing.”

Her mother was starting to take her side. “Darling, I don’t see why she has to stay if she doesn’t want to.”

Simon shot his wife a warning look. “Brenda, it’s important to see theatre. Broadens the mind.” In fact this was mostly pigheadedness on his part. Plus the desire that they should be seen together as a family. The fact was he couldn't stand drama, especially this sort of pathetic nonsense. It was just the sort of silliness that he assumed they all loved down at the Ministry of Heritage.

"Can you please be quiet?" called somebody in an icy whisper from the row behind.

Simon Daviot turned round to face them with a slow deliberation. "If I were you, madam, I'd keep your advice to yourself."

"Dad, you're so embarrassing," murmured Charlotte. "Why can't we just go?"

Five rows behind, Rosamund Westcott got to her feet. The sight of that Daviot family spitting vitriol at one another finally decided her. Plus the fact that for some time the sight of the cast swaying like drunken dancers had been making her feel less than well. If only they'd been able to keep still. She'd have thought they'd be specially trained for this sort of thing. As it was, they were moving so much that it was almost worse than staring at the horizon.

She went out onto the main upper deck, and stood for a moment feeling the breeze. Immediately, she began to feel better.

She had intended to go back to the cabin, but now she had second thoughts. She felt all right. And there was the thought of Patrick. He was bound to be smug about her having given up on the play. Especially after she had tried to make him go.

The very thought of him made her feel slightly sick again.

No, she decided. She wouldn't go back yet. She would take a walk about the ship. Perhaps even pluck up courage for a drink in one of the bars. She might even meet somebody. Live a little.

Sandra Van Horn had already been back in her cabin – and out of her seven thousand dollar dress – for some time, and now she was lying in bed, a glass of scotch in her hand.

Not that she felt unwell. She never had any trouble at sea. If she had, she'd have made a point of avoiding that method of travel too. No, she left the theatre because the play had wholly failed in the purpose she had set it: to distract her. In fact the sight of those silly young actors and actresses trying to look cheerful as they staggered about had only made matters worse. Every time they sang about what the future held the worries came back to her more strongly. She stared at her scotch, then placed it on the bedside table, untasted. She did not seem to have the strength even for that.

Adrian Clarke crouched by the door of the cabin, tapping his fingers on the wood and wishing the workman had thought to place the spy hole a little higher. It was so damned uncomfortable squatting like this.

It was nine o'clock, the ship was heaving and slicing through the water like a mad thing, but nobody had come. People had passed by, of course, including staff returning to their rooms from the rest of the ship, most of them taking their steps in quick bursts, making use of the moments when the ship's movements were the most calm. But nobody had paused in front of Roman Brindle's door, let alone knocked.

A disappointment. Clarke had been fairly sure that if the note-writer was coming, it would be on time. Of course he, or she, might still turn up. But why specify a time and then ignore it?

He hated waiting. Peering again through the spy hole at the blank white of Roman's door, he then got to his feet and walked back into the room, where the security officer and the large crewman were sitting, looking bored. For some time he had been stifling the impulse to call through to the girl. Now he allowed himself to give in.

He picked up the telephone and dialled. Moments later he could hear it ringing across the corridor.

"Hello?" Roman's voice sounded flustered.

"It's Adrian. Just checking how things are going."

She grew calmer. "Fine. But nothing's happened. Have you seen anything?"

"Nothing. He may not be coming. But we'd best keep waiting." He returned to his post, crouching by the door.

Rupert had been smarting at his sister's earlier meanness throughout the performance of *Salad Days*. In fact his bad temper had extended to the play, and he had mentally alternated between rerunning his argument with Julia – adding clever put-downs he could have made – and despising the production before him. It was, he decided, typical theatre. So much fussier and more over-the-top than modern acting of the kind you saw on television. Compared to a good soap it was just crude.

It was during the second half that he saw Julia get up. She had insisted they sit well apart, and he was a good few rows back, but he had still located her easily through the dimmed theatre light, and even saw that she didn't look very well. She never had been much good on ships.

It was too tempting to resist.

He caught up with her at their cabin. She was already lying on her bed, her face showing a look of pained concentration. He sat down beside her. "I saw you leaving the theatre. Not feeling too good, Sis?" The question was asked with just a jot too much concern.

"Bugger off."

He seemed not to hear. "I didn't see your friend the copper in the audience. Did you?"

She gave him a warning look. "I said bugger off."

But he was just getting going. Spilling out the annoyance nurtured during the last hours. He feigned thoughtful reflection. "Shame, eh? You must be disappointed. Especially after all the trouble you went to. Wanting to go alone and all of that. And you thought you were in with a chance tonight, didn't you Sis? Thought you'd get your knickers off tonight."

He had gone too far. She pushed him off the bed and got to her feet. "You are a little toad, Rupert." She reached for the door handle. "Just remember this. Next time you're looking to beg money and desperate for somewhere to sleep, you can damn well look elsewhere." With that she marched, or rather staggered (since ships in storms have a way of spoiling moments of drama) out of the cabin, and slammed the door.

Rupert lay down on the bed, now a touch uneasy, wondering if he had done something he might regret.

"Honestly, Dad," Charlotte complained, "we're about the only people here."

This was quite true. The auditorium was almost empty. Even the stage seemed depopulated. Some minutes ago the leading lady had stopped in mid-speech and run suddenly into the wings, leaving the rest of the cast briefly but intensely silent, swaying and sliding and looking at one another. Then the leading man had started singing what was presumably the next number. The others had soon joined him, with the band catching on last of all, and eventually managing to synchronize quite well. Thereafter the cast had simply jumped from one song to another. A bit confusing, as without the dialogue there was no knowing what they were now singing about, or why. But it kept things running along.

"We should stay," her father insisted. "It's not done walking out of a play before it's over."

"But everybody else has."

Brenda and Sophie said nothing, but both groaned faintly. For some time they had had their eyes shut, and had been tightly clutching the seats in front.

In the event matters were soon settled by forces altogether above and beyond the powers of Simon Daviot. The ship rode into an especially large wave. Five of the cast had for some time been locked in a tight semicircle, supporting one another by gripping each other's shoulders, and the success of this experiment had led them to advance rashly close to the front of the stage. The shock caused by the especially large wave was easily enough. The five flew neatly forwards, landing – still locked together – in the orchestra pit. Fortunately it was virtually empty.

The stage manager soon appeared in their place. "Ladies and gentlemen, I'm very sorry, but tonight's production will have to be abandoned. Weather permitting, there will, of course, be another performance tomorrow night."

Charlotte was the first to her feet. "What a shame."

The family had adjacent cabins, and walked back together. Simon Daviot was the first to peel off. "It's still early. Want a nightcap, Brenda?"

Her expression was an emphatic No.

"I think I might."

Charlotte waited until she and her sister were in their cabin, and her sister was lying unhappily on her bed. "You know, I'm not tired at all. I think I might go for a little walk."

Sophie groaned. "I don't know how you can even say that." She rolled over, hiding her face from the light. "Why don't they just sink the damn ship and get it over with."

Charlotte hurried out into the corridor, and started her journey, heart pounding. Deck C, room a hundred and twelve. Deck C, room a hundred and twelve.

Adrian Clarke had just begun to think seriously of abandoning the watch on Roman's room when a figure appeared outside and hovered furtively in front of the opposite door.

"D'you think I could put on the television?" asked the large crewman. He was very bored, and had been asking about the television with tedious regularity during the last hour. "I'd have it on quiet."

"Shhh," Clarke retorted, with urgency. "There's someone there." He peered through the spy hole, but could see nothing as his view was blocked. The somebody had stopped right in front of the spy hole. He could see nothing but a blue fuzz, denim, probably. After a moment's pause he heard the clear sound of a knock.

Clarke turned round and waved meaningfully to the others, signalling them to get themselves ready. They both got up from their chairs and took their places behind him.

Outside, talking had begun. But it was hard to make out. Two wooden doors were more than enough to muffle Roman's voice beyond comprehension, and it was not easy to make out the words of the new arrival. He seemed to be leaning right against the cabin door, covering the spy hole with his legs – the view was now blank darkness – and was speaking softly. But it was a man all right, and the voice sounded familiar. Clarke tried to fit a face to the sound.

The odd phrase was audible.

"Roman, what is this? Why don't you open the door?"

But then all fell into inaudibility once more. Frustrating. And he had no way of knowing if the arrival had admitted to writing the note. Clarke tried to think, fast. Perhaps he should ring Roman. But the sound of the phone going might scare off their man.

They'd just have to wait, hoping he'd move so that they could see or hear something.

The sound was faint but audible. The clicking of a door catch. Surely she couldn't . . . It was the one thing he had told her not to do. But there was no doubting it. He turned to the others, whispering urgently. "She's opened her door."

The security chief frowned. "What d'you want us to do?"

That was the problem. If they burst out now it might be too soon. What the hell did she think she was doing? Unless she had some reason he did not understand. Perhaps she was hoping to induce the man to acknowledge he had written the note.

But if he was the murderer . . .

No, he decided. It was too much of a risk.

He signalled to the others. "Let's get him." Then he turned the door handle and pulled it sharply in. The fact that the man was leaning against the door was at last useful. With a crash he tumbled into the room between them, and they fell upon him, pinning his arms onto the ground.

"What the hell?" he began.

Roman Brindle was shouting. "Let him go, for God's sake. He's nothing to do with this."

Detective Clark found himself staring into the face of Mike Young, looking as surprised as anybody could.

Slowly the moment calmed. Clarke told the others to let him up and they all recovered their breath.

"Can I ask what you were doing here, sir?" Clarke asked, a touch formally, just in case. He had met Mike Young a number of times, and regarded him as a most unlikely suspect, but you never could tell.

"I just wanted to talk to Roman."

"But you didn't write her a note?"

Again he looked puzzled. "No."

Roman interrupted. "You see, Chief Superintendent . . ." She blushed. "Mike and I have got quite close."

Clarke nodded. "I understand."

Mike still looked unsure. "But what were you doing in here, waiting to pounce like that?"

"Well," Clarke began. "There was a note, you see, sent to Roman. Anonymous. The writer said he was going to visit her tonight. And we couldn't help but wonder if . . ."

He got no further. He was interrupted by the bleep of his radio.

"Mr Clarke?" a voice called out through the crackle.

"Yes."

"Staff Captain Harcourt. Sorry to bother you, but one of the passengers has just called in complaining of a disturbance. A lot of shouting and banging in Professor Westcott's cabin. It's an old chap who called us. Said it sounded nasty. He didn't feel up to going and having a look himself."

Westcott's cabin. Surely not again . . . and right across the other side of the ship. An awful thought occurred to Adrian

Clarke that the murderer might have deliberately set him up. Written the note to get him off the scent. Waste his time. "I'll be right there."

Charlotte Daviot walked down the corridors towards Deck C, room a hundred and twelve, high on her own nervousness and anticipation. She did not want to run into her father – not that that was very likely. She had carefully avoided going near the various bars. And the ship seemed very quiet now. Most people had clearly taken to their beds.

Turning a corner she found herself in the corridor – the corridor. With just a few steps she had reached the room.

She stopped, taken aback by her success, suddenly nervous. Nothing to stop her now. Except, what if it turned out to be something she'd regret? If she just felt squalid? Throwing away something that should be treasured?

But after a moment her courage returned. He had seemed nice enough before. And it would be so feeble to run away now. Miss her chance of doing it on a ship in a storm. The sort of thing she could tell her friends. The thought of her friends settled matters. Most of them had already done it. She was beginning to feel quite left out.

She was just about to knock when she heard a low moan from inside.

Did he have another woman in there? How dare he? How could he do such a thing to her. On this night, when she had been willing to . . .

Temper roaring, she hammered on the door.

"Who the hell is it?" murmured a male voice.

"Charlotte Daviot. Who else did you expect?"

But as the door swung inwards her anger left her. There was no woman in sight. Just Dave, sadly reduced. His face was an extraordinary colour: it actually looked faintly green. His clothes were pulled about and half undone, and even his pigtail seemed dishevelled. From the interior of the room floated an ominous smell.

"Hi Charley," he managed to say. "Good to see you. Come on in." But this effort of speech had exhausted his resistance. With a faint groan he added, "Hang on a sec," and swung himself into his bathroom.

Charlotte Daviot marched briskly and furiously away.

Adrian Clarke was hurrying along the length of the ship. Or trying to hurry. It wasn't easy to move with any speed down corridors that wouldn't keep still. You had to try and time your lurches with the bouncing of the floor, so that it helped you forward rather than knocking you backwards or tipping you against the walls. The chief of security and the large crewman, he saw, seemed to have it down to a tee. Fairly springing along, they were. It was as much as he could manage to keep them in sight.

They were both waiting by the Westcotts' door when he finally caught up with them.

"Shut," the security man explained. "But there doesn't seem to be anybody inside. I knocked." He reached into his pocket. "I have a master key card."

Silence did not necessarily mean there was nobody inside. "Give it to me," Adrian told him. "You two get back."

He stood on the opening side of the door, positioned the electronic card at the ready, then waited until the movement of the ship tilted in the direction the door would open. In one smooth movement he managed to insert the card, turn the handle, and push with all his strength. The door swung open in an instant, pulling him inside behind.

But there was nobody there. Or at least nobody dangerous. On the floor lay sprawled the bloated form of Professor Westcott, amid a pool of blood that was still seeping into the carpet around him. Clarke squatted down to take his wrist. There was no pulse. It looked as if he'd been stabbed close to the heart. He'd never much liked the man. In fact he'd considered him a possible suspect. He couldn't help but feel sorry for him now.

"Better call Dr Patel," he instructed the security officer. "And the photographer."

"Right you are," he agreed grimly and, stepping back into the corridor, he reached into a pocket for his radio.

It was only then, as he stood back from the body, that Clarke noticed the mark. A red smear on the carpet, and fortunately an area not yet engulfed by the spreading puddle, close by Westcott's hand.

The large crewman had seen it too. "He must have done it himself," he suggested. "As he was going."

"Must have," Clarke agreed. He stepped closer, to examine it. It was a messy sort of mark. It seemed the professor had needed to replenish the blood on his finger, with which he was writing, rather like dipping a quill, and consequently the result was rather confused.

"Could be a G," the crewman suggested. "Or an H."

"Yes," Clarke agreed, tentatively. "Or a D."

The crewman stared at it a little longer. "Or even an R and an O."

Adrian Clarke wished that Professor Westcott had made more of an effort to write neatly. He took a step round the corpse, so he could see the mark from a different angle. "In fact, it almost looks a little like a hammer and sickle."

chapter THIRTEEN

It was the last night of the cruise. The great ship headed north, towards England and everyday life. As the afternoon cooled into evening the passengers drifted away from the swimming pools and games decks and headed for their cabins to change. There was an end-of-term feeling in the air. Tonight was a night to break the rules, a night for self-indulgence, a last chance of romance.

Adrian Clarke felt a little sour. There had been three murders during the cruise and he had no idea who might have committed them. And he had met a fascinating, glamorous woman who liked him – yet he had done little to get to know her and had acted like a jealous schoolboy when he saw her with someone else. Perhaps this is what getting old is like, he thought: somehow you lose your get-up-and-go.

"Bloody fool," he said to the mirror as he knotted his tie. "You're not sixty yet. You can solve the murders and seduce Julia Grant if only you put your mind to it." Nothing was going to happen unless he made it happen.

He looked at his tie. It was the navy one with a gold stripe he had worn with his blazer every night of the cruise. He remembered buying six new ties two days before embarking. So far he had not worn any of them. He opened his suitcase and looked at them, still in their cellophane wrappings. He picked out a red one with a pattern of theatrical masks in blue and green: that was a bit more cheerful.

He combed his greying hair, shrugged into his double-breasted blazer and glanced in the mirror again. "Passable in a dim light," he said aloud, and he left his cabin, switching off the light.

They had left the Mediterranean for the mighty Atlantic, and he felt the changed motion beneath his feet as he climbed the stairs. On the Promenade Deck he ran into Julia Grant, barefoot and wearing a towelling robe over a swimsuit. Her hair was wet from the pool, and she had no make-up on, but when she smiled at him she was stunning. He smiled back, then he began to speak without thinking what he was going to say, and the words came tumbling out in no particular order. "Um, I don't suppose you'd care to . . . I mean, are you having dinner tonight?" He felt a fool. He had not done this sort of thing since before he got married, and that was thirty years ago. "Well, of course you're having dinner," he burbled on.

She stopped him by putting her forefinger on his lips, a gesture he found unbearably sexy. "I'll meet you in the Oriental Restaurant at eight o'clock," she said, and then she was gone.

He was embarrassed. It was not like him to speak without thinking, nor to talk nervous gibberish.

On the other hand, it worked, he thought; and he continued up the staircase with a spring in his step.

The Crow's Nest was a popular bar at this time of day. Adrian ordered a beer and looked around. Standing at the panoramic window watching the sun go down was Warren. Adrian carried his beer over.

Warren nodded politely and said, "How's the case going?"

Adrian shook his head. "I'm starting to think I was right to retire when I did. I seem to have lost the touch."

"You don't mean that," Warren said crisply. "You're not the type to give in easily," he added, slightly flirtatiously.

"Perhaps you're right. Let me ask you a direct question."

"By all means." Warren sipped his cocktail.

"Do you think Professor Westcott's death had anything to do with his sexuality?"

"You're asking me if he was gay."

"Was he?"

"Yes." Warren sighed. "I don't think he ever had a lover, poor man; in fact he may never have admitted the truth even to himself – but he was gay."

"If he never did anything about his feelings, it's not likely he was killed by a jealous lover, or a nervous blackmailer."

"No."

Adrian looked hard at Warren. "You seem very certain of that. You do know something, don't you?"

Warren smiled. "So! Straight men have intuition, too."

"Detectives are supposed to."

Warren hesitated, then shrugged. "And your intuition is right. Patrick told me he was an agent for Soviet Intelligence – a spy, in short."

"Good God."

"He was a recruiter, to be exact. He identified idealistic left-wing youths and turned them into KGB informants. I can't imagine that he can have been active for many years."

Adrian swallowed most of his beer, thinking. "I'm glad you told me this."

"Does it help?"

"No. It makes a complicated story even more baffling."

Warren finished his drink. "I must get changed. Got to look ravishing for the last night of the cruise. Excuse me."

Adrian stared thoughtfully out at the Atlantic waves. The notion of a KGB connection was not that surprising. England was full of old professors who had backed the wrong side in the Cold War. But there was another reason why it made sense: Olivia Harman.

Adrian had been lying in his pretence to everyone that he knew nothing about the girl. He remembered her perfectly well. He had guessed that she was working under cover, not knowing what her mission might have been.

She had left the police force long ago. But Adrian knew where she had gone. She had joined the Secret Intelligence Service, popularly known as M16.

She must have been shadowing Patrick Westcott, Adrian reasoned. It was a bit difficult to imagine why. Once upon a time perhaps he might have been of some use to Soviet Intelligence but what importance could he possibly have now that the Cold War was over?

Once again Adrian had the feeling that the more he learned, the less he knew.

Lisa had two of her Davenports back. Phil and Wayne sat on her bed in T-shirts and shorts, sharing a cold bottle of vodka from the fridge, while she touched up her face in the mirror. Wayne was eighteen and blond, a real hunk. Phil was dark and more mature, but just as fit and equally gorgeous. She wondered if they would feel like doing something kinky on the last night of the cruise. She had a yen to take both of them to bed at the same time. Would they go for it? That might depend on how much vodka they swallowed before she put it to them. The trouble with vodka was that a drunk man was ready for anything and capable of nothing. Lisa had suffered many disappointments because of alcohol.

She wondered how to get things started. She could begin by asking them both to rub after-sun lotion on her. Phil could do her right side and Wayne her left. Then –

There was a knock at the door. Lisa frowned. Jazzy was watching a film in the Chaplin Cinema, and anyway she wouldn't knock. "Who is it?" Lisa called.

The door opened and a girl looked in. Lisa recognized Charlotte, the snobby daughter of the MP. "Hello," Charlotte said brightly.

Lisa was suspicious. "What do you want?"

Charlotte came in uninvited. In her Sloane Ranger accent she said, "Um, I don't suppose you've got any skins, by any chance?"

Lisa's attitude changed dramatically. If Charlotte was searching for cigarette rolling papers, that meant she had some dope. A nice fat joint would be just the thing to put Phil and Wayne in the mood for a threesome.

But Lisa did not have any skins. "Jazzy might," she said.

"I've got some," said Wayne, reaching into his pocket.

"Party on, Wayne," Lisa said. "Close the door, Charley," she added. "We'll do a number with you."

Charlotte took from her pocket a small polythene bag containing a few spoonfuls of a brown compound. Wayne handed her a packet of extra-large Rizla rolling papers. She took a cigarette from a pack of Silk Cut on Lisa's dressing table and broke the cigarette open, spilling the tobacco on the paper, sprinkling the brown compound over the tobacco, and rolling up the paper with a skill born of much practice.

"I hope the *News of the World* don't find out about you," Lisa said.

Charlotte rolled up her eyes. "Don't talk to me about the News of the bloody World." She picked up a matchbook and lit the joint.

"Where did you get the stuff?" Lisa said.

"Nicked it," Charlotte said.

Lisa shook her head in mock disgust. "The upper classes have no moral fibre," she said.

"Thank God," said Wayne, reaching for the joint.

Phil stood up suddenly. "I'm out of here," he said. "Pot makes me paranoid. See you later, guys."

Lisa watched him go regretfully. So much for her threesome.

On the other hand, there were still three people in her bedroom. She looked at Charlotte: pretty girl, nice figure, not as snobby as she seemed, and enough dope left in that little polythene bag for several more joints.

"Give us that spliff, Wayne," Lisa said. "This might turn into an interesting evening after all."

Brenda Daviot had bought new underwear for the cruise: a lacy camisole, French knickers and a suspender belt, all in a rather sophisticated navy blue. They looked very sexy on the model in the Oxford Street window. Of course the model was wearing a size eight and Brenda had bought a sixteen.

The new underwear had lain in the bottom of the drawer throughout the cruise. This was the last night: if she did not wear it now, she never would. She stood with a towel wrapped around her, hesitating. Simon was in the shower.

She wondered if she could get it on and cover it with her dress before he came out.

"If I don't want him to see it, why did I buy it?" she asked herself.

But even if no one saw the underwear it might make her feel romantic just knowing what she had on under her dress.

It's the nearest I'll get to romance, she thought.

She dropped the towel. She averted her eyes from the mirror, so that she could not see how plump she was, while she hastily pulled the camisole on over her head. She risked a look in the mirror and was quite gratified. The slip did not make her look thin, nothing would; but it draped her rather elegantly. She put on the suspender belt and the French knickers. Simon turned off the shower just as she was doing up the buttons of her lavender shirtwaist dress.

She handed him a towel as he stepped onto the mat. He took it automatically and began to rub his wet hair vigorously.

Brenda took out a new pair of stockings and slipped one on. She normally wore tights and she wondered if Simon would notice her fastening the stocking-tops. But he did not look at her as he dropped the towel and combed his hair. "I think I'll skip dinner tonight," he said.

Her heart sank. So much for romance. "But it's the last night of the cruise!" she protested.

"I've got a queasy tummy," he said. "You go with the girls. I'll just have a drink in the Crow's Nest."

He was up to something, she knew. Probably he had an assignation planned. She fought back tears. Would he go to bed with that Julia Grant female while his wife had dinner with the children? It would be typically mean of him. Suddenly she felt angry.

She put on the other stocking, stood up, and stepped into her shoes. "You're too cruel, Simon," she said in a shaky voice. "Too bloody cruel for words."

He turned and stared at her in wounded astonishment as she stamped out of the cabin.

Strangely enough she felt better than she had in years.

She made her way down to the Promenade Deck and, on impulse, went into Anderson's, the quiet bar. She sat in a club chair and crossed her legs, conscious of the odd feel of the stockings. A steward came up, gave her a flirtatious smile, and asked what was her pleasure.

Suddenly confident she said: "I'll have a glass of champagne." She was sure Simon bought champagne for his fancy women, the bastard: now he could buy some for his wife, whether he wanted to or not.

A young man with huge shoulders, who looked strangely familiar, walked in and started to look around a little nervously. Brenda smiled rather vacantly at him. He went to the bar and ordered a beer. Brenda tried to remember who he was. After a minute it occurred to her that he was one of the dance troupe, the Davenports: she had seen him in a G-string on the advertizing poster outside the Theatre Royal. She was surprised to see him in the bar, mixing with the passengers.

Her mind turned back to Simon, as it always did in the end. She wished she had not sworn at him. It had given her momentary satisfaction, but she knew he would punish her. It would be his excuse for all kinds of bad behaviour over the next few weeks. If she asked why he cancelled a lunch with her, or forgot their anniversary, or came in drunk at midnight, he would give a sneaky grin and say, "I suppose it's because I'm too bloody cruel for words."

A voice said, "May I join you?"

She looked up. It was the dancer. Brenda was too surprised to reply, but he took silence for assent and sat down. "I'm Phil Peckham," he said.

"Brenda Daviot."

"I know who you are. You husband is the MP, isn't he?"

"That's me," she said sourly. "Always introduced as 'the wife of . . .' And you're a dancer, aren't you? In one of the shows on board."

"That's me," he said. "The body in the show."

"Don't you like it?" she said. "It seems so glamorous . . . sailing around the world and dancing to entertain people every night."

"It's limiting," he said. "I'm thirty years old and I dye my hair to take out the grey."

"Good lord!" she said. He was only just over ten years younger than she was.

"I'm not really supposed to be here," he admitted, "mixing with the customers like this, but I couldn't stand the company of the others for another second. There is a limit to the amount of time you can spend discussing exercise routines and diets."

Brenda laughed, "I guess there has to be a price to pay for everything, particularly physical beauty. I don't suppose anyone will mind you being here, it being the last night and everything."

"Too bad if they do," he smiled, "I like the company too much to leave now."

The steward brought their drinks. Phil raised his glass. "To green eyes," he said.

Brenda was surprised again. It was a long time since a man had noticed the colour of her eyes. She raised her champagne glass and took a long swallow. The bubbles tickled her throat and she felt herself flush slightly.

"I've always been a fool for green eyes," Phil said. "My first ever girlfriend, Pauline, had green eyes."

My goodness, he's flirting with me, Brenda thought; this underwear really works! She suppressed a giggle. Perhaps she ought to get up and leave. But she had nowhere to go. "How old were you?"

"I was fifteen and Pauline was thirteen. It's a long time ago."

Brenda nodded. "I met Simon when I was thirteen. That was . . ." For some reason she told a lie. "That was twenty-one years ago."

"Where's Simon now?" Phil said pointedly.

Brenda shrugged. "He's skipping dinner tonight."

"Would you have dinner with me?" Phil asked.

Brenda decided this was going too far. "Oh no," she said firmly. Flirtatious talk was bad enough. The last time she had dined alone with a man other than Simon was . . . well, never. "No, I couldn't."

He smiled easily. "Why not?" he asked, as if the question intrigued him mightily.

"Well . . . I'm expected to dine with my daughters."

He looked sceptical. "How badly will they miss you?"

She smiled ruefully. "Not much. Still . . ."

"Still, what?" She made no reply and he went on. "I was depressed when I walked in. In five minutes you've cheered me up. Let's spend some more time together. Please."

Brenda felt a little breathless. How nice it would be to spend the evening talking and laughing with an attractive man, instead of feeling bitter about her wayward husband. She felt a sudden excess of daring. "Why not?" she said.

Phil raised a hand to the steward. "Two more glasses of champagne, please," he said.

Annie Young was sitting at the bar of the Crow's Nest talking to Rupert Revell. Adrian Clarke noticed how close together they sat. As they talked, Rupert kept touching Annie's hand, her shoulder and her thigh. They acted like lovers.

Now and again she glanced in Adrian Clarke's direction, and he felt she wanted to speak to him. When he finished his beer he went to the bar and put his glass on the counter.

"Same again, sir?" said the steward.

"No, thanks."

Annie turned to him. "Don't go yet, Adrian," she said. "Let me have a word with you, if I may."

"Sure."

She turned back to Rupert. "Why don't you go and put your tie on," she said.

He smiled, looking into her eyes, and squeezed her hand. Then he left without speaking to Adrian.

Adrian watched him go then turned to Annie.

"Do you disapprove?" she said.

He thought they both looked ridiculous, but he was too polite to say so. "What is there to disapprove of?"

"He's after my money and I'm only interested in his body: that's two things."

Adrian shook his head. "What I really disapprove of is people who pronounce judgement on other folks' private lives."

Annie nodded. "You're a man after my own heart, Adrian." She opened her handbag and took out an envelope. Her face was suddenly older. "Read that, if you would."

Adrian took it from her. It was an A3 envelope with nine or ten folded sheets inside. The envelope was already slit open. He took out a typewritten sheet with the letterhead of the Abbey National building society. It was addressed to Chrissie Young, Annie's niece, the second murder victim. It simply stated that the society was obliged to foreclose on Chrissie's mortgage and repossess her house.

He took out another sheet. It was from the credit card division of Barclays Bank, demanding the return of her card as she had not paid her instalments.

Adrian looked quickly over the other letters. There was a letter from American Express, one from the credit department of House of Fraser, another from NatWest Bank, all asking for repayment of loans.

"I didn't know she had got into such a mess," Annie said. "If I had, I would have tried to help her sort things out. But instead I told her she was not going to get anything in my will. It must have seemed like the last straw."

"She didn't deserve your help," Adrian said.

Annie nodded. "I know that, but I will always regret what I did, just the same."

"Can I keep these?"

"Of course. Do you think this had something to do with her death?"

"I don't know," said Adrian. "I'm as confused as you are."

The gong sounded for dinner.

Jazzy was thinking how great it must have been in the seventies, when the clothes were so glamorous, the music so melodic, and the dancing so sexy. She loved platform shoes and flared slacks and tank tops, and men in white suits and open-neck shirts.

She had been watching Saturday Night Fever in the Chaplin Cinema. She was too sunburned to sit by the pool. Lisa did not like going to the movies in daylight so they had done their separate things. Now Jazzy was headed for their cabin, with the tune of Stayin' Alive echoing in her head.

The scene that confronted her when she entered the cabin looked like the aftermath of a Roman orgy. Lisa was sitting in a chair, stark naked, looking dazed. Another girl was lying on the bed, passed out. There was an empty vodka bottle on the floor and an ashtray with several roaches. From the bathroom came the sound of someone throwing up. Jazzy looked in and saw Wayne, one of the Davenports, kneeling over the toilet.

Lisa lit a cigarette. "I'm getting a very strange buzz off this hash," she mumbled. "It's a bit stronger than usual."

Jazzy had a feeling she knew why. "Did you spew, too?" she said.

"Yeah – but I didn't mind, you know? I didn't feel ill or anything. Just, like, vomited, know what I mean?"

Jazzy saw a crumpled polythene bag on the bedside table. There were a few grains of brown powder left inside. Jazzy picked up a little of the dust on her fingertip and sniffed it. She felt a freezing sensation in her nose. She licked her finger. There was a sharply bitter taste, and a moment later she felt faintly giddy and elated.

"This isn't pot, Lisa," she said. "It's brown sugar."

"I never heard of that."

"It's smack. Heroin. Unrefined, the kind you smoke."

"How do you know?"

"I went out with a smackhead, years ago. He swore he'd given it up. Then he started smoking this stuff, and before long he was shooting up again. I chucked him."

The girl on the bed rolled over and opened her eyes. "What's going on?" she mumbled.

Jazzy could see now that it was Charlotte Daviot. "Where did you get this dope?" Jazzy questioned her.

"It makes you puke, but it's good stuff," Charlotte said.

"It's not hash, it's heroin," Jazzy said.

"Oh, God, that's why."

"Where did you get it?" Jazzy said again.

"It was in this Greek statuette. The old professor used it in his introductory lecture at the start of the cruise. It was stuffed full of dope, maybe a kilo of it, all in plastic baggies."

"You stole this from Professor What's-his-name?"

"No. It's his statuette, but I found it in Chrissie Young's cabin, in her beach bag, and I stole it from her."

"Jesus," Jazzy said. "Don't you realize they probably both died because of this stuff?"

Charlotte suddenly looked scared. "Do you really think so?"

"I'm bloody sure of it."

"What can I do?"

"Get rid of the statuette and the dope, the quicker the better."

"How can I get rid of it?"

"Just dump it, you stupid cow. Stick it back in the beach bag and take it somewhere and just drop it behind a bleedin' lifeboat."

"All right."

"And do it now – before someone murders you, too."

It took Simon Daviot a long time to find Julia Grant. He called her room several times when he was sure she must be changing for dinner, but the phone rang unanswered. He looked into all the bars without success – although he did spot his wife, somewhat to his surprise, drinking champagne with a young man who looked vaguely familiar. He finally saw Julia walking into the Oriental Restaurant with the retired policeman, Adrian Clarke. She was dressed up to the nines, he noticed, in a slinky black frock and stiletto heels. To his dismay they sat down to dinner together.

After dinner she would return to her cabin, almost certainly. Simon went to the Tiffany Court, through which she would have to pass, and sat down to wait.

He knew she was doing this to torment him. She did not want to sleep with PC Plod. She was probably bored out of her skull, listening to him recount the Case of the Missing Pension Book. She would much prefer to be having a tête-à-tête with a glamorous, respected public figure. But she was punishing Simon.

The strains of a string quartet reached him from the nearby Curzon Room, but they failed to soothe him. He lit a cigar and smoked it impatiently, so that it burned too hot.

He nodded politely at people who passed by. Every damn passenger now reckoned themselves a close personal friend of Simon Daviot, the MP. Half of them would write to him as soon as they got home, telling him how the Party should run the country. Being a public figure was all right, but at times like this, waiting for his mistress while she had dinner with another man, Simon craved anonymity.

Two hours went by and at last she appeared. She stepped out of the lift on her high heels. She saw him sitting there, hesitated, then turned away, heading for her cabin.

Simon went after her and caught up with her just as she opened the cabin door. "I've been trying to get a word with you all evening," he said irritably.

She gave him a cool look. "Well, here I am."

He put his hands on her shoulders. "I miss you," he said, assuming the lost-puppy-dog expression that usually worked.

She frowned. "I won't be toyed with, Simon."

He gave her his boyish grin. "Not even just a little bit?"

"No," she said, but he saw her face soften.

"Let me in for a minute," he said, and his hand slid off her shoulder to her breast.

To his disappointment her expression turned sour. "No," she said firmly, and she took hold of his arms and removed his hands from her body. "I have to pee, actually, then I'm going to the Pacific Lounge with Adrian Clarke."

Simon frowned. "But you've spent half the evening with him!"

"I'm going to spend the other half with him, too," she said. "He's good looking, intelligent, kind . . . and single. Excuse me." She went into her cabin and shut the door firmly.

"Well, I'll be damned," Simon said angrily. He walked back along the corridor to the Tiffany Court.

The door to one of the lifts was just closing as he got there. There were two people inside in a passionate embrace: a dark-haired young man and a woman in a lavender dress. As the doors drew together the man stroked the woman's thigh, lifting the skirt of the dress to reveal the top of a stocking. Then the doors closed and the lift was gone.

"Filthy beasts," Simon muttered.

Then he realized there was something familiar about the dress. In fact he knew it very well. It belonged to his wife, Brenda. And the man was the one she had been talking to earlier.

He stared, flabbergasted, at the closed lift door. He did not even know whether it had gone up or down. All he knew was that Brenda was in there kissing a boy.

He stood there, stunned. Both his wife and his mistress were being unfaithful to him – at the same time!

He wondered whether to throw himself overboard.

Brenda lay on a mattress in the darkness beside the deserted swimming pool, looking at the stars, panting. She still had on the stockings and the lavender dress, but she had no idea where her knickers were.

Phil lay beside her, his head on her bosom, breathing hard. "Did I make a noise?"

"Yes – a very loud one." She laughed.

"So did you," he said. "Thank God there's no one about."

She stroked the muscles of his back with her fingertips. He was so hard . . . everywhere. She giggled to herself.

"What?" he breathed.

"I've lost my knickers," she said. She felt about her in the dark. Her hand came in contact with foliage: one of the trees in big wooden containers that dotted the pool deck. She felt around its base. She touched a bag of some kind and pulled it towards her. It tipped over. She reached inside it and found a heavy, cold object. She brought it out into the starlight. Something fell out of its base.

"What have you found?" said Phil.

Brenda stared at it, puzzled. "It's the statuette that poor Professor Westcott used in his opening lecture last week . . ."

"What the hell is it doing under a tree on the pool deck?"

"Goodness knows. I think something fell out of it. A little packet."

Phil scrabbled around on the deck and came up with a polythene bag full of what might have been sugar. "Wow."

"I wonder what it is."

"I think I know. It's dope. Drugs."

"Goodness. We'd better hand it in to someone."

"Yes," Phil said. "In about ten minutes' time."

Brenda frowned, puzzled. "Why the delay?"

She felt his hand on her thigh. "There's no rush." He rolled on top of her.

She giggled. "At least make it fifteen minutes," she said.

"MI6?" said Captain Moore. "Haven't they been abolished?"

"Not yet," said Adrian Clarke. "They're civil servants, remember. You have to move heaven and earth to get rid of them." He spoke scornfully. He had strong feelings about obsolete cloak-and-dagger men who thought they could transform themselves into policemen.

"But what do they do?" said the captain.

"They're trying to gather intelligence on international drug traffic. That, I suspect, was what Olivia Harman was doing on this cruise. And she must have discovered something – that's why she was killed."

The Captain frowned. "Professor Westcott seems a frightfully unlikely dope smuggler."

Adrian smiled. "Doesn't he just. But he's such a good blackmail victim, with his KGB past and his secret sexual longings."

"You think it's possible someone blackmailed him into smuggling these packets of heroin into England inside his statuette?"

"I think someone tried. Perhaps he refused, or got cold feet. Anyway, something went wrong, and he was killed too."

"But the statuette was found in Chrissie Young's bag."

"She was desperate for money. I think she must have stolen the statuette thinking it was valuable, then found the dope inside. I haven't weighed the stuff, but I'd guess this is worth about a hundred thousand pounds wholesale. That would have paid her debts."

"Stupid girl."

"Yes. Whoever took the statuette from Chrissie's room was a fraction less stupid, and decided not to be the fourth person to die on account of it. He, or she, got scared and dumped it. And Phil Peckham found it. By the way, what was he doing on the pool deck so late at night?"

"He didn't say, but I'd guess a lady was involved."

"Ah. That would explain the navy blue French knickers I found hanging from a branch of the tree under which the bag was found."

"Doubtless," said Captain Moore. If there was hanky-panky on the pool deck he did not want to know about it. "So you think you know why the three were killed . . . but you still have no idea who did it."

"Only that it is someone on board this ship."

"Is there nothing more you can do?"

"Nothing," said Adrian, but he was lying.

He put the statuette back in Chrissie Young's beach bag, closed the bag, picked it up and went to the door.

"Are you sure you don't want to put it in the safe?"

"Quite sure. I don't intend to let it out of my sight till it's in the evidence room at Southampton police headquarters."

"Half the ship has seen you carrying that bag, and it's quite distinctive. There's a strong chance the murderer will know you've got it. Three people have already been killed because of it –"

"I'm not an elderly professor or a young girl, and I'm certainly not a bungling MI6 amateur," Adrian said crisply. "Don't worry about me."

"All right . . . Goodnight."

"Goodnight, Captain."

Adrian went out and closed the door.

At four o'clock in the morning the passageways of the ship were lit by dim security lights. A figure dressed in black sweatshirt, jogging pants and trainers padded along the carpeted corridors silently, heading for Adrian Clarke's room.

Clarke was a fool. Half the ship had seen him carrying Chrissie Young's beach bag. The police were so dumb.

The black-clad figure reached Clarke's door, slid a skeleton card silently into the lock, and opened the door a fraction. In the slice of light from the corridor, the bed was visible. A six-foot figure lay motionless beneath the quilt, its head just visible.

The intruder slipped inside and closed the door, then stood listening. There was no sound but the distant swish of the waves and the deep throb of the ship's mighty diesel engines. The black figure crossed the dark room to the bed, drew a carving knife with a six-inch blade, raised the knife, and without hesitation plunged it again and again into the figure on the bed, feeling the blade slice through the bedclothes and into something firm. Death must have been instant: the victim made no sound.

Now for the statuette.

The intruder felt for the bedside table and switched on the lamp.

Light glinted off the silver blade of the carving knife.

A frown began to form on the intruder's face: there should have been blood, buckets of it . . .

A sudden, painful blow struck the arm that held the knife, and it fell to the carpet. The intruder was grabbed from behind and wrestled to the floor by a tall, strong man. Cold handcuffs closed over the wrists. Then the intruder was rolled over and looked up into the face of Adrian Clarke.

"Good God," said Adrian. "It's Mrs Van Horn."

Warren was appalled at the sight of his friend. She was wearing dark glasses when he came into the cabin where she was being kept in custody and appeared almost composed. But once Adrian had gone out and they were left alone together she took the glasses off to reveal bolting eyes that seemed to have gone quite mad.

"My poor darling," he said with genuine sympathy, "what on earth happened?"

Tears welled up and trickled down her face and her normal elegant posture seemed to collapse, as if someone had surgically removed her spine. Warren was horrified to see how old she looked.

"It all became so complicated," she moaned through her tears. "I didn't mean for any of it to happen, it just got out of control."

"Tell me all about it," cooed Warren, pulling up a chair and cradling her trembling hand in his. "Let it all out."

"I needed the money, Warren. I was hit so badly by the crash at Lloyds in London it looked as if I was going to lose everything. I met this man in New York, at a party. I had been telling him about how I loved to travel and to go by ship and all the places I had been to and he started to show a real interest. Eventually he asked me if I would be willing to act as a 'courier' between countries for some friends of his." She had to stop talking to blow her nose.

"Drugs?" whispered Warren.

"Of course it was, and I knew it, but I kidded myself that it might be something else. I had to make some money quickly or I was going to have to start selling off the collection and I couldn't bear that. All I had to do was tell them where I was going and they would have the goods delivered to me. They seem to have people everywhere. They could always contact me when they wanted to. Rich, well-dressed women on cruise ships don't often attract the attentions of customs officials, you know."

"Yes," Warren nodded, "I see. So what went wrong?"

"Just before we boarded at Southampton, I received a warning. There was an MI6 agent on board. They told me I would have to dispose of her before she got to me."

"Dispose of her!" Warren was shocked at the casual way in which his friend spoke of murder, and fascinated at the same time.

"I know." She seemed momentarily calm. "I can't imagine what happened to me. I was just so afraid of losing everything and of going to prison. Anyway, I followed her around, looking for an opportunity. When I saw her go into a cabin without shutting the door after her, it seemed too good a chance to miss."

"Professor Westcott's cabin?" Warren was beginning to see the pieces coming together. "It was him she was after, not you at all."

She looked at him blankly, her mind on the terrible scene in the professor's cabin with all the blood and the overwhelming sense of panic. "In the struggle I knocked over one of the statuettes the professor used for his lectures," she went on. "I was surprised by how light it was. I had imagined it was solid, I don't know why. It occurred to me that it must be hollow and that it would be an ideal place to hide the drugs that I was carrying. I also thought that if I took it, the police would assume the woman had been murdered by a thief. Suspicion would hardly be likely to fall on me for that – a well known art connoisseur stealing a fibreglass model . . . Ridiculous!"

She paused for a sip of water from the glass on the table beside her. "I realized that I was covered in blood so I grabbed one of the professor's shirts from the wardrobe and threw it over me to cover all the marks. Then later, I ditched it overboard with my stained shirt and pants.

"The only person I saw on the way back to my cabin was that Chrissie Young girl. I didn't think she had seen the statuette, but she must have done. I went back to the cabin and filled it with the drugs. I wasn't clear in my mind what I would do with it next. I thought I might plant it on someone else to distract the police, or possibly hide it somewhere where I could collect it later. My mind was racing and I was so confused. I just wanted to move the drugs out of my cabin until the heat was off.

"The decision was taken out of my hands because Chrissie Young must have followed me and later broke into my cabin and stole the statuette. I guessed it was her, because the burglar had gone through my room very thoroughly and that was the only item missing. She was certainly smart enough to appreciate the value of the statuette, if it had been real. If she had found the drugs inside, that must have been a huge bonus for her. Anyhow, I decided to let her hold onto the incriminating evidence for a while so I could formulate a plan."

"But if they had caught her with it she would have said she got it from you," Warren protested.

"I thought of that, and decided that if that happened I would simply brazen it out. Who would take her word against mine?"

"No one, I guess," agreed Warren.

"Anyway, my contacts came back to me and said that the MI6 woman hadn't been after me – she was following Patrick Westcott. No one seemed to be making a fuss about the missing statuette either, so I thought I might as well return to business as usual and that meant getting the drugs back." She paused for a long time, lost in thought, before continuing . . . "Killing her was much easier. I crept up on her from behind. She didn't even turn around as I slit her throat."

Warren felt as if he might be sick but managed to force the bile back down.

"But the statuette wasn't in her cabin," Sandra carried on dreamily, almost as if in a trance. "All I could think of was that someone had given it back to the professor. To make sure that I wasn't spotted, I sent an anonymous note to that girl singer, Roman Brindle. Whilst Adrian Clarke was concentrating on that, I headed for the professor's cabin. I confronted him with all that KGB stuff you told me about."

Warren swallowed hard. God, he could be such a gossip!

"But the blackmail didn't work. He just started ranting and shouting like some half-mad fool and I had to shut him up. I almost took pleasure in killing him. But I still didn't know where the statuette was. Then last night I saw the chief superintendent carrying Chrissie's beach bag back to his cabin.

"How did you know it was hers?"

"It was very distinctive, very ugly. I had seen her with it before," she dismissed his interruption irritably. "So I deduced the statuette must be in it. I went after him." Having finished her story she seemed to snap out of her dream and began to cry. "I didn't mean to kill anyone, Warren." She dug her blood-red nails painfully into the back of his hand. "But it couldn't be helped. You can understand that, can't you?"

Warren stood up, his legs wobbling under him. He had to get some air. "Do you want me to handle the attorney for your defence?" he asked.

"Do whatever is necessary," she nodded.

"Okay." He walked slowly over to the door and knocked for Adrian to let him out. Sandra Van Horn put her dark glasses on again.

The great ship was at last tied up at the Southampton dockside. Thousands of suitcases were being rolled, carried and dragged down the gangways. Suntanned passengers appeared dressed in shorts and dresses with thin cardigans and sweaters slung over their arms, and crew members disembarked in their jeans and blazers.

Sandra Van Horn left the ship in handcuffs, escorted by a detective from Southampton CID. The media surged forward to the barriers which the police had erected, shouting questions and flashing their cameras. Sandra hung her head.

"It's terribly sad," said Warren to Adrian as they watched her walk unsteadily down the gangway. "Poor Sandi. I feel so sorry for her."

Adrian felt sorry for the people she had killed, but he did not say so. "Why did she do it? She's refusing to talk to us until her lawyers arrive."

"It seems she ran out of money, but she couldn't bear to give up her passion for beautiful old objects. So she tried to finance her purchases by drug smuggling. But things began to go wrong."

Adrian nodded. It made a kind of sense. The details would emerge from several days of interrogation, but someone else would do that: he was returning to retirement.

"Goodbye," Warren said. "Thank you for your courtesy. You are a good man."

Adrian shook his hand.

Annie Young came up to say goodbye. She was wearing a panama with a feather in it. "I wasn't a very good Miss Marple, was I?" she said. "Now I'm going home to a wedding and a funeral."

"A wedding?" Adrian said. Surely she was not going to marry that actor.

"My nephew Mike is going to marry Roman Brindle."

"Ah."

Annie smiled ruefully. "Rupert is fond of me, Adrian, but not so fond that he would tie himself to me. And even if he wanted to I wouldn't be such a fool."

"No," Adrian said. "I should have known that. Goodbye."

Lisa and Jazzy walked past with one of the Davenports. They all looked a little subdued, and avoided Adrian's eye. He wondered whether they knew anything about the drugs in the statuette, but he was not going to do anything about it. They were old enough to know the score. If they wanted to risk their lives with dangerous drugs, he was not going to save them from themselves: it was a thankless task.

The Daviots were the next to go by. Adrian voted Conservative but he still thought Simon was a creep. The MP looked especially sour today, but his wife, Brenda, wore a curious little smile, as if she was pleased with herself about something. As they descended the gangway Simon saw the media waiting at the bottom and seemed to grow six inches in stature. A beaming smile spread across his face and he raised his hand in a confident wave.

Rosamund Westcott came up to Adrian, wearing a green mack and black silk scarf. She was leaning heavily on Hilary Brown's arm. "Mr Clarke," she said as if beginning a rehearsed speech. "Can you tell me why my husband died?"

"I think he was an innocent victim," Adrian lied.

"There has been horrible talk . . . something about the Russians, and something about boys . . ."

"True or false, that had nothing to do with his death. He was used – or rather his statuette was – but he probably knew nothing about it." Hilary gave him an appreciative nod of thanks over Rosamund's head.

"Thank you," Rosamund said. She shook his hand and left. She seemed to believe him.

It might even be true, but as she reached the bottom of the steps the media shouted their questions with renewed vigour. She looked like a startled animal as Hilary hastened her towards the exit.

Adrian's single bag was by his side, and he held his raincoat over his arm. He was ready to go, but he was waiting for someone. Now she arrived, in a smart black suit with a brightly coloured silk scarf.

"Julia," he said.

A porter appeared with her two cases. Adrian picked up his own bag and they followed the man down the gangway to the waiting taxi.

As they took a last look at the great ship, Julia said, "You were very clever, weren't you."

"Not in the least. I solved the murders at the last minute, by chance."

"I didn't mean that. You were clever not to sleep with me."

"Was I?"

"Most shipboard romances end at the dockside. But we're leaving together. Because we haven't slept together, we're still intrigued. Most men would have jumped into bed at the first opportunity. But you planned ahead. Clever you."

Adrian grinned. He had done no such thing. But he did not contradict her.

Why spoil a good story?